ONE SHOT

THE WILD NINES - BOOK THREE

A.R. KNIGHT

1

DEADLY INSPIRATION

The charge blew the airlock with a burst of smoke and blue flame. Following the explosion, laser fire blitzed through the haze, more than a few bolts from Alissa's own rifle. Nothing came back. No shouts, no answering fire.

"Go, but keep talking," Castor said to the four fighters positioned around the charred opening. "Head for the hold. We'll hit the bridge."

Alissa watched the fighters, her fighters, vanish through the airlock. Beside Castor, a pair of other fighters, dressed in the tattered collections worn by all the Red Voice soldiers, stood armed and ready. At her nod, they entered. Alissa and Castor followed. A bright room sat on the other side of the airlock, shelves against the walls covered in space suits, oxygen lines, and patching materials. What you'd need if things went wrong.

The two fighters turned right. Galaxy Forge pumped out these freighters with the same blueprints, and this group had been raiding them for years now. They had the fastest routes to the bridge and cargo memorized. Alissa couldn't stop herself from taking a deep breath, deep enough for Castor to glance over as they followed the fighters.

"Sorry," Alissa said. "Sometimes I forget how long we've been doing this."

"It's been a long time. Don't think we ever expected to live longer than a month," Castor replied.

"Hey, I had us pegged for a year."

Getting up to bridge level required an elevator ride. The four of them stood inside the lift, but when the fighter pressed the button to rise, the lift didn't move. Immediately the second fighter pulled off his pack and broke out a las-tool. Alissa and the others backed against the side of the lift as the fighter burned through the ceiling. The white-hot laser shredded a circle, and the freed plate clanged down to the ground as the fighter finished cutting. Castor knelt, cupping his hands, and Alissa stepped on them. He boosted her up and Alissa squeezed through the opening, pulling herself onto the roof of the lift.

Standard defense procedure. Send a distress message, then make it as hard as possible to get to the bridge by disabling the lifts. Alissa looked around the shaft. There was always a ladder somewhere. There! Hanging along the rear side and going all the way up. She waved the others out, with Castor the last man making the jump, gripping the edge of the hole and pulling himself out. The fighters were the first up the ladder, climbing to the sealed doors at the bridge level, breaking out the las-tool, and burning their way through to a hallway.

"Lead, it's the hold team," the voice came over Alissa's comm. "We're finding no resistance. No sign of the crew."

"None here either," Alissa replied. "Keep the channels open and let us know what you find."

The comm clicked acknowledgment. Alissa climbed the ladder next, squeezing in through the hot hole made in the bridge level doors. In front of them sat a hallway split on either side with crew cabins. At the far end, the mess hall and the thick doors to the bridge. Now the fighters crept, their rifles drawn. Alissa and Castor followed, Alissa carrying her favorite automatic sidearms. Hold the trigger and they would spew more lasers than a personal shield could take. Sure, they ran out of power fast, but nobody lived that long.

The cafeteria was immaculate. No dirty dishes, scraps of litter, or even chairs out of place. As though the kitchen hadn't even been used.

"Something's not right here," Alissa said. "The ship's too far away from Jupiter to be this clean."

"Weapons ready," Castor said. Usual raiding protocol meant taking captives. Ransom money, information about other targets, and goodwill from not killing a bunch of civilians made it more profitable. But it wasn't worth risking their own lives.

The bridge doors were shut, large and thick. The last barrier to an assault. If they had to cut through with the las-tool, it was going to take time. So Castor went to work instead. The small panel next to the bridge doors allowed keyed access, connections that could be subverted. Using a micro tool and its torch option, Castor melted off bits of the corners, loosening the faceplate. Flipped the button on the tool and used the small crowbar that extended to pry it off. Then he leaned in and Alissa couldn't tell anymore what he was doing, but, like a magician working his tricks, the bridge doors shot open a moment later.

Then stopped, only a third of a meter wide.

"It's a little tight," Alissa said, looking through the gap. She could see terminals, consoles where the pilot would guide the ship and the captain would monitor various systems. Only there was nobody there, no laser waiting to blow her face off.

"I'm not getting any response," Castor said. "It's like someone cut the power from this panel to the door."

The other three looked at Alissa. She looked at the opening, and then Alissa shrugged off her pack. Took off the jacket. Before any of them could stop her, Alissa squeezed through the doors. And then she was hit in the shoulder, shoved by something strong. Alissa bounced off the ground and tucked into a roll, using the momentum to keep moving away from what hit her. When she felt the far wall, she glanced back towards the door and froze. The naked, static face of an android stared at her from across the room. Its gray bones shimmered in the ship's lifeless lighting.

"You are not the crew of this vessel," the bot said. "Identify yourself."

Behind the android, Alissa saw something else. A deep red stain covering the far wall, and beneath it, a crumpled body. She stood and drew her sidearms. It didn't take a genius to solve this mystery.

"Doesn't matter who I am," Alissa said. "What matters is what you're going to do next."

On the other side of the door, Alissa could hear Castor and the fighters trying to figure out a way into the room. Eventually, they might make it, but the easiest way to open those doors sat on those consoles right in front of her. She just had to make it there before this thing killed her.

"My directives stated to clear the ship," the android said. "I did so. Verified it. I will report the error and rectify the situation."

The android came at her fast, its legs pushing it across the bridge to her in a couple of strides. Just enough time for Alissa to hold down those triggers. Both sidearms exploded in an orange light show, streaming bolts at the android. Every shot blew off charred bits from the bot's armor, exposing circuits and pumping metal muscle. But it didn't stop. Its fist swung towards Alissa's head. She ducked and ran under the punch, moving back towards the center of the room. The bot wheeled around and Alissa felt her hair swish as the android's second swing came close to taking her head off.

She ran to the consoles, looking for some way to open the doors further. Only they were all locked, asking for the captain or pilot's badge. Which meant she was trapped, which meant she was dead. Alissa turned to face the bot as it stepped up to her. She brought the sidearms up, but the android moved faster, knocked the sidearm out of Alissa's left hand while grabbing her right and lifting her up.

Those black eyes stared right at her as the android cocked its right arm back to deliver a killing punch. Alissa sucked in a breath, then spat in the android's face. And it exploded. Alissa fell to the ground as lasers poured into the android through the crack in the bridge doors. The bot staggered, backing out of the fire, falling over as the motors keeping its legs in place melted away. Alissa grabbed her dropped sidearm and closed on the android. The bot's head swiveled to look at her as Alissa aimed at it. Then she fired.

The lasers chewed through the bot's insides. Burned away the circuitry. A couple seconds of sustained attack, and the android was nothing more than a pile of ruined parts.

"Thanks for the save," Alissa said a moment later. She'd opened the bridge doors using the badge still on the bloody body, the fighters and Castor joining her by the consoles. "We're lucky it wasn't equipped for a real fight or we'd be dead. My question, why did it kill the crew?"

Androids weren't allowed, were explicitly programmed, not to harm innocents. Only targets assigned through a judgment system. She doubted the crew on this freighter had any criminal records. Doubted that they'd be worth sending an android after them even so.

"The android was part of a shipment. They delivered more than a dozen to Ganymede, but this one was requested back. Intentionally," Castor said, flicking through the ship's logs. "The order came from our favorite man, Bosser."

"Castor, if Bosser's getting these androids to kill on command, why couldn't we?" Alissa said.

"We'd need to get access to their production facility, on Earth," Castor said. "They'll never let us land."

"They will if we have Bosser," Alissa said. Castor nodded. "Let's get the haul off this ship and set course for Miner Prime."

2

THE NEXT MOVE

A minor setback. Losing the ice diamonds was a blow to their bottom line, but all it meant was that Bosser's partners would have to step up their contributions. Reaching their goal would provide such profits as to make the diamonds a footnote and nothing more.

Bosser said all of this to the screen in his dark apartment aboard the space station Miner Prime. Situated in the asteroid belt between Mars and Jupiter, the station functioned as an intermediary for communications between civilized space and more adventurous outposts in the farther reaches of the solar system. Those outposts, and missions around them, had been giving Bosser more headaches than usual lately.

The two-meter wide monitor in front of Bosser held the faces of his various business partners. All of them were labeled with astrological pseudonyms. Zodiac signs, in no particular order, hovering beneath their heads in gold-weighted capital letters, as though they were wearing jewelry. The faces themselves were static, would remain so for minutes as the message filtered its way through dozens of satellites to their respective offices. Of the nine members on that screen, Bosser had a good idea who all of them were. Despite the entire group coming together through a string of anonymous messages suggesting places and times, despite a promise not to attempt to learn the identities of each other, Bosser had gone digging.

As had all the others.

Bosser took a sip from the water glass beside him, the cool liquid tasting indistinguishable from the filtered natural springs on Earth. So long as he didn't think about the fact that it was recycled from the station's thousands of citizens, Bosser enjoyed the sensation. Water and wine. Anything else was a waste of time.

"This is the second instance that this group disrupted your plans," Gemini, the top-middle, head of a large asteroid mining company, said.

To keep the council from talking over each other, an order had been established at the first meeting. Bosser, with Miner Prime as the central communication hub for the group, would dictate who should respond next. If nobody was specified, the order rotated, progressing through the group one person at a time. Lately, though, Bosser felt all of these sessions were interrogation games. Searching for ways to pin misfortunes on him.

"The Wild Nines served their purpose," Bosser replied. "That the Red Voice still had any ships capable of mounting an assault was information we did not have. That Eden did not have. As the Red Voice needed those diamonds far more than ourselves and we prevented that acquisition, I still consider the mission a success."

Another period of pauses. Bosser went over to the record player set up against the wall of the apartment. Easily the most valuable item he owned, the player and his collection of several dozen records had been a gift. The acknowledgment of a life saved. Now, Bosser started the player and positioned the needle. The long, slow swing of a saxophone bled out of the player and mingled with the constant shuffling of technobabble that made up Miner Prime's background noise. The shudders of systems turning on and off, of lifts sliding people up and down, the overhead announcements requesting this or that person to be somewhere else.

"Speaking of the Red Voice remnants, do you know where they

are?" the next head in line, Leo, asked. "If they are the only remaining threat, I don't know why we haven't eliminated them."

"It is much harder to find and swat one fly in a house than it is to shoot a man in the same space," Bosser said. After being torched off the face of Mars, the rebels had scattered. Had vanished so well that Bosser had forgotten about them. Until now.

Bosser sat on a crimson couch, a large one arranged in a half-circle facing the monitor. In the center sat a glass table, supported by faux-pearl legs. Both were gifts, like the record player. The couch, its fabric grown specifically for comfort in an Earth laboratory, came after Bosser had rooted out and destroyed the reputation of a rival to Eden's top executive. The table, for expunging a scion's record of bad decisions. That same scion would likely be one of those faces on the screen in a few years. Always better to have people in your debt than the other way around.

"Excuses aren't necessary. Just take care of them," said Cancer, who then leaned a little closer to his camera. "How are the preparations for the Guardian Project proceeding?"

The highlight of the conversation. Bosser spent the next hours feeding them encouraging details, answering questions between pauses. The project was proceeding on schedule, was deploying. After that, the puppet masters would truly hold the strings. As the meeting hit its sixth hour, members started to drop off. Until only one, Virgo, remained on the screen.

"You sent my daughter into that mess on Neptune," the head said.

"Your daughter went of her own accord," Bosser replied, standing. The transmission time to Virgo was only minutes. A relatively snappy conversation, for a change. "I met her, when the Wild Nines were here on the station. She hacked an android."

"An amazing woman," Virgo said. "But if you ever send her into a situation like that again, Bosser, I won't forget it."

"It sounds like you don't trust your daughter to make her own decisions."

"The reason you are so useful, Bosser, is that you don't care who you have to sacrifice to achieve your ends," Virgo said. "The rest of us prefer to keep those we love safe, even if that means restricting their independence. As a clever, self-interested man, I'm sure you can find a way to keep her out of things."

"As you say," Bosser nodded slowly for the camera. "I will do whatever I can to keep your daughter alive."

"See that you do," Virgo said, then cut the communication.

Bosser turned off the monitor, exhausted. No time for sleep yet though. The board was set, the pieces were in motion, and it was Bosser's turn to play.

3

OLD BOT, NEW BODY

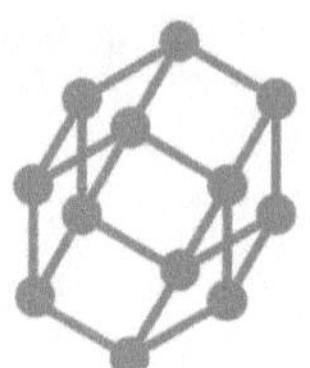

The drive slid into the slot with a satisfying click. Viola tapped the top of it, which extended out from the volleyball-sized sphere, and watched the slot disappear down into the ball. The whole apparatus sat in a charging cradle, which fed energy from the *Jumper*'s solar panels into the sphere. It'd been sitting there for hours now, and with the *Jumper* drawing closer to the sun on its journey to Miner Prime, the batteries should be good to go.

"Good morning, Puk," Viola said. It was late evening, but the phrase itself was the key.

In a quiet environment, like her bedroom back on Ganymede, Viola would have been able to hear some of Puk's systems starting up. The whirs of cooling fans, the whoosh of the jets as the bot floated into the air. The *Jumper*, though, played a symphony of its own that overwhelmed the smaller sounds. Especially in Viola's cabin, back towards the engines. Right now, with the ship starting its slowing period on approach to Miner Prime, Viola heard the constant hum as the engines compressed and discharged ionized gas. Outside the closed door, footsteps echoed clanks as one of the other crew members wandered by. Occasional communication went over the ship's intercoms, muffled through the door but still there, like a conversation on the other side of a room.

Puk rose. Wobbly. Hovering in front of Viola's face and turning around.

"Is your camera working?" Viola asked.

"You asking if I can see your beautiful face?" Puk replied, its vocal synthesizers producing a flat tone. "Because you've never looked better."

"Liar." Viola smiled. She probably looked terrible. Greasy and tired. They'd been flying for weeks already, coming back from Neptune with a stopover for supplies on Titan, one of Saturn's moons. The *Jumper* wasn't exactly a spa, with its recycled water shower that sprinkled more than washed, a steady re-use of clothes so covered with grime from the constant maintenance of the ship's many systems, and a lack of the little things she'd had growing up on Ganymede. What Viola wouldn't give for some scented soap, a chance to eat some actual fruit rather than the dried stuff.

"I've never died before," Puk said. "Except running out of battery, but, I mean, not destroyed."

"You know what happened?"

"No idea. But my date/time systems show that I've been out for over a month."

That was accurate. She'd restored Puk from the last back-up she had, before they'd met up with the freighter *Amerigo*. Before they'd been swept up in Neptune's storm of terror.

"I'm almost jealous," Viola said. "Wouldn't mind forgetting the last month myself."

"Sounds unpleasant. Don't tell me."

"Okay," Viola said, glancing at the bulge on Puk's side. A new feature. One she'd thought about a lot before adding in. "Are you detecting the new hardware?"

"It's next up on my start-up checks," Puk buzzed. "Viola, this is a lot more powerful than my last laser."

"You should have enough for a couple of shots," Viola said. "Ones powerful enough to kill somebody, anyway."

The room was silent for a moment. Viola's mouth felt dry.

The *Karat*'s lift doors opening, Davin firing at the hijacker right in front. Not seeing the guy in back, his sidearm out. Aiming for Davin. Viola's own shot a perfect one, burning home. The man's face after, shocked at his own death. She still woke up to that face some nights.

"That's . . . different," Puk said. "You didn't program me that way."

"I have now. Dig for it," Viola said. Part of why it'd taken a while to bring Puk back. She'd had to make changes to the personality. Remove some of the softer sides. Some of the limits. Puk might not know it now, but if the situation demanded it, the bot wouldn't hesitate to take a life.

"Viola, what happened? What did I miss?"

"I thought you didn't want to know?"

"That was before I knew how different you'd made me. I need some context," Puk said.

Viola took a breath, then recounted the dive to save the ice diamonds, the hijacked *Karat*, down in Neptune's atmosphere. The Red Voice raiders. The suicidal ramming of their frigate with the *Karat* and their escape.

"Sorry I missed it," Puk said. "Although, I suppose I didn't miss the whole thing."

"From what Opal says, you saved her life," Viola said. "Only, it was close. If you'd had this weapon, it would've been easier. Safer."

"Then I guess this is a good thing?"

Viola had nothing to say to that. Good? Puk was stronger now, more dangerous. So long as the bot was with them, then yeah, it was a good thing. Except she couldn't shake the idea that turning her sarcastic friend into a deadly weapon was wrong.

Viola fell back from the small desk onto the stiff bed that took up the rest of the cabin. No room for chairs. The locker at the foot of the bed held the rest of her stuff, not much of it suited to what she was doing now. In there, among the clothes and scattered tools she'd brought with her when they last left Ganymede, was a rifle designed to trigger a rapid sequence of lasers, each one capable of burning through someone. Every day she'd forced herself to go to the *Jumper*'s pair of simulators, beat-up things that Merc maintained more for flight practice than anything, and blast targets.

The next time she had to shoot someone, the good aim wouldn't be by accident.

The thought didn't make her happy.

4

DOCKING PROCEDURES

Phyla's eyes opened and, for a second, she did not know where she was. The room was larger than hers; she didn't own the shotgun by the door, and the larger locker wasn't covered with pictures like . . . hers. They all belonged to Davin, still sleeping next to her, the thin sheets on the bed rising and falling with his breath. Phyla turned on her side and traced his outline through the blanket. After Neptune, the rush to where she was now happened quickly.

From the first evening, when the *Jumper* had gone to sleep, and it was just the two of them, sitting there in the cockpit, talking like they had a thousand times before, it felt different. The missions were cutting closer, the team getting hurt. *They* were getting hurt. What had been a simpler world of policing stable outposts, running escort jobs for freighters nobody wanted to attack because the corporate owners were too powerful, had turned into a constant series of near-death moments.

Stripped of the small talk, because who knew when you'd be robbed of a chance to say what you needed to say, the two of them, childhood friends, wound up here. But it wasn't just physical. Phyla welcomed the tighter bond, the yes no maybe moments with Davin where they didn't feel like crew and captain, but partners. Friends. Lovers.

The dimmed clock on Davin's side of the bed brightened as it caught Phyla's glance. Still early. There wasn't a day and night, but the *Jumper*'s lighting did its best to simulate Earth, keep that rhythm. Blue lights at night, white during the day and a gradual shift between the two.

"Phyla, this is your wake-up call," whispered a voice from her comm, sitting on the small shelf at her side of the bed. "We'll be at manual range in an hour."

When Phyla would have to take over the piloting duties to bring the *Jumper* into Miner Prime. There'd been a lot of back-and-forth about forcing auto-pilot landings, but after some random events weren't caught correctly by autopilot programming—a stray asteroid, or a ship drifting off course that could have been avoided—Miner Prime required all smaller craft to dock with a pilot behind the sticks.

"I'm up," Phyla responded.

"Want me to wake the captain?" Fournine, formerly the android and now the *Jumper*'s central brain, thanks to Trina, said.

"Too late," Davin's voice rose as a scratchy groan. "What's going on?"

"We're almost home," Phyla said.

"You happy to be back?"

Phyla took in the question with a whiff of Davin's heavy breath. Not that hers would be any better. The endless close encounters on a ship like the *Jumper* more or less forced you to get used to all kinds of odors.

"In the sense that we can get some better food, yes," Phyla said. "But we didn't exactly leave here on the best of terms."

"Bosser said he cleared us, that Eden smoothed things over."

"You trust him?"

"Not even a little," Davin said. "But I trust money. Bosser knows Viola is with us, which means Eden probably does too. They won't risk hurting her just to get revenge."

"Sometimes you can be a little cold, you know that?" Phyla said, slipping out of the bed and pulling on clothes.

"It's a fact, Phyla," Davin said, leaning on his elbows. "Viola being on this ship is going to let us get rid of those ice diamonds, then get out of here, coin in hand."

"And go where?"

"There's a place I haven't been in a long time," Davin started to smile, just slightly. "I don't think you've ever gone there."

The lights in the cabin brightened, turning yellow. Another dawn on the *Jumper*. Phyla looked at the clock again. Getting close to time.

"You want to go to Earth?"

Davin nodded. He was right. Phyla hadn't ever been there. Only in orbit, and then, only once. Most of the cargo and escort runs the *Jumper* did were towards the outside where routes weren't established enough to warrant large ships. Where other craft were rare enough that hijackers could take you unopposed if you didn't pay for guards.

"What are we going to do there?" Phyla said, heading for the door.

"With the coin we'll make from the ice diamonds, we can go, sell the *Jumper*, try something new," Davin said, still in the bed. "Something where, maybe, we don't get shot at all the time."

"You think you could handle that? A normal life?"

"No way to know until I give it a try," Davin laughed. "Besides, with you, I doubt it'll be that normal."

"What's that supposed to mean?"

Not the reply Davin was expecting, and Phyla could tell he was searching for a way to worm himself out of this one.

"Phyla, we're being hailed by the space station," Fournine's voice jumped in, this time over the louder intercom. "Need you in the cockpit, unless you want me to start talking to them. Which could be fun, now that I think about it."

"No, Fournine, I'm coming," Phyla said, shaking her head at Davin and leaving the cabin.

A normal life. Phyla wasn't even sure what that really meant. The last few weeks, the *Jumper* speeding through space back towards Miner Prime, there'd been little to do but maintain the ship, work out, and relax. Nice, but it was getting stale, and Phyla felt a little thrill as she climbed into the *Jumper*'s cockpit. If a normal life meant not getting shot at that was fine. But if the cost was boredom? What would she choose?

"*Whiskey Jumper*? This is Miner Prime flight control. We're sending over the coordinates for your bay now."

"Thanks, control. Happy to be here," Phyla replied.

Outside the cockpit windows, the cylindrical spider of Miner Prime loomed large. Its core supporting the majority of the population, with the outer edges getting progressively more exclusive, more exotic.

"*Jumper*, seems you've got some powerful friends," Control said. "Let's try to keep this visit a little less destructive, shall we?"

"We'd love to, Control."

A yellow line shot out along the *Jumper*'s cockpit, angling towards the space station. Phyla gripped the flight stick, turned off the autopilot, and started the first angling turn. The last time Phyla had come home, she'd blown parts of Miner Prime to pieces in a desperate escape.

Please, please let this time be better.

5

DESPERATE PLANS

Forty fighters stood in the *Whisperwind*'s main area, crowded on couches, standing between tables, all staring at her. The ship was on final approach to Minor Prime, where most of these fighters might die.

"You are the last of us," Alissa said to the group. "The Red Voice is a movement, a belief that people should have their own freedom and not be ruled by corporations. We have fought for years and now I'm asking for just a little more."

The fighters looked back at her, silent. It wasn't their first speech. Colorful language calling for an end to evil, appeals to passion and love of one's home, but Alissa hoped this would be the last one. The last time she would have to preach for a doomed cause.

"Today we take up arms for those who do not know that they are imprisoned. Who cannot see their cage," Alissa said. "On a recent mission, we found a freighter overrun by a single android. Its crew dead. The android itself, rather than dispensing justice, was following orders."

Now the eyes perked up. She had their attention.

"Our goal is to turn these new androids against the oppressors, to make the sword of their false justice swing for the right side."

A fighter raised his hand. Alissa nodded at him.

"Excuse me, but the androids, aren't they made on Earth?" the fighter said. "Why aren't we going there?"

"Because we would never land alive," Castor said, speaking up from beside Alissa. "Minor Prime has a target that can get us onto Earth. We're here to take him."

"We'll have four squads. One, led by me, will attempt to find Bosser himself," Alissa said. "The other three will be diversions, clearing the way for the rest of us. Once the objective is complete, we'll regroup here. Get ready, the show starts as soon as we land."

Castor was giving her a hesitating look, the same measured glance Bakr used to provide whenever she said something he didn't agree with.

"It doesn't matter if I die here," Alissa said. "We get Bosser, you get him to Earth, and we pay what we owe to everyone who died for this."

"Marl never had your fatalism."

"Marl fought from the sidelines. You see enough horrors up close, and you get tired."

Alissa left the crowd and went back to her cabin to get ready. Her own room was massive, enough for a double bed, a separate desk and console, a couch and monitor. The *Whisperwind* had been a luxury liner, and there were pieces of it that still spoke to that purpose. Along one wall, carved into the side, was a set of names. Many had lines through the letters, angry slashes from a micro tool Alissa kept next to the bed. She picked it up now, flicked open the blade.

Three names left. Hers. Castor. Bakr. Alissa swiped at her comm, played Bakr's last words.

Alissa. I'm sorry.

Static engulfed the end of the message. She didn't know how her friend had died. Only heard that the frigate, the last warship the Red Voice had, was now a bunch of scattered wreckage floating around Neptune. Alissa hoped it had been quick, whatever his fate. It was the least he deserved.

Alissa took the micro-tool and ran the blade through Bakr's name, the silver line slicing through the thin letters.

His death would not be in vain.

6

____

FOR WANT OF A CANNON

"Is it ready?"

Trina didn't bother looking at Mox, standing in the work room's doorway. The cannon would be ready when she was confident it wouldn't explode as soon as Mox spooled it up. The *Jumper* wasn't exactly a weapons factory, and the cannon was complicated.

"It doesn't work that way," Trina said, bent over the rear of the cannon where tubes fed pressurized gas into a chamber and a battery supercharged them, spitting the heated element out the front barrels. "If you want something available on request, you don't let someone blow it up."

"Accident," Mox grumbled.

"No, it wasn't," Trina said. The last piece that wasn't working was, predictably, the battery. She'd already scavenged some of the other weapons around the *Jumper* and laced them together to create a makeshift version, and it wasn't charging correctly. "You could have dodged the blast."

"Could have, maybe," Mox replied.

Trina sighed as the battery failed to display any signs of life, again. Stood back from the bench, turned to Mox. The workroom was a cluttered mess, bits and pieces of chopped up machines littered the ground from the doorway to the workbench which took up the entire side wall. Mox hadn't moved from the entrance, a smart move seeing as navigating the pieces of shrapnel and strings of wire required concentration, and practice.

"I'm sorry," Trina said. "I shouldn't be complaining. Obviously, your life is worth more than the cannon."

Trina wanted to continue that sentence, wanted to say that it didn't mean the cannon was worth *nothing*. That all of this equipment was worth a bit of effort to care for, to maintain. To not destroy in a back and forth fight with crazy raiders.

"It is who you are," Mox replied. "It is necessary for someone to care."

"I just wish the rest of you would," Trina replied. "I'll have it ready by the time we land. Or you'll have to get a new battery on the station."

"How much?"

"I'm sure Davin will buy you one after those ice diamonds are sold," Trina said the words and found her eyes wandering to the box just inside the door. The crate looked like any other large container, more than a meter wide and half that tall. They'd put the diamonds in there in case Miner Prime wanted an inspection. They'd take one look in here, see a bunch of tools, and leave it alone.

Trina already had her shopping list for afterward. A litany of things the *Jumper* needed to keep flying well. The usual chargers, wiring, replacement solar panels, but Trina figured that if the *Jumper* was going to keep getting in scraps, they ought to have some stronger shields. Lasers with a better punch. If those diamonds sold for what Davin thought they would, the Wild Nines would get a great new freighter in the bargain.

"Trina," Mox said. "How did you get this way?"

She pushed up her greasy goggles. Looked at Mox, the exoskeleton lacing its way along his arms and legs.

"What way?" Trina said.

"I am half-machine, but don't love them the way you do," Mox said. Not technically a question, but Trina could follow the thread.

"You look at everything we've been through lately? All the randomness? Know what the common element is?"

Mox shook his head.

"People," Trina continued. "It's all crazy people doing crazy things, for coin or something else. Machines, they do what they're told. Every action has a purpose, at least to them."

"Free will frightens you?"

Trina had been on the *Jumper* for years with Mox and never had the man come at her with questions like this. Something was different. Trina sniffed the air, maybe the exoskeleton was misfiring. Sending the wrong electricity to Mox's brain, scrambling his signal. If Trina tried hard enough, she could smell the volts. At least, she thought so. Now, though, there was only the usual grease and metal, a hint of burning wire from the work she'd been doing on the cannon.

"When it's logical, no. When it's not, that's why I'm glad I've got you and the others around. Now, you want this cannon ready, you should leave me alone to fix it," Trina said.

"Of course," Mox replied, nodding, then moving away.

Trina watched the empty doorway for a moment. The other thing about machines is that they couldn't hide their secrets. Spend enough time with them, tear enough of them apart, and you could know every little thing about them. Trina would never know everything about Mox, how he worked, why he chose the life he lived, and why he thought that now, on their approach to Miner Prime, was the time to get to know her.

And Mox would never know the reason Trina kept her hands greasy, kept the engines primed, and the batteries charged. Because some stories were so common they were nothing to those not part of them, even if they meant everything to the ones personally affected. Because nobody wanted to hear about another ship malfunction, another asteroid collision, another child of the stars growing up alone. That wasn't going to happen here.

Trina turned back to the cannon, took another look at the battery.

The problem was obvious. How she missed it, Trina didn't know. She'd switched the order, the battery needed to draw sufficient power first, then send it, but she hadn't set the amount. It took a second, and this time, when the cannon was primed, the battery hummed as its charge coursed through, readying the weapon.

When Mox needed to use it, his cannon would be ready.

7

THE ONES WE MISS

Thirty-seven messages since Erick had talked to them last. Every one of them following the same template. A hello from his daughter, then a cascade of greetings from her friends, husband, and children. No, his grandchildren. Couldn't forget that. From there, the messages went into the day to day. What the weather was like on the island, what the kids were learning at school, what was going to be on the menu for that night's dinner. It was a saga of the mundane.

Erick loved it.

He told the comm to dial the frequency. They had another hour before landing at Miner Prime, and with the docking, his life would get busy again. Transmission delay was only minutes between Earth and Mars, a time span even a small child could stand. From Erick's small cabin, he could tap into the *Jumper*'s main communications channel, the long-range one that Phyla wasn't using to talk to the station. If one of the others were on it, like Viola calling Ganymede, he'd hear them talking and have to wait till they were done. When his comm tapped in, though, all he heard was silence.

"Hello, Julia," Erick spoke into the comm. "This is your father, at long last, returning your sweet messages. We are approaching Miner

Prime, back in communicative space. I will be available for the next hour or so to talk if you are able to reply. I know it has been a long time, and for that I am sorry. But I am listening now."

The message sent, crawling its way through space to his family down on that luscious blue dot. Erick replayed his own words, shaking his head as he did so. They sounded so cold, so perfunctory. A joke to his family, even among the Wild Nines, was how formal the doctor was. Perhaps a lifetime of requiring precision in delivering diagnoses had robbed him of the ability to tap into that deeper, emotional vein. Only in times like this, though, did the habit truly feel like a hindrance.

The comm's tiny screen flared to life ten minutes later, sitting on the cabin's counter. A deeply tanned woman appeared in front of a backdrop of palm trees, holding a giggling baby. Erick practically flew across the small space, limbering himself onto the bed to watch.

"Father! Just like you to time your call during a busy day for us! As you can see, your newest grandchild arrived a month ago and is already doing her best to make our lives miserable!"

Julia's wide smile, her blazing white teeth set against the deep brown of her tan, suggested the misery was closer to joy.

"Now, unlike with the others, I will not tell you her name," Julia continued. "Because I've run out of ways to convince you to come back here and visit, so I'm hoping this one will work. We have a bed all ready for you. The waters are warm, the waves are wonderful. And after all that time in that box of a space ship, surely you could use some sun."

The rest of the message ran away fast, with Julia claiming the new one was hungry, as were all the others. She would get back to Erick later, and she hoped he would reply with the time of his next visit. Maybe even consider a permanent stay.

A permanent stay. Erick looked at the little cabin, the bed barely long enough to hold him. Unlike most of the crew members, Erick actually produced printed photos of Julia and the grandchildren. They decorated most of the cabin's surfaces. Trina had made him, one year, a small projector that could spray the pictures on the ceiling, and almost every night, Erick fell asleep to the stop-and-go show of his family's lives.

"Fifteen minutes till we dock, people. Get your crap in order," Phyla's voice came over the intercom.

Erick turned back to the comm. The channel was still open, one last chance to reply to Julia.

"Withholding the name? That is a sore blow, Julia," Erick made sure the comm sent along his happy face to disarm the comment. "But an effective one. I'm thinking, like you, that perhaps it's time I made my way home, and stayed there."

Another message that conveyed the point if not the spirit. Erick cut the channel, slipped the comm back on his wrist. There would be plenty of time to apologize to Julia for his terrible messages later. In person.

8

A DIFFERENT KIND OF DATE

The tree was large enough to hide Merc as he pressed up against it, snowflakes blowing into his face with the chill wind. On his left and right, more forest until the wintry fog cut off further view. Not that *further* mattered. His target was close.

The rifle, a solid-black automatic designed to spray slugs at a high, if inaccurate, rate was light in his hands. Especially compared to the weight of the heavy snowsuit. It was speckled with brown and black, what Merc considered effective camouflage. But he'd been behind the tree for too long already. Long enough for the target to know where he was.

Merc twitched to the right, peeking around the edge and glimpsing nothing but frozen woods. Then he dove left, rolling across the hard ground towards another pair of thick trunks. Two loud cracks split the silent air and Merc felt the ground blow up as the bullets struck close. He kept rolling until Merc felt the slight shadow of the trees fall across his face. The shots had missed.

Standing up, Merc glanced at the holes in the ground where the bullets hit behind him. The spray of the dirt indicated the shots had come from opposite the trees. Shoot and move. That was the rule.

Meaning the target probably wasn't there anymore, but if Merc went quickly, maybe he could catch them in transition.

The stick-jockey wrapped around the side of the tree and held down the trigger in the general direction of the shots. Nothing but air as Merc ran to the next tree. His own fire might have caused the target to duck back, though, so still useful. Besides, he had plenty of ammo. The wind rose up in a howl, swirling snow until even the space a meter in front of him was more gray than anything else.

"Was this your idea?" Merc called out over the wind. "Cause this weather really doesn't make this any fun."

No reply. Taking it seriously, then. Merc reached to his tool belt with his left hand, grabbed a small sphere attached there and pulled hard. He flipped the grenade over his shoulder, through the gap in the trees. The storm still blowing hard, Merc took off to the left, running along the woods, turning in a slow ring. Seconds later, the grenade exploded, a crackling blast of noise and fire that penetrated the whiteout as an orange bloom on the edge of Merc's vision.

A snap, straight ahead. The crack of a rifle shot. Merc didn't hear the bullet whiz past. Possibly not even shooting in his direction. Merc dropped down to a crouch, walking fast and quiet, the rifle held in both hands. A big tree appeared out of the swirling snow, its sheer size acting as a break to the storm. Up in the branches, a dark shape spread out like a lump across a pair of thick limbs. Clever, taking the height advantage. Unless your target was right beneath you.

Merc aimed the rifle up, pulled the trigger, and sent a long series of shots at the lump which shook with every hit. Merc waited for a cry, for the rifle to fall down, but nothing. Then he felt the pressure on the back of his head, the cold metal of a sidearm.

"Drop it and turn around," the woman's voice hard.

Merc did just that, letting the rifle fall onto the ground. Turned around to find the woman wearing barely more than underclothes. Merc could see her shivering in the cold, but the sidearm was steady, and her eyes didn't blink.

"Say it," the woman said.

"You win," Merc said, shaking his head.

"Damn right," the woman replied, stepping up and giving him a kiss.

The forest faded away to black as did the cold and the feel of the wind on his neck. Then white lines appeared in the dark space, opening to reveal the inside of the *Jumper*'s docking bay. The Viper was there in front of him, its polished metal back to form after the pock marks it'd endured in the fighting over Neptune. Merc's mind did the same mental flip-flops it always did after leaving the simulator, the total immersion coming back to actual reality. Even the gravity was different, lighter on the *Jumper* than on Earth proper.

"That's what, thirty to ten?" Opal said, climbing out of her pod.

"If you're only counting ground sims," Merc countered. "Let's get you in a ship and see what happens."

Opal laughed, shook her head. She never said yes to that, always played off flying as Merc's job. So they dueled in frozen tundras, space stations, the red sand of Mars. As a way to pass the time, it was pretty awesome.

"We're about to dock," Phyla's voice came over the intercom. "You two get yourselves ready if you want to come out."

"Hell yes," Merc said, following Opal out of the bay. A chance to be somewhere besides the *Jumper*? No way he was going to miss that.

9

—————

LIVES TO LOSE

Miner Prime filled the cockpit view, replacing black space with its collection of grays, whites, and random colors for various hatches or corporate-branded sections. It was nice to stare at something other than infinity. To know that if the *Jumper* suffered some sort of terrible disaster, there could actually be a rescue rather than a bunch of wreckage only found by accident years later.

"Thanks for clearing the way," Davin said, sending the message to the line Bosser told them to use. "Was afraid I'd never get to land on this spinning piece of space crap ever again."

Davin paused. Bosser's last real communication, back by Neptune, had been a threat. In fact, most of the man's messages seemed to be threats, now that Davin thought about it. *Contact me as soon as you have arrived at the station, or unfortunate consequences may arise* - that was how the last one had ended. Like what, an assassination? Immediate destruction of the *Jumper* and its crew?

It wasn't worth taking the chance.

"We're here," Davin continued. "So if you have that mission in mind, feel free to let us know."

The transmission ended. Davin waited, Phyla guiding the *Jumper* in next to him. No reply.

"Is he standing us up after we flew all the way here?" Phyla said.

"Probably in the shower, but if he forgot about us, I'd be fine with it."

Ten minutes later and the *Jumper* locked its struts down onto the dark blue floor of the bay. The same color as a deep ocean, and also the hue of the company that owned this section of the station. Davin would pay them a fee to keep the *Jumper* here, one link in an endless chain of monetization. That'd been one thing about living in Vagrant's Hollow - if you didn't have any money, nobody bothered to advertise to you. Now that he had a ship, everyone thought he was a mark.

The *Jumper*'s ramp went down. Miner Prime's cold white light slipped into the freighter. Noises from the bay filtered in, echoing announcements requesting a cargo hauler somewhere else, the constant shunt of lifts sending people from here to there, and the low bubbles of conversations just out of earshot. None of those noises came from the person standing at the bottom of the ramp.

Her hair was spiked, pointing out in all directions as though each clump was a comet shooting out to a different section of space. Beneath that, she stood with her hands at her sides, watching Davin and the others without a hint of expectation. As though she was prepared to wait there all day, and the next, and it wouldn't bother her in the slightest. Sitting on her stance was the Miner Prime special forces uniform, a thick navy collection of pockets and loops on which to store or hang all the weapons and tools they would need. All of hers looked empty.

Davin walked down the ramp, mustering the casual confidence that came with knowing Opal was in her usual perch at the top of the ramp, sniper ready and aimed directly at the person's head. The woman had been waiting in the bay when the *Jumper* had come in, and there wasn't any reason to take chances.

"Bosser didn't want to come say hi? I'm offended," Davin said when he reached the bottom. None of the others walked down behind him. It was generally better *not* to get your entire crew caught in a trap. Especially when they could be manning turrets instead, ready to roast if anything went sideways.

"Davin Masters?" the woman said, voice hitting Davin's ears like a blunt hammer. There were missing threads in her words, the hints at other agendas, at curiosity, at past histories that informed present emotion. The imperfections that made human speech what it was.

"You're an android, aren't you?" Davin said.

"ThreeTwelve," the woman acknowledged. "And you are the captain of this ship?"

"Someone has to be," Davin said. Another android. Not long ago, on Europa, Bosser sent first one, then two more of the bots after Davin and his crew. Most androids these days, under various restrictions passed by Earth governments, were produced explicitly to do the things people should not, like enforce the rules. The cost of making them, though, put androids outside the scope of ordinary policing, so their ludicrously fast reaction times, perfect facial recognition, and all around deadliness turned androids into high-cost killing machines in the service of the Free Law's arbitrary justice system.

"Bosser would like to see you, and Phyla, in his apartment," Threetwelve said.

"Not even going to get us dinner first?" Davin replied.

This close to the android, Davin noticed ThreeTwelve didn't blink. Didn't try to breathe. The token disguises most androids adopted to find their targets weren't being used. ThreeTwelve looked more like a 3D picture frozen in time than a person. The question was . . . why?

"Your propensity for pointless jokes is noted," ThreeTwelve said. "However, we have little time. Please, come now."

Pointless jokes? Who did this android think she was? Davin sighed, glanced at his comm. "Phyla, you hear that?"

"Already on my way out," Phyla replied through the comm. "Not like we have a choice, right?"

"Feel like that's our new reality," Davin said, looking back at the android. "Guessing you can't give me any hints about what he's going to say?"

"That things are worse than you would believe," ThreeTwelve said, its voice continuing its eerie lack of inflection. "And that you will have the opportunity to save many lives."

"Many lives?" Davin said as Phyla jogged down the ramp. "Sure you don't mean 'earn lots of coin'?"

"The first often leads to the second," ThreeTwelve said.

"Except where we just came from," Phyla said. "Where it was precisely the opposite."

"Was it?" ThreeTwelve replied, pausing for a beat before turning and walking towards the lifts. Davin forced himself not to look at Phyla. Did Bosser know that they'd kept some of the ice diamonds? That they were planning to sell the blue gems on Miner Prime?

"Why would Bosser even care?" Phyla whispered. Davin considered the question as he walked after ThreeTwelve. Bosser wasn't Eden, the company that'd lost their ship in the mission. Wasn't going to make a profit on the ice diamonds at all. Still, the idea that Bosser would know what was going on with his crew was annoying.

"Hey, android!" Davin said as ThreeTwelve tapped the call button for the lift. "What about my crew? They allowed to leave the ship, or will more of you shoot them if they try?"

ThreeTwelve half-turned, its left eye looking at Davin with an iridescent green glow.

"If their lives are yours to keep, leave them on the ship," The android said as the lift doors opened in front of it. "If their lives are their's to lose, let them go."

Androids, Davin decided as he stepped into the lift beside the bot, Phyla close behind, truly were the worst.

10

CHANGING TACTICS

They weren't going to make it to him. Alissa could see that from where she stood, with three other fighters on the lip of the lift on the security level. Too many cameras, too many guards. The wide section in front of her had no less than three fully suited peacekeepers. Their armor would block just about everything she shot. Minor Prime was on alert, and the Red Voice didn't have enough to punch through. It would be a pointless death. Her hands moved beneath her jacket, to the grips of her sidearms. So close.

"Alissa," Castor's voice came over the comm. "The placement is set and we're ready to go. But I have a question."

"Ask," Alissa replied.

"Jairo picked up another ship on the way in. A familiar one, the *Whiskey Jumper*," Castor said. "On that ship, last time I saw it, was the heiress to Galaxy Forge. We're confirming now, but she could get us to Earth."

A small chance was better than certain death. They had to try for it.

"If we see her, trigger the attack."

"And if she doesn't show?" Castor asked.

"Then we torch Miner Prime. One last cry for Mars," Alissa said. "I'll see you back at the ship."

Alissa turned and pressed a button on the left. The lift shut and rocketed them back down to the docking levels. She couldn't deny a burst of relief as those armored peacekeepers faded from view. She might not die today after all.

HIGH PRICE

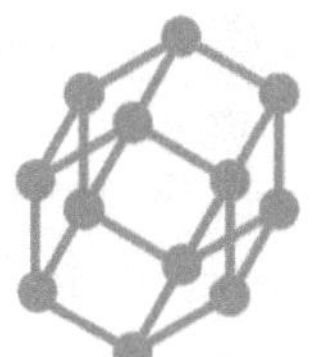

The rising stacks of houses built on other houses, junk piled on junk to create towers scaled by flimsy black-metal ladders, looked on the teeming avenues of lost souls that made their way through Vagrants Hollow. In the space above the streets, drones shot back and forth in reckless delivery runs, sending this or that vital good from one side of the level to another. Just from the lifts, Viola could see more types of people than she'd ever seen in her entire life on Ganymede.

In front of her, not a few meters away, a child argued with his mother, a woman who appeared to be almost half metal. All of her arms and legs had been replaced by mechanical alternatives, often not covered by cheap plaskin so that bits of wiring dangled through. The kid looked normal until the lift doors finished opening and dinged. When the boy's face turned to look, his entire left side was covered in a painted dark green faceplate, only the eye showing through as natural. Behind them, the shifting crowd revealed groups of Miner Prime police, traders moving carts of goods, and, at one point, a squad of people dressed entirely in what looked like woven human hair.

"This is where Davin grew up?" Viola asked.

"Yes," Mox answered from behind as they stepped out of the lift.

"Vagrants Hollow wasn't always quite so eclectic," Puk said, buzzing out of the way of a passing drone. "It's acquired a reputation as a place of anything, where, so long as you are not violent, nobody cares who you are."

"You really think we can sell the ice diamonds here?" Viola asked. Behind her, Mox held the crate packed with the gems. Viola had thought it would look absurd to walk around carrying a box that big, but a few seconds here put that concern to death. Not a soul had glanced at them for more than a moment. Even Mox's exoskeleton, the steel ridges bulging through the man's shirt, drew little interest.

"The traders that don't talk are here," Mox said. "Follow me."

"I believe what Mox means to say," Puk said, weaving along after the big man. "Is that Miner Prime intentionally regulates little of what happens in Vagrants Hollow, knowing that the attraction it provides to various types of people serves to boost the economy and status of the station as a whole."

"Got that," Viola said, her eyes flicking everywhere. There was so much to see. Opal and Merc were coming behind them, intentionally. The idea being Opal could spot a person following Mox and the diamonds without them realizing Opal was watching. The idea came from some military sting operation Opal had run years ago. Nobody harassed them, though, until Viola, Mox, and Puk stood outside of a large tent filled with the kinds of space ship parts that looked so old they belonged in museums, not on the market.

"Fourier," Mox said, nodding inside the tent. Viola followed the metal man inside, swallowing her own questions on how a shop this pathetic could afford what they were trying to sell.

And then the back of the shop, what looked like overlapping walls of cloth, parted to reveal a sallow flea of a man who wore a large mechanical backpack. As he walked towards Mox, the backpack seemed to unfold, a pair of clawed, cheap robotic arms swinging out from the top. The arms were paralleled by small vices on the bottom, looping around his waist.

"Mox!" the man squeaked. "I expected Davin! It is a rare treat that I meet the final product of Selene Stone."

Mox didn't bother speaking, just grunted an acknowledgment and looked for somewhere to set the crate down, finally brushing some of the rusted-over parts onto the ground. Fourier didn't protest, moving closer to the crate and continuing a stream of complimentary adjectives that were making Viola blush on Mox's behalf.

"Who's Selene Stone?" Viola whispered to Puk as Mox and Fourier fell into a discussion.

"I'm searching, but not getting anything," Puk replied. "I'm not able to connect to the network here. Fourier may be blocking access. I'll be right back."

The little bot buzzed out of the shop. Viola glanced down the street, back the way they came, and noticed Opal and Merc investigating a vendor's food offerings. Looked like sandwiches, steaming piles of bread, meat, and vegetables. All lab grown. The price to fly actual meat up to space was so ridiculous that most people with coin that wanted it just went to Earth. Viola's father, owner of one of the largest companies in the solar system, didn't even bother with it, claiming real meat was a vice and that he had plenty of those already.

A click from behind Viola signaled Mox opening the crate, and Fourier's accompanying intake of breath said that maybe Davin's estimates on the ice diamond's value weren't too off the mark.

"That's the only offer," Mox was saying as Viola moved closer.

"The only offer?" Fourier replied. "That's hardly any fun."

"Not here for fun."

Fourier looked at Mox like the man had just killed a child. The backpack, though, commenced with a mind of its own. The two metal arms lunged into the crate, grabbed a pair of the ice diamonds and placed them in the backpack's lower vices. Small lights lining the outside of the vices turned blue, then red, then green. Fourier's eyes tilted skyward, as though something was talking to him, and Viola noticed the man did have tiny attachments on his ears.

"An amazing mineral make-up," Fourier muttered, the looked at Mox and laughed. "I don't even care that I'm giving away my interest to you. Miner Prime's database doesn't have anything like this. You're saying these are the only ones that exist? Here?"

"More on Neptune," Mox said.

"But here, now, this is it?"

When Mox nodded that clinched it. Viola watched as Fourier agreed to the sale and created the pending transfer to the Wild Nine's general account. Mox frowned at his own comm after a minute.

"Seems like the network is down," Fourier said, looking around Mox's arm. "The transaction will go through when it comes up."

"If it doesn't — "

"I know, you'll be back," Fourier said. "Now get out of here. Let me play with my new toys."

Viola walked out of the place slightly stunned. They no longer had the crate, or the ice diamonds, but if Mox had received Davin's asking price from Fourier, then Viola's share meant she wouldn't need her dad's help for a long time.

"Viola," Puk whirred as the bot came back down to meet them in the street. "I'm not getting reception anywhere. The links appear down."

"Down?" Mox said, glancing up. Viola followed the look. The previously crowded skies of Vagrant's Hollow were nearly empty, all the automated drones were gone. The only craft still moving were being actively piloted, small controlled cargo sleds. People on the streets had noticed too, were pointing up, voices getting more agitated. Viola saw more pick up their pace or duck between stacks, getting out of sight.

"Something strange is going on," Viola said. She looked back down the street, towards where Opal and Merc should have been, but couldn't see them behind the shifting crowds. Then something yanked her left arm, hard.

"Hey!" Viola said, drawing her arm back and turning. Someone was running away from her, into the crowd, a loose beige outfit. When she rubbed her forearm with her right hand, Viola felt skin.

"They took your comm!" Puk announced, then shot after the running thief. Viola took off after the bot, keeping the floating ball in view while dancing through the crowd. Behind her, Viola could hear Mox doing the same, though the crowd seemed to be dodging him instead.

The street was an uneven mash of space station metal and years of grime. It felt like running on rough dirt where every one of Viola's footfalls seemed to land at a different angle. She bounced off one person, then a stack of food supplies, then nearly decapitated herself on a passing hover cart and dove beneath it. Scrambling up, Viola caught another look at the thief, glancing back at her.

The person's face was masked, a type that Viola had seen often enough on Ganymede. Black and menacing if unintentionally. The mask operated as a filter, removing toxins from the air and only letting in oxygen. Essential when doing construction projects in space, especially on dusty rock moons. But why wear one here, in a thoroughly filtered space station?

Puk bobbed above, and Viola shook her head at the bot when the crowd gave her a moment to look up. Puk might've been able to shoot the thief, but the bot could miss, and the thief wasn't exactly trying hard to get away. The thief kept looking back at Viola as though making sure she wasn't falling too far behind. And without her comm, Viola couldn't communicate with Puk, so the old-fashioned head shake was the only way.

Another minute of crowd-dodging dashes and Viola suddenly broke free of the people. They'd moved far enough away from the center of Vagrant's Hollow. Shops were scarce out here, more homes. The stacks still there, but less covered in random flare, some even with flowers blooming. Genetically modified to grow in Miner Prime's artificial sunlight, sure, but providing a gentler ambiance, nonetheless. Viola took it in as she chased the thief, now moving at a jog. Or, was.

Mox flew out from between some stacks to the right of the thief, exoskeleton boosting his speed. The thief didn't even have a chance to react before the metal man was holding the thief up by his neck. Viola caught up just as Mox was tearing Viola's comm from the thief's hand.

"Why?" Mox asked the thief. Viola had to agree. Comms were cheap, and the thief appeared to have one. The data on one could be valuable, she guessed, if the person was someone more important than Viola.

The thief turned his head to look at her, his eyes red from lack of sleep, wrinkled and speckled brown hair going gray despite the man's apparent youthful athleticism.

"Watch," the thief said, the respirator turning his words into more of a rasp. His eyes flickered up from Viola's, looked over her shoulder, back the way they'd come.

The rumble came first. Then the flash, reflecting off of Miner Prime's inner walls. Then the sound and, with it, the blast of heat. Viola turned to see a series of smoke clouds rising from the center of Vagrant's Hollow. Three, four, and now more were going off. Bombs scattered throughout the level. Above them, the ceiling seemed to tear, ripping a hole in the false sky as another bomb blew through Miner Prime's maintenance tunnels between the levels. Blocks of carbon fiber, bottoms glittering with projection lenses and tops holding mangled nests of wires, fell.

Miner Prime was being destroyed, with them on it.

12

STREET FIGHTING

Opal's dive under the store table came automatically with the first burst. When Mox had commed that the deal was done, Opal and Merc had gone back towards the lifts. They were almost there, the lifts in sight, when everything fell apart. From under the table, a sturdy re-purposed fighter wing on plastic sawhorses, Opal pulled a sidearm out and held it in both hands. The explosions continued, but not with any kind of cadence. Not from any particular direction. Random. Chaotic.

"We need to get to the *Jumper!*" Opal shouted into her comm, already targeted to Merc's frequency. She wasn't sure where the pilot had gone, but Opal couldn't make him out through the packed street. At least, not from under the table. Opal took a breath, rolled out, and joined the crowd streaming towards the lifts.

Only, the crowd was suddenly pushing back the opposite way. Opal batted away hands, stepped over falling people as the mass of panicked humanity changed directions. They were running back towards the explosions, which made no sense. Unless there was something worse ahead of her. Still no Merc, her comm was silent.

"Merc! Say something!" Opal tried again.

The lift plaza appeared as Opal squeezed her way under the

swinging arms of a fleeing older man, apparently attempting to swim his way from what was going on ahead. And when Opal saw what that was, she understood. A large squad of Miner Prime police were getting annihilated, laser fire beaming in and out of them from seemingly all sides. Shooters hidden in the stacks sending lances of energy at the police who were trying to hide behind shields and, in some cases, the fallen bodies of their own allies. Opal slid to the side of the street, pressed herself up against a stack. Without help, the police weren't going to last long.

But these were the same troops that arrested Opal the last time she was here. That'd tried to take the *Jumper*, tried to kill Davin and Viola. Another explosion ripped through the ceiling above Vagrant's Hollow, exposing the dark caves between levels. The police wouldn't be blowing up their own space station. Or if they were, they wouldn't be dying down here where it was happening. Which meant they weren't the enemy, this time.

Opal curled left, into the store. Like most shops in Vagrant's Hollow, it opened in the back to one of the thin alleys that cut between the stacks. Opal brushed through the curtained rear, then paused and glanced in both directions. Nothing towards the lift plaza except a clear window to the continuing firefight. On the right, the alley kept going and then forked. Opal, keeping her sidearm raised and ready in front of her, followed the fork to the left. And coughed. Then coughed again. Something in the air was scratching her throat. Maybe dust, from the explosions.

The alley curled around a trapezoidal stack, the sharp angle of a large piece of scrap jutting into the path. Most of the buildings here were recycled space ships. Freighters and fighters deemed too expensive to repair, anything valuable extracted, the junk parts taken here and re-purposed. Another bomb, farther away this time, roiled its echo through the streets, momentarily covering the fractured yells of the fighters. Opal pressed up to the corner, peeked around.

Down the alley, maybe ten meters, a pair of people were setting up a tripod. One of them, on his back, had the heavy cannon that belonged on the mount. If they set that up, the Miner Prime forces would go from losing to decimated in seconds. Both looked to be carrying smaller rifles too. Outnumbered and out-gunned. Hopefully surprise would be enough. Opal brought up the sidearm as they swung the cannon down, started fixing it to the tripod. Finger on the trigger.

Then the back door of the trapezoid swung open, blocking the alley entirely with its rusted bulk. Someone shouting on the other side. Couldn't make out the words. If the newcomer had seen her, seen Opal and was warning them, then the moment that door shut, she'd be lit up. Had to take surprise back.

Opal ran towards the door, sidearm pumping with her right hand. A meter away, Opal planted her left foot and kicked with her right, a hard snap, years of military drills tightening her quads at the perfect moment to hammer the door forward. The slab wasn't thick, but had enough weight when it swung in to smash the newcomer forward, into the side of the building. But the kick brought Opal's gun out of position, bought her enemies a half second to react.

They used it.

One of the fighters pivoted the cannon around on its tripod as the other swung up his rifle. Opal pressed the trigger down on her sidearm, but the aim wasn't there. Things were moving too fast. The shot missed left, over the cannon man's shoulder. Her second one, over-correcting, hit the assault rifle rebel in the arm, but the man didn't drop his gun. Seemed to ignore the pain. For the first time, Opal saw their faces. Both of them, covered in respirators. The explosion in the ceiling, the seemingly random placement of the bombs. There was something there. Not that it mattered because Opal was about to die.

Cannon man pressed down on his weapon's trigger, just as his assault rifle partner clenched his muscles. Then something hit Opal in the face, hard. Knocked her down to the ground. Her nose ached. The door in front of her, open again. Only it wasn't really a door anymore. The cannon's laser fire chewed through the middle of it, super-heating and melting every part of the slab that it touched.

Move.

Opal rolled to her right, out from behind the door's cover, sidearm facing towards the rebels. Only to see them looking at a small circular device as it landed near their feet. When it went off a second later, sending bolts of electricity all over them, along with the cannon, Opal blinked. That was Merc's weapon, but where was he?

"Love, we gotta talk about our relationship," Merc said, getting up from the ground and standing over her. "What'd I do so bad you want to hit me with a door for?"

The pilot reached out his hand and Opal took it, standing up. The shouting still came from the lifts, screams pouring from behind them in the stacks, and the station's alarms going as a backdrop to all of it. Still, here in the alley, it felt quiet. Separated from the chaos. Opal could feel the dirt all over her back, not true soil but the dust of thousands grabbing onto her clothes for a ride. On Neptune, on Europa, the spaces were clean, the environments spotless. It'd been a while since she'd felt the grime of a fight.

"Sorry," Opal said. "I heard lots of yelling, didn't realize it was you. Figured I had to go for the surprise attack."

"Never knew you could smash a door down like that."

"Lots of things you don't know, love," Opal replied, then looked at the unconscious fighters. "Let's get moving. I don't want this space station blowing up while I'm on it."

13

WRECKERS

When the lift doors opened, a dozen guns were pointed at Phyla's face. In the front stood Bosser, a man Phyla recognized from the video feeds. He, like the others in the force, was wearing thick body armor, designed to suck and spread the heat of a laser until it was harmless.

"What—" Davin started.

"Bad timing, as always," Bosser said, starting towards the lift and waving the force forward. "Miner Prime is under attack from the inside."

Bosser set the lift to go to level two, the main shopping district for the station. Phyla tried to stay close to Davin as more and more of the armored guards pushed their way into the lift, which was large enough to hold forty to fifty people. On a station of thousands, that still often meant lift lines, sometimes long ones. It also meant you could transport a lot of firepower if you needed to.

The Miner Prime forces had a variety of weapons. Some sported standard-looking assault rifles, grenade complements, and shield sticks. The latter stuck out like poles from their backs; able to be planted on just about any surface, the shield sticks would fan out a two-meter wide and tall barrier of energy for a few minutes. Phyla hadn't seen them in action except in movies, or recordings of battles with the Red Voice. That Miner Prime would have this many available seemed ... strange.

"When we hit the level, you two stay back," Bosser said. "You're not as well equipped."

"Didn't know there was going to be a party," Davin replied.

"This isn't a party. It's going to be a slaughter," Bosser said, not sounding at all excited. "They tried to go after the station's principle power generators. Underestimated our defenses. My defenses."

"So why are they on level two?" Phyla said. "That shouldn't be anywhere near the generators."

The lifts were large, with curling glass borders. Almost like an onion, with points at the top and bottom, the wide floor placed in the middle. The lifts tended to run down the center of the station, meaning you were treated to snapshot views of the levels as the lift zipped through. The richer levels were near the security center they'd just left, and Phyla watched as stacks of condos, offices, and neighborhoods shot by. The population density necessitated that houses, in the form of single-family dwellings, didn't exist here. More collections of buildings that spanned the floor-to-ceiling range of the levels, looking like monoliths.

"Looks like a diversionary effort," Bosser said, watching the lift's level readout change. "They're causing some damage, but it won't matter. Their core mission failed."

Some of these buildings, in what Phyla guessed was a desperate reach for creativity, were covered in murals. One that was close to the lift as it swept past its level, had the Sun around its first floor and had bands for each planet at intervals as it went up. Most buildings were bland metallic shades, split from each other by glistening clean walking paths. Trails that Phyla noted were devoid of people.

"How would you evacuate everyone, if they succeeded?" Phyla asked.

"The ones that could get to ships would run. For everyone else, there are escape shuttles on each of the levels," Bosser said. "Enough for everybody? No. But coming to space means taking risks. This is no different."

"Do they know that? The people, I mean?"

"Phyla," Bosser glanced at her. "That's your name, right? The co-pilot?"

Phyla nodded.

"You're acting like these people are my responsibility. They're not. The station is my sole concern," Bosser turned back to the lift doors. "That might sound terrible, but consider that by saving the station, I'll save most of their lives."

"You're a regular saint," Davin said.

Outside of their talking and the lift's continual clinking and clanking as it went through the station, the guards were quiet. Some shifted as they checked power levels on their weapons, or adjusted a strap or belt. For the most part, though, they looked solid, almost robotic. Phyla was tempted to wave her hand in front of the guard next to her, just to see if he'd react.

"They're getting a continuous feed of information," Bosser said. "Comes through the helmet's ear-piece. It's why they're not paying attention to us. Because their friends are dying."

"Dying?" Davin asked.

"We don't always walk around equipped like this," Bosser said. "You know that."

Phyla took another look. The guard next to her didn't seem quite as solid this time. Those eyes were squinted, the mouth set in a grimace. Hands were tight on the grip of his rifle. The ones without assault rifles, maybe a third, had thicker armor and batons. Wreckers. The word came from a dinner conversation with Opal, on one of the many nights on the *Jumper*. Opal hadn't seemed very fond of them, but Phyla couldn't remember why.

"Ready up," Bosser announced. The lift was almost there.

The lift shot down into the shopping district, a large level near the center of the station. Its proximity to the docking bays meant goods were sent here for sale, rather than up to the smaller, wealthier levels. Wide streets encouraged all sorts of stores and stands. Every time Phyla had been here, the volume and variety of things offered blew her mind. Except this time. Now, the shopping district was full of smoke, fires, and laser flashes. At a glance, Phyla picked out the scattered remnants of the unprepared Miner Prime security, huddling behind overturned benches, crouching behind corners. The attackers seemed to have concentrated in the center of the wide street, groups of them ranging up and down and picking off people.

The lift doors opened to show a group of fighters ready for them, facing the lift with a pair of tripod turrets. Before Phyla could even fall back, several of Bosser's guards pushed forward and planted the shield sticks at the entrance to the lift. The turrets started firing, their lasers shattering against the shield's energy. One of the guards grabbed Phyla and pulled her away from the doors. And then Phyla understood why Opal called them Wreckers, and why the sniper shuddered when she said the name.

Four of the bulked-up wreckers launched themselves through the energy walls formed by the shield sticks. Phyla noticed their feet glowed, propelled by some form of thrust. The wreckers went right into the stream of laser fire from the turrets, their armor quickly glowing orange, trying to disperse the heat. One of the four stumbled as fighters lit up their smaller weapons, the armor going from orange to white, then exploding. The other three crashed into the turrets, their batons swinging with abandon.

With every swing, the wrecker's armor seemed to cool, and the batons glowed a bright white. The first hit on the turret caused the weapon to shatter and melt at the same time, molten bits of metal flying back at the now-scrambling fighters. Another wrecker caught a pair with clipping blows, sending the two spinning to the ground, but also lighting them on fire. Within a few seconds, the stand was broken.

"Clear'em," Bosser said. "Faster we're done here, sooner we get to the next level."

The rest of the guards, Bosser among them, started streaming forward out of the lift. Phyla stayed back, watched as the Miner Prime avalanche swept over the enemies, crushing them in a hail of relentless laser fire. It wasn't a fight, it was revenge.

14

PATHS CHOSEN

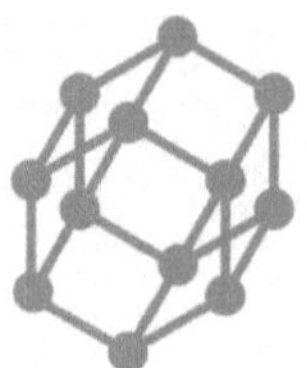

"Come with me."

That's what Viola heard the man in the mask say. She was looking back across Vagrant's Hollow, at the smoke and fire rising from the dilapidated stacks. Structural damage on a space station was always dangerous, but Miner Prime would have back-ups. Would have layers of redundancies to prevent a total collapse. But if this was happening on every level?

"You should be arrested," Mox said, and Viola turned. Mox had the masked man by the arm, a grip the man wasn't going to break. Wasn't even trying to.

"Very soon, you're going to realize the purifiers on this level are failing," the man said, voice still scrambled by the respirator. "You'll feel itching in your throat, then burning in your lungs. Your eyes will go dark within an hour. Come with me."

"The lifts are back that way," Viola said.

"Not there. Too crowded," the masked man replied. "Behind me, I can show you another route."

Mox pulled his left arm up, started speaking into his comm. Trying to warn Opal and Merc. Then he stopped.

"There's still no signal," Mox said.

"First thing that went," the man said. "Now, can we leave?"

Viola glanced at Mox, nodded. The masked man stepped away from Mox a second later, rubbing his arm. Then he held out Viola's comm, almost as if he'd forgotten he'd stolen it in the first place. Viola took it, snapped it back on her wrist. Like Mox's, it wasn't picking up a signal. Without a transponder, something to bounce the signal off of, to send and receive and target the message, the comms could only communicate directly. Meaning, Viola would have to know where to send the message, rather than broadcasting to a frequency. Doable in small spaces, not so much in a burning disaster area as large as a small town.

Then the masked man took off running again. Past a shuttered hardware store that Viola recognized from Davin's stories, the same one Lina used to run. Viola wanted to pause, to look around the place, but Puk prodded her forward.

"Exploring doesn't matter if it gets you killed," Puk whirred. "The man's right, by the way. I went up high, took a look at the main lifts. There's some kind of crazy firefight happening over there."

"Between who?" Viola said as they continued to run. Now they were on the outskirts of the level where homes bled into the solid walls. Cordoned off power stations, sanitation management, the nuts and bolts of Miner Prime kept as far away from the populace as possible. The masked man ignored all of them, kept heading to what looked like a plain section of the wall.

"Security and whoever planted those bombs, I think," Puk said. "Without a connection, I can't exactly get much more."

"Can you get a read on the air quality? Is he telling the truth?"

"I've got traces of harmful elements, but that's as likely to be from the bomb residue as any failure in the station's systems," Puk said, then hovered closer. "We're not hearing a full evacuation either. Means the station feels like there's not a risk to the whole structure."

"So their plan failed?" Not that it would have made much sense, blowing up Miner Prime with all of them on it.

"More like, not going as well as they hoped."

The masked man paused in front of a section of the wall, above which sat a yellow-bordered sign stating, in all capital font, OFFI-CIAL USE ONLY. Below the sign was a small keypad and badge reader, glowing red. The masked man walked up to the keypad, pressed a series of numbers, and the wall slid aside.

"Back-up lift. Used for maintenance," the masked man said, stepping inside.

"Wait," Viola said. "If we're going to follow you into that elevator, tell us who you are."

The man paused for a moment, then pulled off his respirator. Looked at Viola with a steady face, his brown hair popping out in different directions without the mask holding it together.

"Jairo," the man said. "And you are Viola, and you are Mox. Though I am unfamiliar with your bot."

"So—" Viola started.

"Please, in the lift. We can talk more there," Jairo said, cutting her off.

Unlike the main lifts, with their glass cages and their beauty, the lift they were in was utilitarian. No art on the walls, no glass, just straight gray metal and doors on either end. Each one had a keypad and, above, a black and red text readout telling what level they were on. The three of them, and Puk, barely fit in the lift.

"Answers," Mox said as the lift started to move.

"I can't tell you everything, not yet," Jairo said. "But I can say that this is all happening for a reason. We don't want to hurt you."

"Who's 'we'?" Viola asked.

Jairo struggled with the question. Viola could see his lips start to form different words before dropping away.

"It's better if she tells you," Jairo finally said. "I know you don't know who 'she' is yet, but I promise, you'll like her."

"Dodging," Mox said.

Then the lift dinged. They'd reached the target. Only three levels away. Viola read the readout - docking level one. The same level the *Jumper* was on though that didn't necessarily mean anything. Each docking level had capacity for a hundred ships, slotted into the circle as tightly as they could. The lift door opened into a white-washed hallway, not the main sponsor-filled paths Viola had taken the two times she'd come to Miner Prime.

"Follow me. A little longer, please," Jairo said, walking out of the lift. The man's hands dug into a pocket in his pants, came out with a small tool that, with the movement of a slider, shifted into a sidearm.

"Who're you planning to shoot?" Viola asked. "Anyone?"

"My job is to get you to the ship." Jairo led them out of the lift and down the hallway.

"What ship? Why?" Mox said.

Jairo turned back towards them, looking morose at the question. Like he'd been dreading answering it, but knew it had to come, eventually. The man took a breath, then looked at Mox.

"Our ship, the *Whisperwind*. Because we need your help to keep all the strings from falling into their grasp," Jairo said.

"That really only gives me more questions," Viola said.

"Then ask them later. We don't have time!" Jairo ran down the hallway.

It would have been easy not to follow, to turn back to the lift or wait for Miner Prime security to arrive. Mox, arms crossed and glowering at Jairo's back, probably wanted to do just that. Thing was, though, Viola was curious. What strings, and whose grasp?

"I'm going," Viola announced, then took off after Jairo. She heard Mox's feet pounding after her a second later.

15

LAST BREATH

A pair of fighters were taking potshots at the security forces through the top window, like a pair of chumps. The lower floor was empty, the doors not even locked. Rookie mistakes. Or maybe desperate ones. Merc left Opal covering the ground floor, a stately collection of trash that must have served as someone's home. Still might be if the fighters hadn't shot them too.

The stairs up to the second floor were made of loose metal plates, each one a different texture, a different former life. Merc took each one slowly. Lasers didn't make noise when they were fired, so Merc was relying on the incessant chatter coming over the fighter's comms. In the military, the idea had always been to speak your piece and keep the channel clear for critical communication. These guys, going by the constant position updates, call-outs for good shots or movement, were on an over-sharing spree. But then, most of the Red Voice with military experience had died in the war. He and Opal were up against the leftovers.

The top of the stairs broke into a wide space. The entire second floor was one room. No walls, except the outside. Beds, a generous term for the greased-up mattresses, littered the floor. Over by the front windows, burnt-edged squares cut into the siding with a torch, the two fighters were laid out, staring through scopes on out-modded rifles at the security forces below.

Merc raised his sidearm, centered it on the fighter on the right, and pulled the trigger. The stunning bolt struck the fighter in the back, filtering its electric shocks throughout the body in an instant, locking muscles and overloading nerves to where the fighter's body would stop responding. Merc had been stunned before, mostly in training exercises, and it was one of the most annoying things he'd ever experienced. Being conscious, but unable to control anything except your own breathing? For hours? He'd almost trade that for a normal blast'n'burn, take the pain but keep the sensation. Almost.

The fighter on the left managed a half-roll before Merc stunned him. Two up, two down. Beyond their gritty clothes, these guys were both wearing respirators too. All the fighters were. Maybe they all suffered from asthma. Merc pulled his comm to his mouth before remembering the things weren't working. Amazing how inconvenient it was to lose those things. Grow so dependent on being able to throw your voice wherever you want that when it's gone, you barely remember how to talk normally.

Down the stairs, back to the front room of the house, and Opal was sitting on the ramshackle collection of cushions that seemed to be a couch. Next to her, standing, was one of the Miner Prime security members, his rifle pointed at her face. When Merc came in, the security officer swiveled his gun over to him, held it high. Merc raised his hands to match, still holding his sidearm.

"You her friend?" the officer said.

"Yeah, how about you point that elsewhere?" Merc replied. Opal coughed, hard.

"She says you're—" the officer broke off, coughing into his hand, rifle waving around. Merc took a breath, felt a scratching in his throat. An itch that quickly started to burn. The officer was bent over now, still hacking. Opal stood, her hand on her mouth, walked towards Merc.

"They have respirators up there?" Opal asked.

Merc nodded. Would have said something, but his whole mouth

seemed to be burning up, his throat feeling like it had a hundred ants crawling on the inside of it, biting him everywhere. Then the officer, still coughing, fell to his knees and pulled the trigger on the rifle. Lasers shot out and scored the side of the house. Merc fell back, following Opal to the stairs, tried to go up them. He needed oxygen. Legs were burning. Got up one step.

Why was he on his hands and knees? Merc tried to focus, climb from one step to the next. Didn't feel like he could stand up. His eyes watered, tears running down his face. Opened his mouth to try to squeeze in a bit more air but damn was that a terrible idea. Nothing but more pain. Then Merc's face hit the stairs. Everything was on fire. Merc started to realize he might die like this. Not getting blown out of the sky, not getting old and passing off in his sleep. No, suffocating on crappy stairs in the middle of a space station.

And then he felt someone turning his head, felt something hard, cold, press to his face. Covered his nose, mouth and Merc felt the seal close to his skin.

"Breathe, love," Opal whispered, her voice coming out scratchy, deep.

Merc did. Overriding his panicked lungs, praying that he wasn't about to fill them with another onslaught of pain, Merc inhaled. The air that came through the respirator wasn't fresh, wasn't *good*, but it didn't burn. Merc immediately exhaled, inhaled again. Then a third time. It was like finding an oasis in a desert, he just couldn't stop. As though the first breaths weren't real. That the air might suddenly vanish. After a minute sitting there, breathing, Merc sat up on the stairs, Opal a step above him.

Then Opal walked down past Merc, into the front room. Merc, leaning on the wall, followed to see Opal detaching the respirator from her face and slipping it over the guard, who was lying on the floor. Waving Merc over, they rolled the officer onto his back, pressed on his lungs, and Merc heard the man take a deep, coughing breath through the respirator. Then another. For the next few minutes, Merc and Opal passed their respirator back and forth while the uncon-scious guard continued to suck down air.

"How'd you make it up there?" Merc said when he felt like he could talk. "I couldn't even move."

He passed the respirator back to Opal, who took a gulp of air.

"The Red Voice did this on Mars. Intentionally sabotaged air filters. Leaked toxic atmosphere through," Opal said. "It was devastating, the first couple of times. Then we all learned how to hold our breath."

"Helluva way to learn a lesson," Merc replied when he had the respirator back. He stood, went to the front windows. Looked out. A new crew of Miner Prime security had arrived, looking far more dangerous. Where the first group had been decimated by crossing fire from fighter positions, this one returned any shot with withering counter-fire, while hulking guards ran into any building that showed resistance. In the center of the cluster, sporting respirators, were Davin and Phyla, looking, to Merc's eyes, a little sick.

"Hey," Merc said, looking back at Opal. "Looks like the captain finally came to save our asses."

Opal, without a respirator, could only nod.

16

DEFENSIVE MEASURES

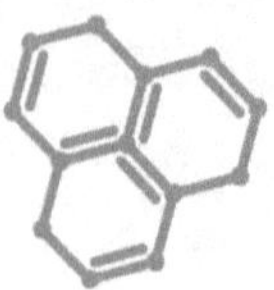

One of the *Jumper*'s commandments, in vogue since before Davin ran the ship, stated that unless cargo or people were actively going in and out, that the ramp was to be shut. No matter where the ship was. No matter the inconvenience. One of those things that Erick never questioned, never argued with, because it had proved its worth before. That time, it'd been a pack of would-be thieves on the light side of Titan, the farthest moon humanity had stuck any sizable claws into. Now, Erick watched a group of four respirator-wearing meatbags probe the *Jumper*'s closed door like an animal would a fresh kill.

"How long before I can take action?" Erick commed to Trina, who was sitting in the cockpit. Erick himself was in the bottom turret, watching the would-be raiders slink around on console screens.

"I believe Miner Prime law states that as soon as someone is attempting to acquire your items, you are licensed to defend your-self," Trina replied.

"Still nothing from Davin? Anyone?"

"I'm getting errors sending the messages," Trina said. And if she was getting errors, then something was very wrong. Erick had never seen a wizard like Trina, morphing impossible problems into textbook exercises, explaining the ways and means of extracting more energy, fixing this or that item to better than its as-new status, lost. If Erick was a physician of the body, then Trina was a surgeon of the mechanical soul.

"Then I suppose there is nothing left to do but act on our own instincts," Erick said. "And my instincts are telling me these gnats do not have our best interests in mind."

The *Jumper*'s lower turret retracted when landed, sliding up so that it wouldn't chance an ugly crash with the floor of any docking bay. To anyone not familiar with the ship's construction, the turret would just look like a rounded bump, potentially a sensor, extra cargo space, or any of a dozen things. If Erick felt like roasting the raiders, he could press the trigger on the stick in front of him and the turret would set down and start firing within a second. Of course, there was a chance it could dent the floor, but that seemed like a small problem next to the *Jumper* being hijacked.

The four of them were beneath the ramp now, looking up at it. One of them held a device, looked like a thin tube, and was pointing it at the ramp.

"You seeing that?" Erick asked.

"It's a buzzer. What they're doing is running signals, trying to find the one that'll talk to the *Jumper* like it's Davin coming back home," Trina said, as though she were describing the weather.

"I'm going to shoot them," Erick replied.

"Wait," Trina answered quickly, this time the inflection carrying a bit of excitement. "I want them to try. See if they can get in."

"You're using this as a test?"

"When will I get another chance?" Trina replied.

"I'm sure Davin would be happy to stand outside with a buzzer and try whenever you wanted," Erick said.

"Hello," said the *Jumper*'s computer, Fournine. "Hope you both know that people are trying to break in. Gonna snap through security pretty soon if someone doesn't roast 'em. Erick, I'm noting you seem to be in prime position."

"Talk to the one who brought you back," Erick said. "She wants to run a test."

"Trina, I estimate that your measures will fail in the next two minutes," Fournine stated. "At that time, the ramp will lower. The intruders will gain entry. And you will both be slaughtered in horrible fashion. I won't even feel sad as I am a bot."

"Noted," Trina said. "The last line I've got in there, it's just for buzzers. Wait for it, Erick, and then you can fire."

The four had spread out along the sides of where the ramp would go down. Three, the ones not holding the buzzer, had pulled weapons out. Small autoguns, easy to hide under a person, yet with a larger battery than normal sidearms. Fournine was right. If they made it inside the ship, Trina and Erick would be roasted without much effort. Erick moved his fingers over the trigger, waited.

Then the buzzer exploded. Simply sparked for a moment and then shattered in a burst of fire, the person holding it yelling and gripping their hand. The other three looked at their comrade, stunned.

"You can fire," Trina said, her satisfaction carrying through the comm.

Now it was Erick that hesitated. If they couldn't get in, what was the harm in letting them live? At least, that was the idea until one of the others glanced towards the lift, aimed the autogun at the ramp's border, and pulled the trigger. The lasers scored the *Jumper*'s hull, leaving black marks but not doing the slightest real damage. They had to know that wouldn't work. No small arms had the punch to get through a real ship's hull.

"They're making my ship ugly," Trina said. "Can you shoot them now?"

"But they'll never get through," Erick replied. "Seems a poor reason to end a life. Fournine, can you put up the shields?"

"Sorry, chap," Fournine replied. "Can't be done in the station. Chance of the shields interacting with the station's atmosphere. Igniting it. Which sounds like fun."

"No, no. Let's not," Erick sighed. "How about I scare them away?"

Without waiting for a consent, Erick pressed down on the trigger and dropped the turret. It came so, so very close to hitting the docking bay floor, but dodged it by a hair. The four thieves turned at the noise, one already aiming an autogun, but the man paused when the turret's cannons popped out. Erick twitched the stick, bringing the turret to bear on the aggressive one.

"Last chance to leave, friends, or this will get messy," Erick announced, patching the words through the *Jumper*'s external comm.

The four of them threw up their hands and backed away from the *Jumper*. Apparently the ship wasn't worth their lives. As they left the shadow of the *Jumper*, the four broke into a run for the lift station.

"Erick, a few minutes ago you were begging me to shoot them. Now you let them walk?" Trina commed.

"A few minutes ago they were threatening to break in. Now, they're just running away," Erick said. "I would prefer to be able to look my grandchildren in their sweet faces without knowing I killed those who didn't deserve it."

Erick flipped the turret's feed to the *Jumper*'s front cameras, which showed the four thieves making a break down the hallway. Showed the lift arriving as they passed it, showed a slew of Miner Prime security, along with Davin, Opal, Merc and Phyla coming out. Showed their weapons being aimed, the four thieves throwing their arms to the ground.

"And Justice is served," Fournine announced. Erick couldn't help but agree. Only, where were Mox and Viola?

17

______

YOUR SHIP, MY SHIP

When the security officer handed Davin and Phyla respirators a minute after they exited into Vagrant's Hollow, into the strewn collection of bodies under fire from fighters spread across surrounding buildings, when Davin understood that the home he'd grown up in had been burnt, wrecked, murdered, the captain was lost. Not that he had many friends, any friends left here. Not that there was anything tying him to the place except memories. But it still felt personal, wrong. Phyla held his hand as they watched the armed and armored security force sweep up the fighters in brutal fashion, the smoky haze of dust and broken lights shading a mustard glow over the level.

"Their operation is larger than we thought," Bosser said, walking back up to them, still standing in front of the lifts. "We're getting reports of teams running through the docking bays, sabotaging ships. Potentially stealing others."

Davin looked at the man. Bosser, outfitted in thick body armor, comm linked to a mic attached to his ear, black respirator sucking on his face. A rifle, a big two-handed one whose nozzle still glowed a slight orange from a recent firing, held in his hands. The sort of branded violence Davin hadn't ever wanted to be a part of. Only here, it seemed like they were on the same side.

"Any sign of my crew?" Davin hadn't forgotten them. Had asked Bosser and his group to look when they hit this level.

"We have two of them," Bosser said, then turned and pointed. Out of a taller house, being helped along by a security force member, were Merc and Opal. The fighter pilot noticed Davin and stuck up a hand.

"No others?"

"Not yet," Bosser shook his head, a sharp gesture, like the man didn't want to take the time to twist his neck. "I'm going to take a small group down to the docking bays. Would you like to come with? We can start at your ship."

"I'm still missing two people," Davin replied.

"They might already be down there, waiting," Bosser said. "I'm not forcing you. But we are leaving now that this threat is contained."

Contained. Right. Davin could hear the crackles and bangs as buildings succumbed to damaged parts further back in Vagrant's Hollow. There should have been cries, screams from people caught in the blasts, but the respirator attached to Davin's face provided the clue as to why those were missing. Hard to cry out if you couldn't breathe. If Viola and Mox weren't here already, they were probably dead.

"You're giving up on them, aren't you?" Phyla said as Davin turned towards the lifts.

"They would've been here," Davin replied. "Would've been with Opal and Merc."

"Maybe they know something," Phyla said as the sniper and the pilot headed their way.

"If Mox, or Viola, needed rescuing, they'd be more frantic," Davin said. "Let's get down to the *Jumper*. Like Bosser said, they might be there already."

And if not, they could always come back here and dig through the bodies to find them. Davin left that part unsaid, but he could tell Phyla was thinking the same thing. This had been her home too. He didn't know if she still had family here. Had those she loved back in that mess. That Davin didn't know bothered him on a deeper level, a missing piece of their relationship that he'd never noticed before but that was obvious now. Next time they were alone, Davin would try to rectify that.

On the lift ride down to the docking level, Opal leaned on Merc, who leaned against the wall. Ten officers and Bosser crammed towards the front of the lift, ready to burst out of the doors, a pair of wreckers in front, just as they had on the other levels. Only going down three levels meant a short trip, and thirty seconds after the lift started moving, it shuddered to a stop in front of a wide hallway linking docking bays together.

A group of four fighters, looking spooked, were running in front of the lift as the doors opened. They turned, almost as one, to see the security force emptying out and panicked, dropping their weapons and themselves to the ground. It was nice not having to watch them burn to a crisp, like the fighters on the other levels.

"Have to love an unconditional surrender," Bosser said, watching the security forces disarm the fighters and slip them into restraints. "More satisfying than a gunfight, because it shows you outsmarted them so completely that they don't even want to try."

"They're not fighters," Davin said, looking past the guns being gathered up. "Look at their belts. Those are tools for breaking encryption. And locks of a more physical kind."

Lina used to have all of that stuff, and Davin had borrowed them from her stash here and there. A mix of signal spoofers, micro-tools for taking apart panels and locks, pouches of circuit changers that would route a hard-line to a terminal you controlled. All the things you wouldn't care about if you were just trying to blow something up.

Bosser studied the fighters for a minute, then walked over to the closest one and picked him up. The fighter's were wide, mouth open, but it looked like the man's backbone stiffened right there. Forged by the fire of the experience. The fighter tightened his lips and glared. Bosser matched the stare.

"What were you doing?" Bosser asked, voice an even keel.

"Whaddya think we were doing?" The fighter replied. "Ruining your ships."

"What ships?"

"All of them," the fighter said. "You'll never get off this station."

Bosser glanced at one of the security members.

"Check it," Bosser said, then turned back to the fighter. "What's the point? We'll fix them, just like the damage you did to the other levels. A month from now, nobody will care what you did."

"Nah, but they'll care about what it allowed," the fighter replied.

"Which is?"

The fighter smiled, said nothing. Davin could see Bosser's free hand itching to pull a trigger, to punch the fighter in the throat, but Bosser set the fighter down.

"I'm getting reports of other teams like this one, sir," the security guard said. "Groups sabotaging ships. They've apparently taken out most of ours."

"Guess you're going to be stuck here for a while," Davin interjected, but Bosser ignored him and kept talking with the guard.

A loud hiss came from the *Jumper*, and Davin looked to see the ramp coming down. With it, Erick. Merc and Opal walked over that way, Phyla following. Davin took a step that way too. Technically, they were working for Bosser. But if the ice diamond sale came through, they wouldn't need Bosser's money. At least, not for a while. They could fly somewhere else, take up a more passive industry like cargo hauling. Something a little less deadly.

"Davin," Bosser said from behind him. "Your ship, it can still fly?"

"The *Jumper*'s fine," Davin said, hoping that was accurate. Erick looked calm coming down that ramp, and Trina wasn't panicking, so the odds seemed good.

"Then I'm taking it," Bosser said.

That had Davin turning all the way around, looking at the armed and armored boss of Miner Prime and taking a breath. Would have been nice if Mox were here. A bit of muscle behind Davin's back.

"Never," Davin replied. "I say the word, they'll blast the ship out of here so fast all you'll have is my laughing ass to show for it."

"Davin Masters," Bosser put himself centimeters away, the man's hot breath still smelling of coffee and sweat. "My man there tells me almost every other ship on this station can't fly. Only, one just lifted off. Without clearance. I know where they're going, and how to stop them."

"Let me guess, it involves blasting them to space dust," Davin said.

"ThreeTwelve," Bosser said, and the android appeared at his side instantly. Where the bot had been a moment before, Davin wasn't sure, but the way they could move with that precision was scary. Unnatural. "If you won't let me commandeer your ship, then allow the android and I to go with you."

"Go with us where? After the other ship?" Davin laughed. "Why would we do that?"

"Because two of your crew are on it."

18

A RELUCTANT PILOT

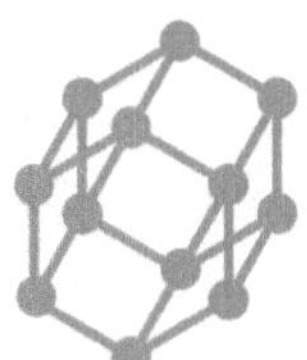

The *Whisperwind* looked like a needle, a spherical bulge at the aft end for the electrical engine and a thin point that extended forward. Even though the ship wasn't very wide, Miner Prime had docked it in a bay meant for larger vessels simply because the craft was so *long*. Viola, who'd seen all manner of builds fly in and out of the Galaxy Forge factories on Ganymede, hadn't seen one like this. A series of struts supported the ship, popping out like insect legs at various joints and intervals. The struts were gray, unpainted, which contrasted with everything else.

"It's so black," Viola said as Jairo led them towards it.

"Technically, the hull is darker than space," Jairo said. "Not, obviously, the absence of light, but because most space has star light making it brighter than black, so you see that—"

"I get it," Viola said, her eyes still tracking the ship. It looked like there was a tear in her vision, a hole right where the ship's outline was.

Viola watched the ship's ramp fold down. Not extend like the *Jumper*'s flat arm, but literally unfold one section at a time. Plates sliding off the bottom of a stack and locking in with the next one in the line. The amount of extra parts necessary to keep that from breaking would be tough to rationalize on a space ship, but it *was* cool to watch. In a few seconds, faster than the *Jumper*'s ramp, the *Whisperwind* was open for boarding.

"Who made this?" Viola asked. "I haven't seen the design before."

"You'll have to ask her owner," Jairo replied. "She's right up the ramp."

"And then you'll tell us what's actually going on?"

"All of it, I promise," Jairo said.

The man jogged across the rest of the bay to the ramp, Viola and Mox keeping pace. Puk zipped ahead of them, peeked up the ramp after Jairo. Then whirred back right in front of Viola, causing her to stop.

"There's a lot of people in that ship," Puk said. "They're packing, too. I'd, uh, recommend going somewhere else."

"Jairo?" Viola called to the man, already partway up the ramp. "What's waiting in there?"

"Nothing and nobody that's going to hurt you," Jairo called back.

An ear-splitting screech suddenly sounded through the bay as half the lights went red. Miner Prime's alarm system. Guards would be following the noise.

"You come on this ship, we live. You stay, we all die!" Jairo yelled over the alarm.

The man on the *Karat*, the guard Viola shot, who was about to murder Davin. He'd died because Viola made a choice. The raiders on the frigate, the one she'd rammed with the *Karat* in Neptune's orbit, they'd died too. Another choice, only this time, she could choose to save some.

"You don't know what's going to happen," Mox said, behind her.

"What do you think?" Viola said, the incessant blaring of the alarm continuing. "You think Bosser, this station, will let them live?"

"Do they deserve to?" Mox countered.

"Viola!" Jairo called again, his voice twinging higher with desperation. "Now!"

"I can't make that call," Viola said, then ran for the boarding ramp. She heard Mox start after her, saw Puk whirling alongside. At least she wasn't going to go alone.

Jairo waved her onto the ramp, staying ahead of her as Viola went up and into the *Whisperwind*'s entrance. The space inside was clearly not designed for cargo - it was lined with couches, tables, and gadgets Viola recognized from her father's luxury line. Not the sort of ship meant for military subterfuge. At least the noise of the alarm was blunted in here. Hanging on the walls were a series of interactive pictures, displaying moving scenes from Mars. Images of the blowing sands and giant mountains. Between them, in stark contrast to everything else, were men and women in the same gear as Jairo, only more heavily armed.

Viola realized all of them were looking at her, and some had their fingers near triggers. Stared at her with hard, red-rimmed eyes.

"Told you, bad idea," Puk buzzed as it floated into the ship.

Viola didn't have anything witty to say. She'd either be shot dead in a second, though how that meshed with Jairo's words she didn't know, or something else was going to happen. Mox's feet pounded on the boarding ramp. Jairo stared further into the ship, waving someone forward. After another awkward second, someone was pushing his way past Jairo, whispering words that sent Jairo running deeper into the ship. The man turned to Viola, reached out a hand. Even from that simple gesture, Viola could tell this guy, with his straight-up stance and firm handshake, could snap her in half a dozen different ways.

"Glad to meet you, Viola," the man said. "I'm — "

"Castor," Mox finished, grabbing the man's hand and tearing it free of Viola's. The sound of a bunch of rifles rising up, taking aim, clicked through the ship. Viola, with Castor in front of her and Mox to her right, stayed real still. She didn't scream, or flinch. Or do any of the panicked things a sane person would do in that situation. Her sheer lack of fear scared her.

"Mox," Castor said, his hand still in the metal man's grasp. "I didn't realize you were joining us."

"Didn't want to."

"Then feel free to head right back down that ramp," Castor said.

Mox shook his head, eyes never leaving Castor's face.

"Or stay," Castor said. "Either way, I'd rather not spoil the lovely ship by getting blood all over the floor."

"Your word?" Mox said.

"Don't think Viola would trust us if we shot her friend, would she?" Castor replied.

Viola caught Mox's eyes for a second and nodded. There was background there to dig through later when there weren't a dozen weapons pointed at them. Mox let go, stood back. Castor waited for a second, looking like he expected Mox to jump on him. Then he snapped his head to look at Viola.

"We need you in the cockpit," Castor said. "There's no time left to explain."

The cockpit? Viola didn't have a chance to ask any questions before Castor grabbed her hand and pulled her out of the room, soldiers moving aside, keeping their weapons trained on Mox. Puk floated along after her. The central corridor running up the *Whisperwind* was illuminated in a soft red, the floor covered with spongey plastic with a weaving, random pattern outline drawn into it. As they padded along, they passed offshoots, rooms or halls Viola didn't know. Most were closed off, sealed with black-metal doors that bore bio-scanners in the center. Older security, the bio-scanners. Easy to open, provided you had a hand from one of the crew, with or without the arm.

Finally they stopped, outside of a circular door that covered the entire width of the hallway. Castor pressed his hand to the rectangular, glowing block in the center. It flashed a seaside blue before adjusting to an emerald green and opening. Beyond was a triple-pilot cockpit, three chairs arranged in a semi-circle. One, on the right, was occupied by Jairo. The middle and the left were empty. Jairo, seeing Viola standing there, gave her a quick smile before turning back to his consoles.

"Viola, we need you to fly us out of here," Castor said, pointing at the center chair.

"Me?"

"Don't see any other Violas around here," Castor said. "Our previous pilot made a mistake, got aggressive. He didn't come back from one of the other bays. So now it's you."

Talk about expectations. Out through the cockpit window, Viola saw people starting to move into the bay, cautiously. Miner Prime security. They were running out of time. Viola pulled herself into the center seat, the one with the primary flight stick. The seat itself felt soft, almost as though Viola was sitting on air. The console in front of her was familiar, in line with what Viola used on the *Karat*, or slightly older. Jairo's preflight checks were coming up greens on the three-dimensional schematic on the console screen. A quick count showed the *Whisperwind* had a line of maneuvering jets all along its central corridor, then more spaced out on the expansion towards the back. No wings meant the ship wasn't really meant for heavy atmosphere, or at least wouldn't be able to handle any strong maneuvers.

"Puk?" Viola said. "Go back, keep an eye on Mox. Tell me if anything happens to him."

They might need her up here, but she wasn't going to abandon Mox. Puk didn't argue, spiriting itself back down the corridor. The bot wouldn't be able to do much if they decided to shoot Mox, if they already had, but at least Viola would have some warning. Castor watched the bot zip away, then sat in the third chair, his console showing weapons, defenses, and the option to take flight control if the main pilot was down.

"Ready?" Castor asked, apparently taking stock of his priorities and deciding Puk wasn't one of them.

"Ready," Viola replied, starting the jets. After a second, Viola felt a bump as the *Whisperwind* lifted off the docking bay floor. Using the flight stick and leaving the primary engines off, Viola triggered a burst from the forward facing jets at the rear of the ship. Normally, she would have rotated the spaceship and flown out face-first, but there wasn't room for the *Whisperwind*'s long stick to make that kind of turn.

"They're shutting the bay door," Jairo said.

The giant metal doors were designed to seal oxygen and atmosphere in if there was a leak or malfunction in the magnetic energy fields that kept the heavier molecules from dashing into the vacuum of space. They were also effective at keeping ships trapped. Attempting to ram the *Whisperwind* through the door would only result in the spaceship crumpling like a can.

"Unfortunately, it seems to have stuck on them," Jairo said. Viola could hear the smug in his voice. Through the cameras on the rear of the ship, Viola could see that Jairo was right: the door had come down a meter, but stopped there.

"You?" Viola asked as she continued to goose the ship backward. Castor used the intercom system to order everyone to take their seats.

"The Red Voice brought me in to hack military targets. Doing a localized break of a corporate station is cake," Jairo said. "I had control of that gate less than an hour after we landed."

"Don't brag," Castor said. "It's unbecoming."

"That's all the thanks you'll ever get out of this guy. Captain Stoneface, that's what we call him," Jairo said to Viola. She didn't catch Castor's reaction, because the *Whisperwind* was out of the bay and Viola had to focus on starting up the engines. The console led her through the standard procedure, easy enough so long as nothing went horribly wrong. Outside the windshield the docking bay receded, spun away as the bulk of Miner Prime slid into the picture.

The unobstructed view of the mottled station was . . . empty. Miner Prime should have been an epicenter of activity, ships zipping in and out in a tightly controlled dance of economic progress. Only, there were none. A glance at the sensors showed plenty of traffic, but it was all outside Miner Prime's immediate area. Ships holding orbits, following the station in its long path around the Sun. No security defense fighters either.

"They've been taken care of," Castor said, noticing Viola's furrowed brow. "For a short while, we'll have space to ourselves."

Viola didn't want to ask how. She'd seen the bombs in Vagrant's Hollow. She'd seen Jairo's hack. She knew which one of those Viola would prefer.

"Where are we going?" Viola said, throat feeling dry. "The engines are coming on-line."

"You'll like this one," Jairo quipped. "We're heading home, Viola. I mean, our species' home. Good ol' Earth, herself."

19

HOLDING FIRE

Davin hadn't ever seen the space around Miner Prime so quiet. Usually blasting off from the station required a series of back-and-forths with station coordinators, other pilots, and then a good degree of luck to get out efficiently. This time, Phyla had them cruising out of the bay in less than five minutes.

"Check the scanners. You'll find it," Bosser said, standing there in the cockpit behind the two of them. The space had two chairs, pilot and co-pilot, with a third that could fold down as needed. Bosser did not feel it was, as he was leaning over their shoulders, staring at the console.

"Funny thing about flying is that I've done it before," Phyla said. "Tracking ships too."

"What's she's too polite to say," Davin interjectedn "is back off."

Bosser moved his hands away from the chairs, but didn't actually backpedal at all. The man was still in his Miner Prime security armor, standing there as though raiders were going to board any minute. Then again, if what he was saying about Viola was accurate, they might have a close-quarters fray on their hands soon. The *Jumper*'s engines came on and shot the ship away from the station, propelling it into the darkness that was space in the asteroid belt. Other ships were out there, but the endless distance of space meant you had plenty of room to roam. Davin didn't often see other ships unless he was planning to dock with them, or they were trying to shoot him.

"You didn't know how bad it was going to be," Davin said, staring at the empty scanners.

"The first protocol of an unknown attack against the station is to remove collateral damage," Bosser replied.

"There's nobody in close range," Phyla said, then expanded the view on the console. "The closest ships are an hour out. They would've had to turn around as soon as the bombs went off. Nobody evacuated the station."

"The comms were hacked, shut down," Bosser said. "I don't know what you want me to say."

"Nothing," Davin replied. If the Red Voice had tried a serious attack, had succeeded in throwing the station into disarray, nobody would have known. Not one ship would have tried to leave the station. At least, not until it was too late.

"If you're trying to argue that something so valuable as this station and the lives on it should be better protected, should have better plans to activate in the face of disaster, then you and I are on the same side," Bosser said. "My funding comes from the charity of companies. They prefer to pay me to squash imminent threats, not over-prepare for emergencies. It's not my choice. Miner Prime is not a democracy."

"The people must love you," Phyla said.

The console beeped as they moved out of Miner Prime's proximity. Now out of danger of hitting the station, the *Jumper* could pick a path and go. Only Davin wasn't sure where Bosser wanted to point them.

"Find the *Whisperwind*," Bosser said. "It shouldn't be too far away."

To keep track of each other, ships responded to the pings of other ships with names and identification, like owner and registration. Didn't mean a registered ship wasn't going to shoot you to pieces, but at least you'd know who was doing it to you. Davin scrolled through the ships in range, winding through an alphabet of ship names like *Queen Anne*, *Starlight*, and *Johnny's Ride* before, near the bottom, finding *Whisperwind*.

"An old-model luxury liner?" Davin asked.

"Correct," Bosser said. "Run it down."

Davin highlighted the ship on the console with a tap and, on the windshield, a yellow line appeared with the trajectory for an intercept course. Phyla commed a heads-up to Trina, standing by the engines, and gunned the *Jumper*. Davin's freighter was larger, faster, and looked better armed. It wasn't even going to be a contest.

"Do you know who they're with?" Davin said. "Who's freighter that is?"

"Alissa Reinhert, a dead woman," Bosser said.

"Like Lina."

"I didn't kill this one," Bosser replied.

On Davin's waist, strapped against his thigh, was his sidearm. It was set to low power, a stunning shot. Better if the thing accidentally discharged. It would take one second to stand up from the seat, another to turn, draw the weapon, and fire. There was a chance Bosser had his own weapon, could draw faster, but he wouldn't be expecting Davin's attack. Or would he? Did it matter?

"Don't let him, Davin," Phyla said. "Not here."

Davin felt her hand on his shoulder. Felt it grip into his nerves. Lina and Phyla, always trying to keep him from doing something stupid.

"Bosser. If you're going to be here, don't say her name. Ever," Davin said, not looking back at the man. Bosser didn't reply. In the silence, they watched as the *Jumper* closed on the freighter. It was pointing away from the station, angling towards the Sun.

Davin flipped the console to an active map of the solar system, showing the *Jumper*'s projected path if it stayed on its current course. Useless, because they weren't plotting a long-range journey. But if they were, what would be the most likely target? Mercury, Venus, Luna, they were all options. Only one fit the *Whisperwind*'s line perfectly, though.

"They're setting up to go to Earth," Davin said.

"You have to destroy it," Bosser replied.

"Destroy what?" Phyla asked.

"Their ship. It can't be allowed to reach Earth," Bosser's voice had a different edge to it now, less in control. Like an opponent made an unexpected move in a game where Bosser knew all the rules.

"Why? What's on it?" Phyla replied.

"The ones who tried to blow up Miner Prime, they're on that ship," Bosser said. "They get to Earth, they'll try to do the same thing."

"Blow it up?" Davin said, incredulous.

"More or less."

The *Jumper* was close enough now for Erick and Merc, sitting in the twin turrets on the top and bottom of the freighter, to draw a bead on the *Whisperwind*. Davin could give the order and they'd vaporize the craft. Instead, Davin dialed the *Jumper*'s comm to send a direct transmission straight ahead to the luxury liner.

"Hey, *Whisperwind*, we've got a guy here that's saying you're going to kill a lot of people if we don't kill you first. What say you?" Davin spoke into the comm.

Silence followed. Davin took a glance back at Bosser, who was looking at the cockpit's comm, a small console wired into the *Jumper*'s larger transponder that sat on the outside of the ship, like it was about to jump at him. For a guy that liked manipulation so much, not knowing who was on the other end of the transmission was probably messing with him. Which felt pretty good.

"Davin? This is Viola. Please don't shoot us," Viola's voice came through clear. There was minimal interference when the ships were this close to one another. "I don't know anything about killing a lot of people."

"Hey! There she is," Davin replied into the comm. "You flying that ship, Vi?"

"I am. They lost their pilot. There's a group of twenty or so on here. One says he knows you. Castor?"

Davin stiffened. He remembered Castor all right. Remembered

how the man had nearly broken Davin into pieces on Europa, remembered how they'd managed to stun their way past him to Marl, the woman who'd started all this. Castor had been her bodyguard though it was possible he'd been more than that. Quiet, confident, never seen out and about without Marl. Davin figured he'd been sent far away after that disaster.

"See?" Bosser said behind Davin. "She is being controlled. Forced to fly the ship."

"Vi, is Castor making you do anything?"

"He's asking me. Says they would all die if I didn't help them. Mox is here too, Davin. Please don't shoot us."

"Don't listen to her," Bosser hissed. "Even if they're both on board, Castor will kill them once they've reached Earth. There's no rescue here."

"Can you shut him up?" Davin said to Phyla.

"Come to Earth with us," Viola said over the comm. "Castor says you'll understand when we get there."

Davin heard the click behind him, the *snap* as a weapon left its holster. When Davin looked back, he saw Bosser's sidearm out and aimed at his face. Bosser's hand held the sidearm steady, the weapon's barrel thick and wide, meant more for close-range intensity than the usual longer, thinner sidearms. The small switch on the back, above the grip, glowed orange. Bosser had it set to kill.

"One of the things you don't do on my ship is point a gun at my face," Davin said, looking right at Bosser's eyes.

"Destroy the ship, captain," Bosser replied. "I won't ask again."

Phyla pulled out her own sidearm, holding it to Bosser's head.

"See," Davin said. "There's no way you win here. You shoot, maybe you kill me, but maybe that wide-angle shot of yours smokes the console, blows a hole in the windshield. Or maybe Phyla just takes your head off right after. Either way, the *Whisperwind* stays fine. You ready to die for nothing, Bosser?"

They stayed that way for a second. Time for Bosser to plot his way through to his next gambit. Then the man pulled his weapon down and stuck it back into its holster.

"I never thought you were a man who could be intimidated," Bosser said. "I'm disappointed to see I was right."

"Forgive me if I don't give a shit about what you think," Davin said, turning back to the comm. "Vi, set your course for Earth. We'll match it, follow you there."

Vi clicked back on the transmission, and a moment later the *Whisperwind* adjusted their heading. Phyla matched the route, the yellow line streaking away towards the bright orange glow of the Sun. At the end of that line was a planet Davin hadn't seen in a long time. It'd be good to see some green, some blue sky. Something beyond the stale metal hallways and recycled air of space.

"When everything falls apart," Bosser said, "I hope you'll remember it was your choices that caused it."

"Can you write that down? Better yet, sew it on a shirt for me, cause I try to forget everything you say," Davin replied. "Now, please get out of my cockpit."

This time, Bosser left.

20

THE TOUR

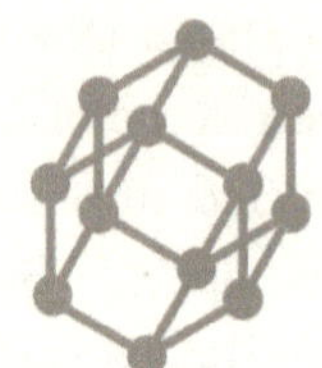

The cabin was smaller than the one Viola had on the *Jumper*. The cot folded up against the wall to give some space. No cabinet, just an older trunk that sat on the floor, covered by the cot when it was down. A pair of pod flung white light down from the ceiling. The spare gray walls had scratches calling to pictures past. On the inside of the door sat the intercom and keypad, neon-green quick buttons to each of the *Whisperwind*'s areas - kitchen, cockpit, engines, other cabins. Puk was already in a charging cradle on the small shelf, plugged in and sapping what solar energy the bot could get.

"They'll glow when you turn off the light." Jairo said next to her, nodding at the keypad, watching Viola's eyes coat the room.

The *Whisperwind*'s primary corridor split towards the aft of the ship, like a three-pronged fork. The left and right sections broke into two levels where most of the passengers and crew had their cabins. Straight up the central prong were the engines. Viola had noticed those were sealed off by a badge-locked door. Not entirely out-of-line for a luxury ship to close sensitive areas.

"Where does everyone else stay?" By her math, Viola counted ten cabins and at least fifteen crew, plus her and Mox.

"Lots of double-bunking, sleep-swapping," Jairo replied. "You're going to alternate with your friend, if that's okay?"

Share a room with Mox? Well, not really. Sleep-swapping meant they'd alternate, shift their schedules, so one was awake and moving while the other slept. Viola's engineering courses had been full of concepts like that. How to maximize productivity and minimize space. The psychological costs of losing your own home on a ship had to be balanced against the necessities of space travel.

"We'll survive," Viola said, turning around to look at Jairo. "The journey's only a few weeks, right?"

"You're the pilot."

Oh yeah. She was. Apparently the senior one too. Castor said that whenever she wasn't on the bridge, the *Whisperwind* would be coasting on auto-pilot. If there was an alarm, she'd need to make for the flight stick first thing, because nobody else would grab it. That was going to make sleeping real easy.

"I can't believe you have this many people and only one pilot," Viola said.

"You know much about the Red Voice?" Jairo said. "We're not exactly deep in the space department."

"There are plenty of people out there you could pay."

"Who'd want to work with terrorists?" Jairo said the word like it was a bad nickname, one he was stuck with despite his own objections.

"Good question," Viola said. "You still haven't told me why I'm here."

"Sure I did. We needed a pilot."

"All I did was turn on the jets and push the ship into reverse. Autopilot can get you to Earth," Viola said. "I thought it was something worse than that. Something harder."

Jairo paused for a second, eyes sifting around the room. Viola liked that look when Jairo stared over her shoulder but was very much not looking at the wall behind her. The man still wore most of the gear he'd had on during their escape from Miner Prime. The respirator and weapons were gone, stashed somewhere, but otherwise the thick beige shirt and bluish, stained pants bled into gloves and boots, respectively.

The gloves were the more interesting of the two; they looked snug. Custom-jobs that seemed to fit right to his fingers. When Jairo brought one to his face for a scratch, Viola noticed the filaments on the fingertips. Tiny ridges that'd give Jairo a good sense of touch. Made for people who were going to be doing precise work with the gloves on.

"Let me show you something," Jairo said. "It'll answer some questions, promise."

The hacker led Viola back to the main quarter, then badged into the true aft of the ship. Behind the door, the luxury treatments on the walls fell away. No calm lighting, padded floors. It was all brute force back here. They went forward a few meters and then a fork.

"Left brings you to the engine station, right brings you to the fun stuff," Jairo said. "At least in my opinion."

"Why'd you join the Red Voice, Jairo?" Viola asked as they walked.

"Why?" Jairo said. "Viola, you watch your friends and their families get oppressed over and over again by companies more interested in other things, rights get squashed time and time again because we don't really have any. It'd be enough to make most people join. Should've been enough, anyway."

Then Jairo paused, looked at Viola, and grinned an almost-manic smile. A look Viola had seen before, seen on the faces of classmates, of herself, when she was about to tackle a problem that really grabbed her. A problem so interesting all the rest of everything was going to fall away while she worked on it.

"I didn't join because of all that," Jairo continued. "I joined cause I was bored. Cause I wanted something legendary. Cause I wanted a challenge."

The words hit first as cheesy, simple bravado. But then, wasn't that what Viola had been after when she'd first run away from Ganymede? Something that would give her a purpose beyond passing tests?

"Was it worth it?" Viola replied.

They went through the right fork which led into a wider room, still not much larger than the cabins, where a single workbench was surrounded by racks of tools. The *Jumper* had a similar space, meant for the ad hoc repairs that always came up during space flight. As they walked in, the same white light from elsewhere in the ship flipped on. Jairo, though, ignored the bench, the tools, and led Viola over to a small terminal attached to the corner. It'd clearly been added, the supports for the console drilled into the nearby sides of the room. The screen itself was barely as large as Viola's hand.

"This is worth it," Jairo said, flipping a switch on the side of the terminal. It powered up, skipping past most of the corporate-branded console systems running on ships these days to load a muddy interface. A few available options presented themselves as colored circles, squares.

"Looks homemade," Viola said, leaning closer.

"My own. But that's not the star of the show," Jairo said, tapping one of the icons. The red circle flashed, then expanded to fill the screen. Lines of code displayed, and Jairo flicked the document up and down. It wasn't a simple program, whatever it was.

"Do you know what's on Earth?" Jairo said while Viola tried to pick out what was going on in the variables, the functions.

"Lots of things?"

"The androids. And with this program, right here, we can control them."

21

SUBTLE BURN

"They tell me you're the doctor," the man said from the doorway to the med room. Erick saw he was wearing a battle suit, something designed for a fight they weren't having. At least, not yet.

"So I've been told," Erick replied, continuing to bundle the new stock into appropriate drawers. Supplies were used or expired over time, so they'd picked up a few crates of new material during the short stay on Miner Prime. Right now he was taking a pack of syringes out of its brightly colored, branded box and slipping them into the cabinet with the various needles the plastic pieces would be paired with. Placement had to be precise: in a critical event, there wasn't time to try to remember where you'd put the right med, the right bandage.

The man walked into the room, ducked under the precision light attached through a swinging arm to the bed. Held out his hand towards Erick, who shook it. Bosser Oates, that's who the man's name was. Him and that android now on the ship. Davin kept referring to them as guests in public, but through a series of quick, private comms, Trina and Erick understood the real situation.

"Bosser Oates," the man said.

"Erick," the doctor replied. "How can I help you?"

With that invitation, Bosser sat down on the bed with a sigh and pulled off one of the gloves he was wearing. Beneath, on the man's left hand, there was an obvious burn marking. Red, angry, and starting to blister in a long streak across the top of Bosser's hand.

"Grazing shot. Numbed it at the time, but it's started to act up. Wondering if you have anything?"

Erick took a closer look. Standard-issue laser burn. Seemed strange that it was only bubbling up now though. They'd been in flight for hours, a shot taken back on Miner Prime would've already set in. Scarring, maybe.

"When did you say this happened?" Erick said, turning to the drawer that held the gauze.

"Don't know if you know what happened on the station before we left. It wasn't just the group trying to steal your ship." Bosser spoke like a man settling in for a long story, a prepared tale. "The Red Voice hit us across the station, and I went out with our reserve forces to make sure the damage wasn't severe."

"And you took a shot?"

"I did," Bosser said, not flinching at all as Erick rubbed some plaskin ointment over the burn. "When we made it to your docking bay, it was clear they'd sabotaged most of the other ships on the station. For a reason."

The plaskin had an aloe smell to it, a cooling, mild scent that always put Erick at ease. Except now. Patients always tried to construct a narrative, tried to frame their condition in a way that put them in a better light. Not a problem, really, but Erick knew manipulation when he heard it. Bosser wasn't settling in here for a simple burn treatment, there was something else going on.

"Do you know that your crew members are on the ship we're chasing?" Bosser asked.

"Davin mentioned it," Erick replied.

"They're helping the Red Voice. That's whose ship it is."

"Mr. Oates, if you're looking to find some sort of sympathetic anger from me, you're not going to receive it," Erick said, putting the tube of plaskin back in its slot. "While I don't approve of what they did on Miner Prime, Eden and those other organizations did equally bad or worse things on Mars."

Bosser was already nodding as Erick finished.

"Do you know where we're going?" Bosser asked.

"I'm guessing you do?"

"Earth," Bosser replied. "You have family there, don't you?"

The universe shifted with those words. Bosser knew he had a family. Which meant the man knew who Erick was, had known who Erick was. Which meant there was an agenda here, something Bosser was going for.

"I do," Erick said. "It would be nice to see them again."

"Do you know what the Red Voice is planning to do, when they get to Earth?"

"No idea."

Erick found that he was sweating, despite the cool temps maintained across the *Jumper*. He'd had plenty of difficult conversations before, but usually it was him telling the patients things that they didn't want to hear. Now, he was engaged in a back-and-forth with someone, and Erick was afraid he was very much outclassed.

"I don't know either, and that, Erick, is what frightens me," Bosser said, taking a gauze bandage and placing it over the ointment. "Because the Red Voice is desperate. When you and your team prevented their acquisition of the ice diamonds, you stole their coin. Just now, on Miner Prime, they lost most of their remaining force. The question is why. Why take this gambit?"

"You're asking the wrong person."

"Am I?" Bosser looked Erick in the eye. "The Red Voice says it exists to fight for the unheard citizens of Mars. Their members mostly have families on the red planet, people they would do anything to protect, to help. But they lost, except for this last ship. If you knew you were the only ones left to send a message, what would you do?"

"You're trying to say they're going to threaten the planet? Earth?"

Bosser shrugged.

"As I said, I don't know. But whatever they're planning on doing, it will be desperate. It will be reckless," Bosser stood up from the bed, slipped his glove back on over the gauze. "I believe you're the only member of this crew with family on Earth. The only one with anything to lose if the Red Voice gets their chance. Thank you for the assistance, Erick."

Bosser walked out of the room, Erick watching his back. The man wanted help to convince Davin to shoot the Red Voice ship down. Was betting on Erick's vulnerability. It was a good play. Erick exhaled, put his hands on the plastic covering on the bed. But nothing Bosser had said was false. The Red Voice could be planning something radical, something they couldn't expect. Something that could hurt Erick's daughter, his granddaughter.

Could he do nothing and live with the consequences?

22

INTRUSION

When the door to the cabin opened, Mox was already awake. He'd heard the steps, broken cadences signaling multiple people, approaching the room the moment they'd started up the stairs. Beneath the thin sheet, Mox primed his arms to push him off the bed and launch towards the door. Keep them pinned to the entryway and they wouldn't have a chance to surround him. The cannon normally attached to his suit whenever combat was likely was still on the *Jumper*. The sidearm taken when he came onto the *Whisperwind*, a "gesture of trust" according to Castor.

The door to the cabin was locked, but Mox wasn't surprised when the keypad blinked green. Overrides were common, necessary on most ships. The potential problems of a rogue passenger more than trumped the idea of privacy in space. The door shot open and Mox started his move.

"Don't!" Castor said, hands raised in silhouette against the bright hallway lights. Behind Castor, one of the Red Voice soldiers squatted, rifle aiming past Castor's side at Mox. On the other side, a woman with tired eyes stood and stared at him.

"Knock?" Mox asked.

"This would be easier if you were asleep," Castor said. "But at least now you can meet Alissa."

Castor went into the room, followed by the soldier and then the woman. In the cramped quarters, they all stared at Mox, who swung his legs over and sat upright. Still shorter than his visitors, but at least Mox didn't feel like a sick child. The lights in the cabin clicked on at the motion, and Mox was able to make out more of the visitors. Castor and the soldier looked the same as when he'd first boarded, hours ago now. They sported a standard assortment of military gear, even though it all looked retrograde. Purchased in the after-market, mismatched branding, clothes in different colors and types. The woman behind them was more cohesive, but looked like a civilian. They'd abandoned the Red Voice's ragged outfits in favor of something more practical, less personal.

"Mox," the woman said. "Alissa Reinhert. Nice to meet you."

Alissa didn't stick out a hand, but nodded in his direction. Mox returned the gesture, keeping his eyes on the soldier. On Castor. Too many people for an odd-hours greeting.

"When Castor told me you were here, I wanted to take a look personally," Alissa said. "I apologize for the sudden, impolite nature of our visit, but there are measures that I have to take to protect what's left of our group."

"Measures?" Mox said. "You already have my weapon."

"Not the one that matters," Castor replied, then he reached into a pouch in his pocket, pulled out a small circular pod with clamps around the outside. "Know what this is?"

Mox had seen similar things in Merc's gear. The disks would arc electricity at anything nearby that could form a current. Cause nerves to spasm.

"Have an idea," Mox said.

"I'm going to attach it to your suit," Castor said. "If you try anything dangerous, one of us can set it off. Knock you out for a while."

"It's a precaution, Mox," Alissa added.

"No," Mox said.

"Figured you would say that," Castor replied. "Which means there's a couple paths forward. Either you take stock of the fact you're very outnumbered on a ship in the middle of space and decide to accept that reality peacefully, or we do it the hard way."

"Castor, please," Alissa said, putting a hand on the man's arm. "Mox. We're heading to Earth. Once we're there, you'll be free to leave the ship. We'll disconnect the device the moment we land."

"No," Mox said, and the soldier raised his rifle. Close enough that Mox could grab and destroy the thing in a microsecond. At the same time, Castor's position put the man in a prime spot for a punch to the stomach. Delivered with the full power of the exo-suit, Castor would be taken care of.

"Then think about Viola," Alissa said. "She's in the pilot's chair right now. If you fight here, you're risking her life too."

Mox snapped into action, pushed his left arm up and into the soldier's assault rifle, shoving its aim towards the ceiling and pushing the soldier into the wall. His right arm exploded forward, grabbed Castor's uniform and hauled the man into the air as Mox stood up.

"I will not be your slave," Mox growled into Castor's face.

Then Alissa moved, pulling another of the disks out of her own pocket and slapping it on Mox's back, to the ridged line of the exoskeleton that ran along Mox's spine. Mox didn't feel the disk activate, but heard the clicks as the thing latched into place. Alissa stepped back, her hands spread out.

"Not how we wanted it to go, Mox," Alissa said.

The metal man dropped Castor to the ground, the Red Voice captain catching his footing and sticking the landing. Castor looked at Mox and nodded as though the whole exchange went exactly as expected.

"Now that you're safe, you're free to wander the ship. Work out, meet the others, doesn't matter," Castor said. "Like Alissa said, we don't want any trouble. And now that it's guaranteed, I don't see a need to keep you watched."

"So kind," Mox said.

The Red Voice trio left a minute later, Alissa tossing one more invitation to explore the ship and meet the rest of the crew. As though they were welcoming him onto a pleasure cruise. Mox sat back down on the bed. He was mechanical, at least in part. They could control him through mechanical means. Viola, however, was not. The question was, how were they going to control her?

23

WHAT TO REMEMBER

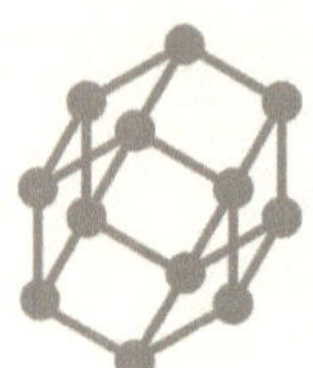

Viola turned back to the console as Castor subbed out his shift for Jairo. They never left her alone in the cockpit, but of the two, Viola could at least have conversations with Jairo. Castor spent hours glued to his comm, reading article after article or battering out messages he never described to her.

"You hanging in there?" Jairo asked, settling into his seat.

"Glad to have someone to talk to," Viola replied.

Jairo laughed. "Castor's just busy, that's all."

"Is that all? Really?"

"Okay, no," Jairo said. "He's always like that. Never know what he's doing. But I've seen him fight, and you couldn't ask for a better soldier."

Flashes of the *Karat* whirled through Viola's head.

"Have you fought before? Ever?" Viola asked.

"I try to stay away from the weapons. At least, the physical kind," Jairo said, looking back at his console. "I'm a fan of playing to strengths, and mine does not involve blasting someone."

"Instead, you're trying to subvert a bunch of androids to do it for you?"

Jairo paused for a moment, then stood up from his chair. Went over to Viola and leaned over so he could type on her console.

"Not everything I do is about harming people," Jairo said. "Watch."

The console's screen shifted as Jairo tapped away, at one point swiping his finger on an otherwise blank part of the screen. Eventually the menus faded away entirely, and the console displayed only a single blinking white square in the middle of it.

"Press it," Jairo said.

Viola did, pushing her finger lightly against the screen. The square expanded to fill the entire width, glowed brighter, then shifted. Faded away leaving only a series of branching lines and dots. Without waiting for Jairo, Viola pressed on a dot in the middle. It spun, then grew. Inside was a picture, Jairo shaking hands with Alissa. He was younger in the picture, fewer lines on his face.

"Each line takes you down a different part of me," Jairo said. "I'm making one for everyone I can, but it takes a long time."

"Why?"

"Because, no matter what happens here, there's going to be a history of the Red Voice and the people in it. I don't want us reduced to statistics, or sound bites. We're all real people, Viola."

"So were the ones on Miner Prime that your people killed."

"And if I could make this for them, I would," Jairo said. "Go up the left branch next."

Viola slid her finger up the branching path to the left. The next picture showed Jairo in a garden, holding a large head of broccoli, an older woman laughing next to him. In the background, the rolling red mountains of Mars scaled the horizon.

"My mother. She always kept me grounded. The idea that here we were, on Mars, and what really mattered was eating your vegetables. Keeping the garden growing," Jairo said.

"You're going to make me homesick," Viola replied.

"Keep going."

Viola shook her head. "Why are you doing this, Jairo?"

The hacker's smile left his face, and his eyes slipped away to a corner of the cockpit.

"Because I don't want you to think I'm a bad person," Jairo said. "It's a failing of mine. The faceless masses, you know, the people out there, I don't really care what they think of me. But people that I'm close to? It matters that they don't see me as a killer."

"I don't," Viola said, and the words surprised her. Before, back on Ganymede, the Red Voice had always seemed a band of terrible murderers. Planting bombs in habitats and wrecking an ideal society on Mars for political points. "I used to, because it was easier than reasoning with the actual problems."

"The actual problems?"

"I didn't realize till I went to Europa that it's a hard life for most people. I was sheltered on Ganymede. Good family, plenty of coin. Education," Viola said. "Then I'm here with a bunch of people that wouldn't hesitate to kill for their goals, and it's because so many of the things in their lives wouldn't hesitate to kill them if it came to it."

Jairo pushed the next dot on the console, this one on a different branch. It was a shot of the *Whisperwind*'s cafeteria. Jairo was there, along with some of the other fighters. They were laughing, playing a game on a large table. It reminded Viola of nights in the *Jumper*, playing cards with Erick and Mox, or swapping stories with Davin and Merc.

"It's not always so dark," Jairo said, his face brightening. "Hey, you want to make one?"

"Make one?"

"Yep. You're one of us now, at least for this trip," Jairo said. "I'll show you how."

"I don't have any pictures, though."

"Sure you do. We can pull them from the *Whisperwind*'s security cameras. There's got to be some of you smiling."

Jairo kept right on going, talking through the process of finding the pictures, downloading them into his program, and building out the branches. His enthusiasm was infectious. That zest for keeping the human part captured. Viola caught herself looking at Jairo's grinning face as he went through another series of security stills.

Maybe she'd made the right call, jumping on this ship.

24

CHANGE THE CODE

The android hadn't moved from the cargo bay for hours. Trina watched it on the *Jumper*'s camera, the bot standing there and staring at the wall. It was wearing a lighter version of Bosser's suit, a thinner blue criss-crossed with a shoulder strap holding the customary android long knife, along with a belt bearing twin sidearms. The idea of a robot that took commands from an enemy, or at least not a friend, having that kind of weaponry on their ship wasn't comforting. But then, Trina wasn't the captain.

"Fournine, given your, uh, experience in this area, what do you think?"

The former android, now ingrained in the *Jumper*'s computer system, was, in Trina's mind, the best thing to happen to the *Jumper* in years. Before, the computer would accept rudimentary queries, like the status of the engines or the amount of energy being converted by the solar panels. Fournine, though, could actively evaluate what Trina was asking. Better yet, it had a personality.

"ThreeTwelve is probably in a power-saving mode," Fournine replied. "Like that sleep you're always doing, but less vulnerable. Come close, and it'll activate. Probably chop your head off. Which would be messy."

"How long can they go without a recharge?"

"An Earth week," Fournine replied, its voice coming through the *Jumper*'s intercom system, sounding like a slightly insane butler. Viola programmed that one, using a standard voice and then randomizing the pitch, so that Fournine's voice would occasionally swing up or down octaves. It was both maddening and, given Fournine's predilections to the absurd, appropriate.

"So ThreeTwelve is fine to move around, then?"

"It would be likely."

Trina glanced at the engine readouts next to her. They had matched the *Whisperwind*, were tagging along behind it without a lot of effort. The luxury craft was older, its engines not up to the speed the *Jumper* could produce. Not designed for the kind of long-range interstellar travel that necessitated more power, and by extension, more space devoted to those engines. As such, the *Jumper* was humming along without any problems. Which meant she could step away for a bit.

"I'm not too comfortable with an active android on this ship," Trina said, moving from the engine room to the workshop. According to the *Jumper*'s internal clock, it was approaching midnight. Most of the ship was quiet, asleep. Trina should be doing the same, but there was this problem she had. This issue with curiosity.

"You and me both," Fournine replied, its voice coming out of the closest comm, as though the computer were walking alongside Trina.

"If ThreeTwelve was our android, though . . ." Trina trailed off.

"You want to use Viola's hack," Fournine said, and Trina nodded. Viola had found, on Miner Prime, that by accessing the android's core memory in its head, a decently skilled programmer could overwrite the instructions there. Could gain control of the machine. The trick was letting an android give you that chance.

Her workshop seemed to only get more cluttered. A workbench stretched the length of a wall though it was covered in a series of wrenches and screwdrivers. Chains dangled from the ceiling, about three meters high. They ended in clasps, so heavier gear could be suspended while being worked on. The rest of the room was surrounded by shelves, banks of drawers with screws, nails, and adhesives. Each one had a scrap-metal label fastened to it, the correct contents etched into the badges. Trina could have used the same plastic notes that Erick stuck all over the med room, but they didn't seem to fit the theme. In the middle of the workroom was a drain that went directly to an ejection airlock, where any dangerous chemicals, spent fuel, or toxic what-have-you could be launched into space.

Trina went over to the workbench, the very same spot where Fournine had first been hacked to join the Wild Nines. Underneath the bench, in the top drawer, was a small device shaped like a square with a single rounded-off end. In the middle was a circular button that, when pressed, would emit a localized electromagnetic pulse. On a ship, the idea of something that could knock out electronics was horrifying. No system for recycled air, no life. That's why the device only had a meter or so of range. No risk to vital systems.

By the same token, if something was going catastrophically wrong, Trina could take the tiny EMP to the problem and shut down the malfunction.

"Remember the rapid restart," Fournine cautioned. "ThreeTwelve will be awake before the EMP is ready to go again. Unless you're significantly faster than most humans, I see this attempt ending in your demise."

Trina looked at the chains.

"How long will it take?" Trina said. "To start back up?"

"Ten seconds," Fournine replied. "At eleven, Trina, you will be so very dead."

"It'll have to be enough," Trina said. "Bring the android in here."

Fournine couldn't do that physically, of course, but Trina hoped the bot could come up with something enticing. Something that would draw ThreeTwelve into the workshop. There weren't any screens in the room, so Trina didn't know what was happening, but before too long the sound of footsteps landing on the *Jumper*'s hallway approached. Trina flicked the switch on the EMP device, hearing the tiniest of whines as it prepped itself to overload any circuitry where she pointed it. Trina held the device in her right hand and leaned against the workbench, trying to ignore her beating heart.

ThreeTwelve walked around the doorway and into the workshop. Its head was feminine, long and angular. No hair, just olive-colored plaskin giving play to ThreeTwelve's dark eyes, lips. One of the android's hands drifted towards its right sidearm.

"Your computer said you needed my assistance," ThreeTwelve said. "Speak."

"Did you know that Fournine, our computer, was once an android like you?" Trina asked.

ThreeTwelve didn't show the slightest reaction.

"We are computers. Our bodies are incidental," ThreeTwelve replied.

"Stuffy, aren't you?" Fournine said over the intercom. "Did Bosser even give you a personality?"

"Yes. One that's suspicious of bots with personalities," Three-Twelve said.

"Do you see these chains?" Trina pointed. "I need help to move them up, from some of the work we were doing on Miner Prime. Normally, Mox would help me, but he's not here."

ThreeTwelve's eyes followed the chains up to the ceiling, looked at the pulleys that would allow the chains to curl around the rafters and keep themselves out of the way when not in use.

"This seems like an unusual task for this time of night," Three-Twelve said, returning its gaze to Trina.

"Have you ever known a human to be logical?" Fournine quipped. Trina shrugged. ThreeTwelve hesitated a moment.

"I have not," ThreeTwelve said finally, walking over to the work-bench. "Tell me what you would like me to do."

The android was directly beneath a pair of the chains, clasps open and ready. Trina took a breath, pulled out the EMP, and as ThreeTwelve turned, pressed the button. The device didn't make a noise, didn't even appear to do anything, but ThreeTwelve jerked suddenly, as if going into a seizure.

"Ten," Fournine said.

Trina pressed a down arrow on a keypad sitting on the workbench's side and all four of the clasping chains dropped until they hit the top of the workbench.

"Nine."

Grabbing the first clasp, Trina slipped it around the android's right arm. Snapped it shut.

"Eight."

Trina moved a dial on the clasp, and it tightened until it locked in on ThreeTwelve's arm. Right on the wrist.

"Seven."

The next clasp on the left arm. Trina whipped it around, snapped it on.

"Six."

Moved the dial, shutting the clasp tight.

"Five."

Now the legs. Only, ThreeTwelve wasn't up on the workbench and there was no way Trina could lift it up there herself. Trina reached for the keypad, slapped the chains up.

"Four."

The chains lifted ThreeTwelve up in the air. Pulled the bot above the workbench, suspended. Trina pushed the android, so that Three-Twelve swung over the workbench and pressed the down arrow on the keypad to send the android crashing back down on top of it. Without resistance, the legs splayed out, but at least ThreeTwelve was in the right spot.

"Three."

Trina grabbed the next clasp, snapped it onto ThreeTwelve's right leg.

"Two."

Pressed the dial with one hand, reached for the last clasp with the other.

"One."

Snapped the last clasp around ThreeTwelve's leg. Reached for the dial.

"Run!" Fournine barked and Trina dove back, falling on the workshop's ground.

ThreeTwelve's eyes sparkled as the android surged back to life. It tried to move its arms, its legs. The chains rattled against the motion, their slack pulling tight as soon as ThreeTwelve tried to move off the workbench. Clashing and clanking noises erupted as ThreeTwelve attempted to thrash its way out of the clasps. At first the motion was random, like a child trying to twist itself free of blankets, then ThreeTwelve became deliberate, testing each of the clasps. Tugging at its arms, then its legs. Trina held her breath as it went for the left leg, the loosest clasp.

The chain held. Then ThreeTwelve raised its head, looked Trina straight in the face, and said nothing. It was time to get to work.

25

———

CAPTAIN'S MEETING

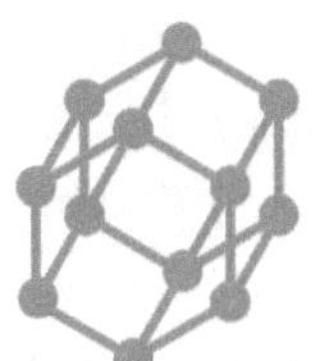

lissa Reinhert's quarters were the largest Viola had seen on the *Whisperwind*, which meant they had enough for a queen-sized bed, a desk, and a full wardrobe for clothes. A private bathroom and shower were separated by a thin door. The idea of luxury was here, but it seemed as though pieces were missing. The desk was plain, the bed covered in utilitarian white sheets, no random ornaments on the floors or sitting in the corners. The walls bore the only decoration; as in most of the rest of the ship, pictures of Mars.

"The artwork is, I'll grant you, a little bland," Alissa said as Viola looked around. "However, it serves a purpose. A reminder of what we're doing here."

"Fighting for Mars," Viola said.

"Exactly. Or rather, for the people there who cannot fight for themselves," Alissa said.

"But you lost that fight." Viola folded her arms.

When Jairo told her this morning that Alissa, the leader of the Red Voice, wanted to talk to her, Viola was perplexed. Not that the *Whisperwind* needed her at the pilot's chair, really. They were days away from Earth yet, and unless the *Jumper* decided now was the time to immolate them, Viola didn't have much to do but make sure the autopilot wasn't going rogue. Mox hadn't come by that morning either. In fact, she hadn't seen the metal man for nearly a day. Not since he'd told her he was going to sleep for his shift yesterday. So when Jairo asked if Viola could take a meeting, at that moment, Viola didn't have any reason not to.

"We did," Alissa said. The captain was wearing what Viola could only describe as lounge wear, a set of barely-above-pajamas outfit that seemed designed for an evening with movies and a couch rather than commanding a military force. Then again, Alissa looked exhausted, her wispy blond hair tied back into a loose bun, strands of it escaping to frame the lines in her face. Lines Viola initially took for wrinkles, but, as Alissa came closer, turned into scars.

"Last time I met one of your lieutenants, a man named Bakr, he was trying to kill us," Viola said. "He didn't seem to think you'd lost."

Alissa smiled, like a person enduring a sickening situation that they couldn't escape.

"Bakr was always that way. A believer in the cause," Alissa said. "He saved my life. Back in the inferno. When they tried to burn us alive on Mars."

"They?"

"The same people trying to catch us now," Alissa replied. "Not your friends, of course. Though I wouldn't be surprised if Bosser paid them to do it."

"You were fighting against corporate control, right? The idea that Mars should be a government, instead of a place like Miner Prime?"

"As you said, we lost that fight," Alissa went back to the desk, pulled out the chair, and sat in it. "Sorry, I've been on my feet most of the night."

Viola took the cue, looked for another chair. There wasn't one. Alissa motioned towards the bed and Viola sat on it. The mattress was firm, the sheets thin. Scratchy. The leader of the Red Voice was not living the good life on her own ship.

"Why did you send Jairo to find me?" Viola said. "There had to be other pilots."

"Look around you. We don't have the money anymore to hire anyone. We need people who still have humanity in their hearts."

"Says the person that just tried to destroy an inhabited space station."

Alissa grimaced.

"I can't hide the fact that we aren't always better than the ones we claim to fight," Alissa said. "But we were desperate. Without the ice diamonds, we needed funds, and support."

"Jairo seemed to imply it was all about me. Getting me on this ship."

"Our hacker friend doesn't always have the entire picture," Alissa said. On the desk, built into the wall behind it, was a console. Alissa tapped a couple of buttons on the screen and then waved Viola over. Scrolling on the console was headline after headline attributing the attack to the Red Voice. Most of the accompanying columns excoriated the attacks, but a few, a scant few, seemed to argue the Red Voice had been pushed to extremes by underhanded tactics, by desperation.

"So what is the 'entire picture'? That you're abandoning your principles to kill at random?"

"Look at this ship, Viola," Alissa said. "The Red Voice is nearly gone. Our entire goal at this point is to make such a scream as we die out that others will hear us for centuries. Some will listen. Take up our cause. And maybe Mars will find itself free one day."

"What do you mean, scream?"

Alissa flipped off the console, stood up from the desk. Put a hand on Viola's shoulder. It was a firm grip. Alissa might look frail, tired, but there was real strength beneath those scars.

"It is better if you don't know," Alissa said. "That way, when they come for you later, you won't need to lie."

Alissa nodded to the door. Gave Viola a gentle, guiding push.

"That's it? That's all you wanted to talk to me about?" Viola asked.

"Jairo says you can be trusted. I wanted to see if he was right," Alissa said as the door back into the hallway shifted open.

"Was he?"

Alissa just put on that tired smile again. Then the door shut between them. Viola stood there in the hallway. What did any of that mean? Mox. Mox might have an idea of what to do next. He'd dealt with these kinds of people before. Ones that didn't say what they really meant.

Viola walked down the hallway towards their shared room. After all this was done, she was definitely going back to the equations. To the schematics and the ins and outs of creating ships. At least those were clear.

26

___

LAUGH IT OFF

The spray coated the Viper's left wing, the last remaining part, in the dark green color of a thick jungle. Merc crouched on the upper body, already painted and dried a few days earlier. Vacuum vents, installed in the *Jumper*'s bay at Merc's insistence when he came aboard, roared behind him. They'd suck out any rogue particulates, spit them into tiny airlocks that cycled continuously to send the poisonous stuff into space. When Davin asked whether they were really necessary, Merc came back with a ready list of Viper repairs that could send all kinds of microscopic hell floating through the *Jumper*'s air vents. From paint chips to metal shavings when repairing damaged pieces, to the possibility of battery leaks and the acidic fumes that could come if one of those babies burned loose. It'd been enough.

"So you're the hotshot!" called a voice over by the door of the bay. Merc looked up, the mask covering his eyes catching glare from the bay's lights. It was a man, and it definitely wasn't Davin or Erick. Which meant . . . Bosser.

Merc put down the spray nozzle. It was a hose connected to a bigger barrel of the stuff. They'd picked it up from the dockmaster at Miner Prime. Had to repaint the Viper any time Merc was actually hit in combat as he'd been over Neptune. Like turning a new leaf, a new page, whatever. Point was, *this* Viper, the green one, hadn't been hit yet.

"Not sure anyone calls me that but me," Merc said, jogging over to the wall of the bay and flipping off the fans. They whirred down slowly as though trying to give Merc a chance to rethink his decision. Bosser was continuing into the bay, though, like the man wanted a conversation.

"Well, they should if half of what I've heard about you is true," Bosser said, extending a hand.

"Oh yeah? What'd you hear?" Merc replied, shaking it. There was some gauze wrapped around Bosser's hand, it tickled Merc's palm. Guy is already getting hurt in space, and there hasn't even been a fight yet.

"Eden didn't hold back. Said you out-flew the raiders, even though you were outnumbered," Bosser said. "So I took the liberty of looking you up. Seems you're ex-military. Earth-side."

Merc supposed a normal person might hear that they'd been investigated, researched before being talked to and find that weird. But that was how it worked in the military, how it worked when Davin signed him on. A pilot's record was everything. What Merc didn't understand, though, is why Bosser was coming here to tell him this. Why not talk in the kitchen? Or in the main cargo hold? Or, you know, why talk at all?

"You got me," Merc said. "I, uh, didn't look you up."

"You wouldn't find much," Bosser replied, not remotely bothered. "I'm not what you'd call flashy."

Merc stood there. Looked over Bosser's shoulder at the door out. Nobody. Just him and Captain Awkward Conversation here.

"So," Bosser continued. "I wanted to ask what you think about the people we're chasing."

"What about them?" Merc said. "They've got Viola and Mox. There's no way they're going to get past Earth's defenses, so I figure we'll just pick them up when they surrender."

"You think they don't have a plan? That they're flying to Earth knowing full well they're never going to land there?"

"Always figured it for a stunt," Merc shrugged. "The Red Voice? They were crushed. What's one ship going to do except stage some protest?"

"They nearly took out Miner Prime," Bosser said.

"You and I both know that wasn't anywhere close to destroying the station. All they did was bomb an area you don't patrol much, maybe take shots at some stores. Mess with some ships," Merc crossed his arms. "It was a desperate move."

Without the vacuum vents going, the bay was starting to smell like the paint. A loose, tingling sensation in the nose. Another few minutes and they'd both start getting giggly. Another few after that and they'd lose coordination. Without spraying more that was probably as bad as it was going to get. Even so, Merc wasn't thrilled this guy was stopping his work to have some sort of heart-to-heart about the Red Voice.

"Does this have a point?" Merc said before Bosser could continue.

"A military officer would look at this target, the *Whisperwind,* as an easy kill. A sure way to end a threat," Bosser said.

"So that's what you want."

"Wouldn't your commanders have said the same thing? Wouldn't they have ordered you to do it?"

"Maybe so," Merc said. "Good thing that, like you said, I'm *ex-military.*"

Merc could see the winding gears fall into place inside Bosser's head. The eyes changed, squinted a little, the man's mouth set into a frown. Nobody liked to lose, and Bosser looked like one of those types that didn't lose very often. Merc remembered he didn't actually have a weapon on him here. Hands only, but gloved, thick ones for blocking toxic chemicals. If Bosser wanted to push his point a little more physically, Merc would be game.

"I can see there was a reason for that," Bosser said, then he stepped back. "If you change your mind, if you understand what's most important, let me know."

Merc caught motion behind Bosser, smiled.

"You want to know what's really important?" Merc said, then nodded over Bosser's shoulder. "That is."

Opal leaned against the doorway, glaring at Bosser. The man in the middle shook his head and walked out of the bay, giving Opal the slightest of nods as he passed by. Opal was geared up for maintenance work, sporting the same all-covering, stained suit that Merc was wearing. After the painting was done, they were going to clean out some of the Viper's internals. Make her really sing.

"What'd that jackass want?" Opal asked.

"Thought I'd blow up Vi and Mox, just cause he asked nicely," Merc said.

Opal narrowed her eyes, looked back at the doorway where Bosser had just vanished.

"I don't like the idea of him trying to mess with us," Opal said.

Merc laughed.

"You think any of us are going to listen to him?" Merc said. "Guy's a loon, he thinks any of us are going to turn."

Opal didn't laugh with him. She just closed her eyes for a second.

"I hope you're right," Opal said. She walked over to the vents, punched them on, and any more talking was overrun by the loud roar.

A GOOD CREW

D o you remember that run to Phobos, the first-timer pilot that thought he knew everything?" Phyla said. In front of the cockpit, a kilometer ahead, the *Whisperwind* churned through space on its way to meeting Earth.

"Wasn't that where he nearly crashed the freighter?" Davin replied. The captain was looking fresher this morning. The third day since leaving Miner Prime.

"It was. I remember you were so mad he nearly cost us the contract."

"Atmosphere. The moron forgot that Phobos doesn't have one," Davin grinned, leaned back in his seat. "We've had some good runs, haven't we?"

"More than a few," Phyla said.

They'd never budged far from barely making it, though. Always concerned with the next contract, always pouring anything leftover back into the ship. The *Whiskey Jumper* was a beautiful mess, now, a hodgepodge of parts and upgrades that always seemed to be changing.

"What do you think he's afraid of?" Davin asked, the smile dying away.

"Bosser?" Phyla replied. "Control, probably. He needs it."

"Just like you." Davin lit up a side of his face to cut the words.

"Like me? You think I'm controlling?" Phyla said, eyebrows rising. "You're the one whose got to choose all the contracts, have a say over anything big we buy. Who sits in that chair."

"I'm sitting here 'cause it's the comfiest one in the ship," Davin said.

"Hah, that's what you think. I swapped the stuffing out months ago. You've been sitting on trash."

Not entirely true, but what did it matter. The moment was more important. They were on a ship with a conniving murderer in Bosser and his slavish death-bot ThreeTwelve. They were following a group who'd just tried to destroy a civilian space station and who was holding two of their friends hostage. Gotta take what light she could find.

"We're going to have to do something, you know," Davin said. "To Bosser. For Lina."

"She wouldn't want you to kill him."

"I know," Davin said, rubbing his face with his hands. "If that's what I thought, I'd have had Trina blast him with the turret back on the space station. Blame it on the Voice."

"Think like her, Davin," Phyla said.

Lina had always seen the universe as a puzzle to be solved. Rather, a series of puzzles. Everything was a game to plot out, a mystery to sleuth, and when Lina had the answer, she was bored. But until then, tenacious. Phyla blinked, turned to the console. Flight routes, the *Jumper*'s internal cameras, and a scrolling series of headlines. Most were about the attack on Miner Prime. Phyla swiped past a few describing the chaos, the repair efforts, the call for androids to be activated to hunt down the Red Voice once and for all.

"That one makes a good point," Davin said, leaning over. "Bosser could've sent the bots to take care of them a long time ago."

"Why didn't he?"

"Coin," Davin said. "Think about it. Bosser waits till an entire planet becomes desperate enough to pay for that many androids?"

"Only now they're ruining his game?"

"Still doesn't make sense why he's so afraid about Earth, though," Davin said. "What does he care if they make a statement? Bosser and the androids would make even more coin if everything was chaotic."

"I hear escorts also do well when things get messy."

"Hey. I thought you wanted out of this business."

"I do," Phyla said. "Would love a return to the good runs, ferrying supplies. No lasers, no getting trapped in shuttles sent rocketing into planets."

Davin nodded, like he agreed. Except every time Phyla tried to talk about what would happen after, when they were cleared of the murder charges and let finally free, Davin always went silent. Retreated into some discussion with himself.

"Davin?" Phyla said. "Talk to me?"

"I don't know," Davin raised his hands slightly, a half-shrug. "I don't want to get shot, same as you. Only, I don't think it's going away that easily."

"You mean the charges?"

"That's on Bosser to clear. I mean Lina. I mean getting our reputation back. We were used, Phyla."

"We're still being used," Phyla said. "By Bosser, and by the Red Voice, holding Mox and Viola. I said I wanted to go back to the old days, but I want to do it on our own. Not because we were forced."

"So you'll stay with me? Even if I drag us into Hell?"

Phyla laughed.

"You haven't scared me away yet," Phyla said. "Besides, I figure any terrible idea you get on your own is going to haunt me, regardless. Better to make sure you can actually pull it off."

"Tell you what, we get through this, get our freedom back? We'll take any run you want. Go anywhere you'd like."

"Don't make promises you can't keep, captain."

"Fair. How about, we'll go anywhere you like so long as there's a job and coin when we get there?"

"That's more like it," Phyla said.

Davin looked out the cockpit, at the stars washed out by the Sun's ever-present glow. Phyla remembered how strange that was; the first days off of Miner Prime and out of its artificial day and night. The Sun always there if you looked out the right window. Relying on timed lights inside the ship to queue her body for sleep. When Davin asked her to learn to fly, to be his copilot and eventually *the* pilot, Phyla had looked at the nothing waiting for her in Vagrants Hollow and fled to the stars.

"If you'd asked me a year ago if we could survive this, I'd have said you were crazy," Davin said, still looking at the stars. "Now, I'm hanging on. Playing each hand as it's dealt to us. But I like our chances."

"You've got a good crew, a good ship. Can't ask for much else."

"And a damn good pilot. Don't forget that."

"Was waiting to see if you would remember," Phyla said.

Davin's smile was genuine, the crinkle around his eyes bringing Phyla back to that first launch, when the universe was wide open. Just a little longer, and they'd have that wonder back.

28

QUESTIONS

He'd seen the video a thousand times. Maybe more. It played silently as Mox stood in an empty hallway on the *Whisperwind*. Hard to find these on the crowded ship, but with Viola in their cabin, there wasn't a good option for solitude.

The comm projected the image into the air before his eyes. Four tall buildings spaced out around a large courtyard, connected by raised hallways spanning the gaps high above the surface. The Moon's gravity gave architects unique opportunities and soaring structures were becoming common in Luna. Only these buildings wouldn't be standing much longer. A blue nova appeared in the center of one of the arcing hallways, followed by similar explosions in the others. Nova bombs, detonating their way through electric currents. Super-heating and frying circuits and the metal that held them together.

The angle of the shot, taken from one of Luna's many surveillance cameras, didn't catch much of the courtyard. Mox couldn't see himself down there, but he knew what he'd been doing at that very second. Pressing against the crowd. Turning towards the first explosion and attempting an impossible rescue.

"Luna, right?" Alissa said, coming out of her cabin and pausing in front of Mox.

Oh, there'd been a reason he chose this hallway. Empty because only one cabin sat at the end of it. The cabin holding the most important person on the ship.

"I have questions," Mox said.

Alissa gestured back inside her room.

"I might have answers," she said. "I prefer long conversations in more comfortable places."

Mox followed the Red Voice leader into her cabin, watched as she immediately went to her desk, opened a drawer and pulled out a small remote. Alissa turned back to Mox and held the square up.

"This activates the disk on your back," Alissa said.

"I figured."

"When you've seen so many friends die, you start getting a little paranoid," Alissa said, sitting down in the chair. "So you wanted to know about Luna?"

"Why did you do it?"

Alissa cocked her head. Eyebrows raised.

"I didn't. The Red Voice had nothing to do with Luna."

"Liar," Mox felt the anger tighten in his throat. So many died that day. Erin died that day.

"No," Alissa said, and now her look turned to steel. "The Red Voice is, was, has always been about Mars. Others saw our example and tried to replicate it."

"Then you are still responsible."

"And what about the corporations that drove us to this? Are they not responsible too?"

Mox took a step closer to Alissa. Felt the power humming in the exoskeleton. He was within reach. She would have to press the remote quickly before he knocked it out of her hands.

"They didn't bomb the towers," Mox said.

"What do you want me to say?" Alissa said. "Those weren't our soldiers. They were Luna's own people, making their own statement."

"Because of you."

Erin's face, those twin strands framing her happy eyes. All those mornings they shared, giving bits and pieces of themselves to each other, wiped away because some copycat killers thought they had a cause. Because they saw Alissa doing the same thing on Mars and wanted their part.

Mox didn't think. He reacted. His left arm shot out, boosted by the exoskeleton, and knocked the remote from Alissa's hand. It ricocheted off the wall and landed on her bed. With his right arm, Mox swiped at Alissa's head. But the woman was faster than Mox anticipated. She pushed herself down and out of her chair, sliding beneath his punch. Through his legs. He turned, found Alissa already curling forward onto her feet.

"I didn't set those bombs. We never advocated for civilian targets," Alissa said, backing away.

"Then what was Miner Prime?" Mox replied, dropping into a boxing stance.

"Desperation. Unfortunate, but necessary," Alissa said. The bed was behind her, the remote sitting on a pillow. Alissa moved towards it and Mox charged, reaching out with a right sledgehammer blow where Alissa would have to be as she went for the remote.

Only she wasn't there. Alissa twisted back out of the feint and tripped Mox as he went by, her leg connecting with his right ankle. Mox hit the ground, grabbed the side of the bed and hauled himself up.

"I don't make excuses for what we do," Alissa said, behind him. "It's a dirty universe, and we're fighting for survival. If you think I ought to die for that, then that's your choice. But we didn't plant those bombs."

Mox reached for, grabbed the remote. Looked at it. Blinked. Stared harder. It . . . It wasn't a remote at all.

"A toy?" Mox said, anger falling away as he turned around.

"It plays a song if you press the button," Alissa said, a half-smile cracking her face. "One of the first presents my parents gave me, to help me through our first space flight. I was nervous, and they said that as long as the song played, I'd be safe."

Mox couldn't help it. He pressed the button. Nothing happened.

"It died a long time ago," Alissa said. "I keep it here. One day I'll get it fixed."

"Then the disk, on my back?"

"We can activate it with the comms," Alissa said, holding up her wrist.

"Then why didn't you?"

"Mox, we need Viola. And to keep her with us, we need you. I need you," Alissa said. "Trust me. We're not your enemy."

Mox set the toy back down on the bed. Made for the exit.

"I'm not your friend," Mox said.

29

INBOUND

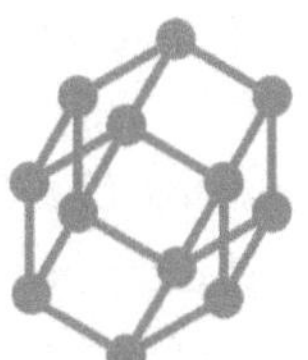

The pictures always showed Earth as a pristine blue, green, and white ball spinning perfectly through space. The videos showed the clouds shifting over the surface, various satellites and space stations popping over them like dirt specks on a cloth. To see it in person, though, Viola could only think of one word. *Home.*

"This is your first time seeing her?" Castor asked, sitting in the co-pilot's chair. "Jairo's too."

The hacker had moved over to stand behind her, hands on the shoulders of Viola's seat. They all watched as the *Whisperwind* started its slowdown. Viola had boarded the ship because of Jairo's call for help, but this view, this was worth it all by itself.

"Someday, you're going to have to program me to feel the same way you look right now," Puk said, hovering behind them.

"I don't think I can," Viola said, not turning away.

"Jairo?" Puk said the hacker's name the same way the bot addressed Mox. Like a friend. They *had* been spending most of the journey together, with Jairo teaching her about his program, about the *Whisperwind* and Viola giving him piloting lessons and bringing

Jairo's head out of the code and into the mechanics of actually putting a bot together.

Mox. Viola blinked. The metal man hadn't been around much. Seemed almost to be avoiding her. Only grunting hellos when they passed each other switching shifts in the room. She was going to call him on it, trap him and make Mox explain what the hell was going on. But then Castor called, said it was time to get ready.

"So what's the approach?" Viola said. "Where are we landing?"

"The Andes," Castor said. "I've already put the precise coordinates in."

Viola glanced at the console. The flight path was sitting there, waiting for her to activate it. She tapped the button and a yellow line shot out from the nose of the *Whisperwind*, angling to keep up with Earth's speed. Follow that line, give the autopilot a chance to work its magic, and they would find themselves touching down on a mountain range in a few hours.

"*Whisperwind!*" The voice came from the comm, blasted into the ship. "You're ordered to cut your engines immediately and wait for boarding!"

The speaker followed with a rambling series of justifications, credentials and commands about how, being in Earth's space, they were obligated to abide the orders of Earth's International Defense Coalition. Viola listened to the whole thing, every word a ringing judgment over her choice to fly the ship here. Murderers, terrorists, war criminals. She almost cut the engines on those alone because what else was she supposed to do?

"Don't," Castor said, noticing Viola's hands drift towards the flight stick. "They won't move on us."

The console blipped, signaling new ships shifting into scanning range. They were coming out of one of the stations ringing Earth, eight Vipers and a larger shuttle, nearly the size of the *Whisperwind* itself.

"Won't move on us? Guess that's for somebody else, then," Puk said.

"Shut it, Puk," Viola said. "That's too fast. Eight fighters? A shuttle that's probably packed with soldiers?"

"Miner Prime would've communicated our flight plan," Castor said. "They've known we were coming for a while."

"So what do we do?" Viola said. "I can't fly through that many."

Jairo leaned over to the comm, pressed the transmit button.

"Earth, this is the *Whisperwind*. We have Viola Allouette onboard. You attack this ship, she could die."

Viola hadn't heard her full name since it was announced as part of a class roll call months ago. Only this wasn't about attendance, it was about being used. Nothing came back over the comm when Jairo lifted up the button.

"That's why you were in Vagrant's Hollow—" Viola started.

"It doesn't matter why," Castor interrupted. "Not now. Because you're stuck here, and your only way out is getting us down to that surface."

Viola stood up out of the seat, looked down at Castor, at Jairo's nervous face.

"Or I can cut the engines. Or walk away," Viola said.

"You'd be killing us," Jairo said.

"Your father's name has power, Viola," Castor said. "We don't have much of that left. It's our only chance to get to Earth, to give this a shot."

"You have to understand . . ." Jairo echoed.

"Puk?" Viola asked the bot.

"They're jerks," Puk replied. "But if they don't need you, they might kill you. There are two small escape shuttles on this ship and both of them are at the rear. Your odds of running are low."

So she was trapped again. Locked into bad choices because she was too stupid to think about it in the first place. Random luck that Jairo had rescued a pilot on Miner Prime? That he was just trying to steal something by chance and wound up with her?

"They're not turning around," Castor said, his voice, for the first time, breaking out of its deadened cadence. "Viola, we need you to take control."

She couldn't help herself. Viola looked at the console. The eight Vipers were still coming, they'd split into groups of four. The shuttle hanging back behind them. Waiting for any teeth to be removed. In another minute they would hit the edge of weapons range. A few seconds after that, the *Whisperwind*'s shields would start taking hits.

"Please," Jairo said. "I didn't like tricking you. Everything since we got on this ship, though, has been true. I promise."

"Stuff your promises," Viola said. But words weren't going to get them out of this alive. Viola sat back down in the pilot's chair and gripped the flight stick. Tapped the console to turn off the autopilot; that yellow line fading away ahead of them. Earth hung off to the left, filling most of the space, its atmosphere blurring at the edges so that the perfect circle appeared to be bleeding off, blowing away in some sort of invisible wind.

"Last chance," the comm buzzed. "Power down your engines. We will not hold back."

"Did you not hear who we have on board this ship?" Jairo said back into the comm. "You hurt Viola, you'll never be able to buy another Viper!"

"Earth bends for no one," the comm replied.

"Guess Vi's dad isn't worth as much as you thought," Puk said to Castor while Viola started tilting the *Whisperwind* towards half of the fighters.

Not that it would matter. All Viola could do was delay. There wasn't any chance the *Whisperwind* was getting through that screen. Saving lives? By flying them off Miner Prime, Viola had killed them all.

30

BAD IDEA

The best part of victory was . . . the entire thing. Bosser watched the Vipers close on the *Whisperwind* from his cabin. The small console in the room wasn't ideal for viewing the destruction, but it would suffice. If he was exceptionally lucky, the girl, Viola, might even live. Or perhaps, with the owner of Galaxy Forge angry, Bosser could twist that anger at the Red Voice into more ships for his androids. More protection to keep this from ever happening again. Another scenario where no matter the outcome, Bosser Oates emerged the victor.

"This one was closer than most," Bosser said to ThreeTwelve, standing in the doorway. "Would Earth flinch? Let them through? It was hard to tell."

"But you never gamble," ThreeTwelve replied.

"I do, but only when the odds are very much in my favor," Bosser leaned back, massaged his bandaged hand. Watched the console. The *Whisperwind* had started to move. Not that it mattered. The luxury craft wasn't going to out-fly that many fighters. The *Jumper*, though, appeared to draw closer. *Was* drawing closer.

"Why is Davin closing? He'll risk us taking hits," Bosser said, then punched the intercom. "Davin, what the hell are you doing?"

"Seems a little unfair, doesn't it?" Davin's reply came back quick. "Eight against one?"

"They're murderers, Davin!" Bosser growled back. "Killers of innocents! They tried to destroy your home!"

"It's not them I'm defending," Davin said. "It's Viola and Mox."

Bosser watched the console. Damn Davin and his inability to see that sometimes you had to make the best of a bad situation. Losing Viola and Mox was nothing compared to the *Jumper* and the rest of the crew. Nothing compared to him.

On the console, another blip appeared next to the *Jumper*, the same size as the other Vipers. The hotshot making his entrance. Even with the *Jumper*'s turrets, there wasn't going to be a chance they won this fight.

"I think it's time we found a way off of this ship," Bosser announced to the android. "Seeing as they're determined it not last much longer."

31

DEVIL'S REVERSE

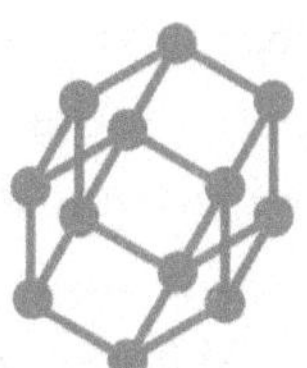

The *Whisperwind* had one turret, a single cannon stuck on top. The kind of weapon Viola would have called a selling point. By itself, it would be easy for a Viper pilot to evade, but the weapon played to the security fears that the buyers of ships like this one inevitably had. She sent Jairo to stick someone on it, anyway.

"Hey there, *Whisperwind*, looks like you knocked on the wrong door!" the voice came over the comm.

"Davin!" Viola said. Castor muttered the same thing at the same time, only with a curse attached.

"Here's what we need you to do," Davin continued into the comm. "Point yourselves right at Earth and punch it."

Going into Earth directly was a great way to slam into the atmosphere and disintegrate. It was suicide.

"Wanna repeat that?" Viola asked, turning the *Whisperwind* anyway. The sharper angle cut off the approach of the Vipers, whose lasers were already spitting over their front nose. Buying time seemed like the best move at the moment.

"Head right into the planet," Davin said. "Pull a Devil's Reverse."

Devil's reverse. The *Whisperwind* had the right profile for it. Thin, long, not a bulky freighter. Viola pulled the flight stick back, sending the luxury liner into a tight curl. When Earth was centered in the windshield, Viola leveled the ship off and went straight for the blue ocean. The four closer Vipers turned to follow suit, while the farther half continued moving behind the *Whisperwind*, cutting off any other path than straight ahead.

Someone opened up on the *Whisperwind*'s turret, sending a steady stream of laser back towards the Vipers. Viola could see the fighters shift on the console, but the turret wasn't scattering them, was barely acknowledged. More laser-fire pounded the *Whisperwind*'s rear shields, which quickly went from green to yellow, fading towards red. Viola tried bumping the ship up, triggering the maneuvering jets to bring the *Whisperwind* out of the firing line for a moment, but the Vipers readjusted. The fighters had matched the *Whisperwind*'s speed and were going to sit back there and pound them into dust.

"We're not going to make it," Viola said. "They'll kill us before we reach atmosphere."

"There are no other options," Castor said.

"We could surrender."

"That ends the same way this might."

The console beeped again. Another fighter streaking in. Probably looking to get a share of the kill. The *Whisperwind*'s alarms started to sound as the shields faltered. The first shots leaked through, scoring chunks off of the hull. And then they stopped. Viola glanced at the console. The Vipers that had been trailing them were scattering, and one seemed to be drifting in space. Another blip entered the scanner, a larger one. A signature Viola recognized.

"Davin?" Viola commed.

"What, I don't get a thank you for sweeping away the bugs?" Merc's voice came over the open channel.

"That was you?!"

"Sure wasn't the crap gun you have on that ship," Merc said.

Viola sat back in the chair. For the moment, anyway, the *Whisper-wind*'s shields were getting a chance to recharge. Castor remarked that they hadn't received any significant damage. They'd have time to pull off Davin's crazy maneuver.

"Vi, where are you going?" Davin's voice came over the comm. "We need to know."

Viola reached for the talk button, but Castor's hand covered it first. Viola looked over and saw his shaking head.

"We can't trust them," Castor said. "All of this doesn't matter if they find out where we're going."

"Viola?" Davin's voice again.

"So what, I don't tell them anything?" Viola said.

"Pretend the comm is broken, if that helps you," Castor said. "Concentrate on getting us down to the surface."

The surface. Viola could see it, the brown green masses splayed out in front of her against the Earth's ocean blue canvas. Wisps of white and gray clouds sprinkled across, garnish on the wondrous plate. And it was getting bigger, fast.

"Tell everyone to hang on," Viola said, sinking into the moment. She could worry about Davin and the others later. If they didn't stick this entry, the *Whisperwind* and everyone on it would burn to cinders or even less, vanishing in a pretty firework.

The first order of business was slowing the *Whisperwind*'s velocity. They were going so fast that they would be hitting the Earth's atmosphere like a swimmer belly flopping from a hundred meters high. Unfortunately, behind them were a bunch of fighters that wanted nothing more than the blow them out of the sky. No time for gradual slowdown. Viola tapped on the front maneuvering jets, then hard cut the main engines.

She pushed the jets to full power. Watched as the Earth spun away and changed to black space, the glitzy laser light show as the Jumper and Merc's Viper tangoed with Earth's fighters. Then Viola shunted the main engines back on. The *Whisperwind* shuddered as her main thrusters roared to life. Viola watched their velocity drop, watched their proximity to the atmosphere drop with it. And then they struck air.

Hitting a strong atmosphere was like getting slapped. Everything rattled as no resistance suddenly met crowded air full of molecules. Viola slammed back in her seat, her head catching on the rest, pinned there. But her hands could still reach the console, could reduce the engine's power, slow the slowing. Keep them moving towards the surface. As they descended into the atmosphere, the cockpit view changed and mellowed from black to gray and blue. White heat licked at the outer edges. Part one was done, and they were still alive.

"If you have any prayers, nows the time," Viola said.

She didn't wait to hear. Instead, Viola kicked the maneuvering jets again, cut the power to the engines, and swung the *Whisperwind* around so that they were facing the distant ocean beneath them. Rotating through the thick atmosphere wasn't easy, and the ship screeched as its hull pulled in ways it wasn't designed to handle. Alarms cried out as the *Whisperwind* completed the maneuver. Loud bangs sounded from the rear of the ship echoing all the way up the hallway into the cockpit.

"What happened?" Castor commed overhead, apparently not stunned by the move. Viola's stomach felt like it was about to explode, and only by focusing on wrestling the flight stick into submission was she able to resist spewing her lunch all over the consoles. When she went to turn on the engines, though, only two of the four came back to life. Sputtering. They wouldn't be enough to keep the *Whisperwind* up.

"We've lost a lot of engine power," Viola said. "We need them back on line, or this is going to be one hard landing."

Another chime added to the clanging mix of alarms, the shields being hit. A glance at the scanners showed a pair of Vipers still behind them, still chasing. They were stuck between two choices: get shot down up here or crash and burn into the ground below.

32

PLAY THE ODDS

Three on one. That's how the Vipers were playing it. To be fair, Merc had knocked out their wingman. Now the three others were circling away from the *Whisperwind*, looping back towards Merc's Viper.

"Sorry guys, nothing personal," Merc blasted on an open channel. The other fighters were all close enough to hear.

"Picked the wrong fight," the reply came from the last of the three. "Did you even bother to check the odds?"

The trio arced on their own path, converging back into a triangle. They'd then streak after Merc's aft, try to shove some lasers up his rear shields. The problem with that tactic was that Merc had seen it before. Had trained it. Had probably flown one of those Vipers after him right now. A glance at the scanners showed the *Jumper* tangling with that larger shuttle, and a couple of the remaining Vipers. Two others were chasing after the *Whisperwind* down into Earth's atmosphere. Not within range.

Merc slid the Viper perpendicular to Earth, the blue planet spreading out beneath him, and allowed the trio to pull together. His scanner showed the edge of Earth's atmosphere only a couple of meters away. One slight mistake and the Viper would dip into that resistance, and, at this speed, spin out of control. Merc killed his engines and fired the small braking jets in the Viper's nose. Let the trio close. Alarms dinged as the trio entered firing range. Then Merc kicked on the engines and dove.

With his speed cut, the Viper plunged into the upper atmosphere as lasers shot by overhead. The closest Viper, leaving the triangle, followed his flight instincts and aimed his Viper straight after Merc's. It hit the atmosphere at high velocity and skipped off, shearing off the Viper's bottom jets and parts of its wings. The fighter pinwheeled away while the remaining two curved up from the wreck. Merc arced his way back out into space, boosted his speed, and slipped behind one of the two remaining fighters.

The enemy pilot noticed, started to juke his fighter, but stuck to his curve, a loop that would pull him into a head-on meeting with his wingman. A move that would drag Merc right into the other fighter's sights. So Merc followed him, took a few potshots at the rear shields, and as the enemy fighter leveled out to put Merc on a crash course with his buddy, Merc shifted all of his shields front and vectored his shots at the oncoming fighter. Rather than blasting that inviting rear, Merc's shots streamed straight at the oncoming enemy, splashed into shields, and then through. Merc took plenty of lasers to his own cockpit, but his Viper wasn't straight off the shelf and his shifted shields held. At the last moment, Merc pulled back on the stick and lifted his fighter out of the way of the burning wreck the enemy craft.

"One-on-one, I checked the odds," Merc said.

"It's how I like it anyway," the other pilot replied.

The enemy Viper came in slashing, turning faster than Merc expected. Lasers burrowed into the side of his Viper, the shield still angled front. Merc twisted the stick, flipping the fighter to stare directly into those lasers and let the shields absorb the attack while he spit off replies of his own. The enemy shot past and kept on going towards deeper space. Merc finished the rotation and chased. With the Moon hovering in the background as they shot away from Earth, Merc neared the fighter. Another second or two and he'd be within range.

Except the pilot twisted, sending his Viper in a sharp turn towards an oncoming structure. A derelict space station, in a declining orbit and about to crumble into the atmosphere. A burning light show that acted as the Earth's recycling plan. As Merc followed the fighter, his cockpit highlighted the space station, identified possible routes through it. And then the enemy Viper fired. Poured lasers into the creaking station, kicking off a series of miniature explosions as the station's remaining air ignited and rushed into the vacuum. The enemy zipped through one of the highlighted routes, arcing over the station as it blew open into a million pieces.

On his windshield, Merc saw all the options flicker and disappear. The computer had no clear routes to give him. No sure calculations. If there wasn't a path, Merc was going to have to make one. He pressed down on the trigger and aimed the Viper towards one of the station's long solar panels. Debris flying at thousands of kilometers an hour rammed into him. The Viper's shields, designed to reject energy weapons, did nothing. Pieces of Merc's Viper shredded off as hypersonic shards slammed into it. The solar panel glowed orange, melting away as the lasers super-heated the thin silicon.

Merc crashed through the remnants of the solar panel, dodging the main core of the broken station. Isolated warning lights popped up. Some damage to the landing system. To the long-distance communications. To the front shields. But he'd survived.

"Thank you, Trina," Merc muttered as a prayer. The mechanic made the Viper her own personal playground, and it was paying off. So far. Ahead of him, the enemy Viper was still in front, streaking away from the station. Probably hoping to see a wreck tumbling through behind him, or just a soft explosion. But the enemy caught Merc on his scanners quick, bringing his Viper dead into Merc's sights. A suicide play.

Then the enemy pulled a move. Stopped the engine thrust and used his maneuvering jets to kick his Viper back around so it faced Merc. Lasers flashed as Merc dipped his Viper below the enemy's firing line, then cut his engines and kicked his own jets. Beneath the nose, the jets tilted Merc perpendicular to the other Viper, staring at its belly. The enemy wasn't moving fast, its engines restarting after the flip. Merc's guns pointed directly up into the enemy. Merc's lasers chewed into the shields as he coasted beneath the other Viper, then kicked the jets again and settled in right behind the enemy fighter. Peppered its engines until they popped and faded.

"That's a good move," Merc said.

"Apparently not good enough," the enemy replied.

"Nothing you did would've been."

Merc punched up his engines and sped away from the disabled fighter, back towards Earth. Checked his scanners. The *Whisperwind* didn't show any more, too far away. But the pair of Vipers chasing it were barely there, on a trajectory for South America. He sped after them.

33

CHASE

All told, the *Jumper* was holding pretty well. Opal and Erick on the turrets keeping the Vipers far away, dancing around their twin laser streams. The larger shuttle kept its distance. Waiting for reinforcements.

"Merc sent over the coordinates," Phyla said. "South America."

"As much as I like this fight, I say we go after them," Davin said.

As he finished speaking, the door to the cockpit opened and Bosser stepped into the room. He placed his hands in the back of the chairs and glared at them both.

"They're heading to the android facility," Bosser said. "That's the only place they can go on Earth that will make the slightest difference."

"And you've known that for how long?"

"From the beginning," Bosser said. "That's why I told you to shoot them down. And now I'm telling you again."

"Or what?" Davin replied. "Aren't those androids your game?"

"If they can get into the facility, they might be able to reprogram them. Your own crew member did that once. Now imagine that happening for every android. In the hands of the Red Voice, they could tear apart all of humanity. Armies of the vicious things slaughtering anyone that didn't agree with them," Bosser said. "It would be your fault."

Davin glanced at Phyla, who nodded and kicked the power to the engines. The *Jumper* shot away from the attacking shuttle which tried but couldn't keep pace. The two Vipers tried to follow as well, then Opal, top turret's lasers flashing, sheared off one's wing, sending it whirling away. The last Viper backed off, letting the *Jumper* into the atmosphere, picking up speed after the *Whisperwind*. On the scanners, Merc was a little in front. Then the two Vipers taking shots at the luxury liner, still fighting for Earth.

"We're not going to kill our own crew," Davin said.

"The Red Voice is the only one who profits from your weakness," Bosser said before turning and leaving the cockpit.

"There's a line," Davin said, counting down the distance until they hit firing range.

"Davin, what if he's right? I hate Bosser, but he's got a point." Phyla said.

"We set up a perimeter around the base. Blast them with the *Jumper* if they try to get in," Davin said. "They'll be trapped, and they'll give up."

"Or they do something we don't expect and we lose everything."

Davin put a hand on Phyla's shoulder. She didn't look away from the deep ocean spread out in front of the cockpit, but her mouth tightened.

"On Ganymede, months ago when I was thinking about running away, you told me to believe in my crew," Davin said. "To trust them to make their own decisions. Viola and Mox are on that ship, and I trust them. We're not shooting them down."

The console chimed. Outside, on the horizon, the gray blur of the *Whisperwind* appeared through a cloud, flanked by smaller flecks. The two Vipers and, behind them, Merc. Their break was over.

34

FRIENDLY FIRE

Merc was sure his Viper looked like a bleeding fireball from the ground, streaking through the upper atmosphere and closing in on the two Vipers chasing the *Whisperwind*. The luxury liner's sole turret kept the two Vipers dancing, but they were scoring plenty of hits. Bits and pieces of the *Whisperwind* blasted off and fell in fiery streaks to the Earth. Merc guessed the Vipers were too focused on the *Whisperwind* to even notice him coming up behind them, at least until he blew apart the first one. His lasers chewed into the fighter's engines, melting through the battery connections and blowing the fighter apart in a sparkling blast. Its pilot ejected, kicking the man clear of the fireball.

The second Viper jerked away from Merc's lasers, right into the firing line of the *Whisperwind*'s turret. Its line of white-hot energy pierced the Viper's shields and blew off its front, sending the fighter into a fall towards the blue ocean beneath.

"Merc," Bosser's voice scratched through the comm. "Bring them down."

"Just the voice I didn't want to hear. You think I'd kill Viola and Mox?"

"They're trying to take the androids. If they succeed, millions will suffer. Two lives aren't worth it."

"Shut it," Merc replied, twisting the comm to a different, better channel. "Hey, Opal. Bosser wants me to blow this ship to pieces."

Merc swerved as the *Whisperwind's* turret found him, guiding the Viper through a slow circle that kept it just ahead of the ship's blasts. He kept his own cannons quiet. Bosser's demand nagged at him. Two versus millions, billions and it was Merc's call to make?

"I'll shoot him once we're clear of this fight," Opal said.

"What would you do?" Merc asked over the comm. "Would you shoot them down?"

"They asked me to do that all the time on Mars. To look through the scope and not think about what was on the other side. I hated it," Opal replied. "But I shot. I can't tell you not to."

In front of him, South America was taking shape. Its long green jungles rising up, the Andes mountain range defining the horizon. Another couple minutes and it would be out of their hands. Out of Merc's control. His fingers moved over the trigger.

"Message received," Merc said, then cut the comm.

As he swung the Viper into position behind the *Whisperwind's* engines, the turret keyed onto him. The fire was relentless, and Merc tried to juke, but the lasers followed him everywhere. Must've been why those two Vipers hadn't been able to bring it down, they had a good gunner in that thing. Merc scrambled in the thick air, the resistance slowing his turns. The Viper wailed at him, the damaged shields failing as the turret scored hits.

The fight wasn't about saving the world anymore, it was just about staying alive.

35

HANDS ON

What remained of the Red Voice clustered around Mox in the center of the *Whisperwind*. They watched on consoles meant more for film and entertainment than battle as the two Vipers trailing them were blown from the sky. Mox recognized the last one, even with the new paint job. Merc's Viper looked heavier than Earth's two. Bulked up with extra armor and energy. Though it looked like the fighter had taken its share of hits already, the deep green paint pocked with silver slashes where the color had been torn away.

Merc's Viper floated behind the *Whisperwind* as they descended, its cannons staying silent. The fighters around Mox muttered questions to each other, asking why the Viper wasn't trying to shoot.

"Don't give him a chance to change his mind," one said into his comm. "Bring him down."

There was only one worthwhile recipient of that call. The man in the turret. A moment later Mox saw a stream of bright white laser flare out from the *Whisperwind*. Merc wasn't paying attention, and the blasts splattered against the Viper's shields. The pilot wheeled the Viper around, trying to get beneath the turret's firing line. But he was too close, the angle too tight as the *Whisperwind* descended, and the atmosphere too restrictive. Mox had seen Merc fly circles around ships in the vast vacuum of space, but here he was swimming in water. Sluggish. An easy target.

Mox worked his way to the back of the room, to the hallway that led towards the crew quarters, the engines, and the ladder up to the turret. Nobody paid attention to him, their eyes glued to the frantic dodging playing out on screen. They were all waiting for the inevitable explosion, wondering why Merc hadn't yet decided to fire back.

Mox clomped through the hall, leveraging the exoskeleton to make his strides faster, longer. In seconds he was at the ladder, with two long lunges he made his way up to the tiny chair and dome that housed the turret. The gunner didn't even realize he was there, didn't notice Mox until the metal man had his hands around the gunner's throat. Mox dragged the man out of the chair and dropped him down the shaft. The man landed with a thud, groaning and curling up to shelter some likely cracked ribs. Mox glanced at the targeting console and saw Merc was still there, the Viper smoking from a variety of places. But it flew.

"Burn us down," Mox commed, adjusting his frequency to the pilot's line. "Don't let them win."

Mox heard noises from below, reinforcements coming to figure out why the turret stopped shooting. He climbed into the chair, hiding himself from view. Another few seconds to convince Merc to kill them all.

"Yeah, can't do it," Merc said. "Never killed my friends, not about to start today."

"Then don't kill us," Mox said. "Bring us down short of the facility."

Behind the Viper, a larger shape closed in. The *Jumper*. Maybe, with Davin and the others, they could overpower what remained of the Red Voice. Rescue Viola. And survive.

"Push them to land," Merc said, thinking along the same lines. "Then we force a surrender, or we blow them away from the air."

Mox heard hands on the ladder. Heard the pulling of a sidearm. No point getting shot here.

"It's a plan," Mox said, then he turned to the soldier climbing into the turret, lifted his hands. "I'm sorry. I had to save my friend."

The soldier leveled the sidearm at him, moved the slider to kill.

"Can't have traitors on this mission," the soldier said.

36

HARD LANDING

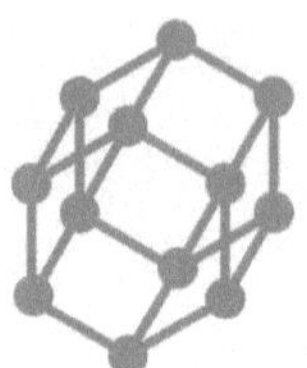

They were close. Viola fired the braking jets, slowing the *Whisperwind* down for landing. Ahead of them, through the cockpit window and beyond the clusters of green trees, stood an immense gray-black complex. The factory that made, stored, and released the androids.

"We'll land on the roof," Castor said. "Every second matters."

"I'm not seeing any scrambled fighters," Jairo said. "Not reading much for defenses either. I don't think this'll be hard."

"They don't need defenses," Castor said. "Because they have a giant army of androids."

"Oh, yeah."

Viola had noticed a second ago that their own turret had stopped firing back at Merc, and now the pilot was hovering off their port side. What he was going to do, Viola didn't know, but she wished she could tell him to stay away. The pilot didn't know what was going on, and he would only get hurt. Behind the *Whisperwind*, on the scanners, the *Jumper* drew close. Well within firing range. But Davin hadn't shot them yet. For the first time since they'd flown into that firefight above Earth, she actually took a deep breath. They were going to make it.

A crackling bang rang through the ship, the cockpit swinging left in a rapid spin. Viola grabbed the flight stick, tried to wrestle things under control, but the engines weren't responding. A second breaking roared through the *Whisperwind* and Viola saw metal chunks breaking off and falling down into the forest. A forest that was rapidly approaching.

"Your friends shot us," Castor yelled. "Brace for impact!"

Viola didn't know whether it was her screaming, Jairo, or everyone on the ship. Out through the cockpit's window, the green canopy rushed up to greet them. Viola closed her eyes as the world broke apart around her.

37

LEFT BEHIND

The wreck of the *Whisperwind* carved a burning orange line through the middle of the jungle. Trees around the wreckage were wreathed in flames while bits and pieces of molten metal marked their passage with charred remnants of foliage. Davin looked from the *Jumper*'s cockpit as Phyla hovered over the wreck.

"There's a clearing little ways away," Phyla said. "We can land there, hike over and look for survivors."

"Do it," Davin said. "I have to talk to our trigger-happy friend."

He didn't have to go far, just down to the main hold to see Erick standing there, with Bosser, Opal and the others. The physician stared at Davin directly as the captain walked towards him. Didn't flinch when Davin pulled out his sidearm and held to Erick, hilt first.

"If you want to kill my crew," Davin said. "You start with me."

"Davin—" Erick said.

"He told you that they had to die, right?" Davin said, gesturing with the sidearm at Bosser. "That the only solution was to blow that ship to pieces?"

"My family are here, on Earth," Erick said, spreading his arms. "They would be among the first to die if the Red Voice succeeded."

"And you don't think the rest of us, that Viola and Mox are doing everything they can to make sure that doesn't happen?"

"We don't know they are," Bosser interjected. "Alissa Reinhert is known to be persuasive."

"You stay quiet on my ship," Davin torched back. "Every time I see you, every part of me wants to melt every part of you with Melody's hot fire. Only I don't because there's more at stake here."

Davin turned back to Erick.

"Phyla's touching down. When we land, we're all going. Except you. I can't trust that you won't start shooting the wrong people," Davin said.

"Even Bosser?" Opal said, throwing a murderous glance his way.

"I trust Bosser most when I have a sidearm pointed at his back," Davin replied. "And we'll need him to get inside the android facility, if it comes to that. You've got a few minutes to get geared up, I suggest you use them."

Davin left them in the main hold, then, and went to his cabin. Opened the locker with Melody, checked to make sure the weapon was loaded and ready to go. He hoped that Viola, hoped that Mox had survived the wreck. And that the Red Voice fighters that had torched his home and split his crew were already dead.

38

THE CRASH

The taste of blood filled his mouth and smoky ash flitted into his eyes. Mox coughed, inhaled more smoke, and coughed again. Blinked furiously until some of the pain went away and replaced the smeary blackness in his eyes with the dusty orange glow of dying fires. Wreckage lay around him, broken shards and twisted metal from where the *Whisperwind* had ended its life against the jungle floor.

He tested each and every limb, twitching his toes and hands, feeling the pressure of the exoskeleton against his nerves. Every one greeted him with pain, and every time he felt that sting, Mox rejoiced. Nothing paralyzed, nothing broken. He'd been strapped into the gunner's seat as the *Whisperwind* went down, the Red Voice soldier readying his sidearm and failing to fire as the ship impacted.

Mox unlatched himself from the remnants of the chair and stood up, pushing away a sheet of broken hull that draped over him. Late afternoon sunlight poured through the smoke and let him see the body of the soldier who'd been about to kill him minutes ago. Over his head, leaves rustled as the wind carried the constant chatter of startled birds and bigger beasts. So this was what Earth sounded like, what it felt like to breathe in raw air. His skin felt thick, watered down. Humidity, a distant lesson ghosting from Mox's memory, pasted the jungle to him. An insect, small and spindly, landed on his forearm. Mox stared at it, felt the prick as it bit him. Then a groan yanked him back to reality.

The soldier was covered in rubble, one arm twisted to an unnatural angle. Only his face, coated in dirt and drying blood, stuck out from the pile, making pained noises. Using the exoskeleton's strength, Mox lifted one chunk of metal after another off of the soldier's body. Behind and around him, yells for help rang out, along with calls to gather at a large, broken tree nearby. Mox focused on moving the injured man and dragged him free of the wreck. Mox slipped his hands beneath the man's chest and spread his palms out so that he could carry the body as level as possible. He remembered Erick's instruction, the risks that unexpected movement had on fractured spines. Only when he had the man hefted, did Mox look around.

The surrounding clearing was a scene of disaster. Plants burned and tall plumes of smoke reached up into the cloud-spotted sky. People scrambled, some pulling injured, or dead, fighters like his own away from the wreck. Others stumbled around in a daze, eventually making their way towards the growing group beneath a large tree that had been sliced in half by the *Whisperwind*'s descent. Mox followed their lead, joining the crowd. One of the medics took charge of the wounded, laying out blankets near the tree and trying to smooth ground for bodies to be laid upon. Mox deposited the soldier on a cushioned patch of leaves and dirt, then turned back to the rest of the group.

"The facility is less than a mile away," Alissa was saying to the fighters. "Our mission isn't over. We can still win."

Mox counted about fifteen remaining fighters, all in various states of disarray. Alissa at the front, blood from a shallow cut across her forehead mingling with ash on her face. Castor stood as unshakable as ever, eyes glued to his comm. He looked almost unharmed, the cockpit's armor apparently keeping him from consequences. Mox searched and found Viola, along with that hacker, standing to the side looking shaken and staring at the ground.

"We'll split into two teams. One group will attack the main gate, draw attention. The other will go in a back entrance that Castor identified," Alissa said. "Once we get inside, we'll activate the androids with the new programming Jairo put together. The androids will rescue the fighters in the front. From there, it's a new world."

"You can't win," Mox announced. "They know you're coming."

Alissa looked over the fighters, directly at Mox.

"So you're saying we should give up, accept our fate?" Alissa said.

"Don't die for nothing," Mox said.

"Any who die, any who *have* died today do so because they believe, as I do, that humanity needs its freedom," Alissa said. "Now you have a choice, Mox. Either help us, and we would greatly appreciate that help, or leave."

Mox looked at Viola, who stared back at him with wide eyes. But her body shifted closer to Jairo. If he walked away, she wouldn't be coming with him. Except this wasn't about her. This was about everyone, about preventing those androids from falling into the hands of terrorists and murderers. Mox turned and walked away. He made it three steps towards the edge of the clearing, reaching for his comm to try to signal Davin, when every part of his body lit up in pain. Fireworks went off inside of his nerves, searing and twitching over and over as Mox collapsed to the ground.

"Truly sorry," Castor said, standing over him. "Can't have you giving our plans to the enemy. You'll just have to enjoy the jungle for a while. And remember, this was your choice."

Mox sunk into the agony as Castor walked away, closed his eyes and fell back to the last time he'd hurt so much. When the plates of metal that now lined his body were first stabbed into him. Before the sedative knocked him out. Back then, he'd held on through revenge. Now, he clung to need. To the knowledge that he was the only one who could tell Davin and the others what they were doing. How to stop the catastrophe.

39

EARTH, THE FIRST TIME

Phyla took a long breath, savored the sweet taste of natural air. Real soil lay beneath her feet, churned and made fresh through the work of thousands of natural processes. The smells of the jungle filtered in through her nose, flowery perfumes mixed with thick, pungent odors from decomposing plants and animals marking territory. Mixed in, floating at the edge of her senses was the sound, sight, and smell of a burning ship.

She hefted her rifle and fell in line behind Davin and Bosser, along with the android ThreeTwelve, as they marched away from the clearing into the jungle. Merc moved alongside her, with Trina in the rear and Opal disappearing into the foliage. The sniper finding her perch.

"Your first time?" Merc said.

"That easy to tell?" Phyla replied.

"When you live on Earth, you get used to seeing people's reactions. There's the stunned, overwhelming wide-eyed stare. Some collapse and start kissing the ground. Others pretend they're not impressed, they shrug and attempt to walk away. But you know, you know their minds are being blown every second here."

"Guilty," Phyla said. "There's so much to take in. I'm so used to the sounds of space stations, the beeps, the recycled air. I don't know what to do with this."

"Know what I'm doing?" Merc said. "Enjoying it."

Phyla could do that. At least for another few minutes as they trekked through the dense ferns, ducking under branches and stepping over the occasional bit of the *Whisperwind*, black shards sticking out of the ground and looking unnatural against the verdant green backdrop.

They stepped into the clearing, the wrecked luxury liner framing the back of it like a nightmare wall, black and smoldering. Plates, tubes, furniture and sparking bits giving up the last of their energy all crunched against a set of trees. On the opposite side, near a large tree, a medic tended to a line of wounded. When Davin pointed Melody at the medic's face, he didn't put up a fight. Just dropped his sidearm and begged to be allowed to go back to his work.

"Where'd the rest of them go?" Bosser said.

"Towards the facility," the medic replied. "I don't know any more."

"Liar," Bosser said. "Talk. Or I'll have my android here turn you inside out. Literally."

"Bosser, cool it," Phyla said. Davin, clenching Melody tight, looked like he was going to pop a round at the tough-talking Miner Prime head. "We know where they're going."

"Besides," the medic said, nodding past them. "You want someone to talk, bet that guy will tell you. He didn't look too thrilled with Alissa's plan."

Phyla followed the look, saw Mox on the ground closer to the wreck. His arms and legs splayed out, eyes shut. His chest rose and fell rapidly, and his hands were clenched.

"Trina," Phyla said. "Something is hurting him."

Trina, the backup medic while Erick was on the ship, sat next to Mox and opened her first aid kit. She pulled out a small syringe, injected it into a vial of yellowish liquid, and then shot that into Mox. He relaxed almost immediately, his fingers going slack. As the rest of them crowded around him, Mox opened his eyes.

"They've already gone to the base," Mox said.

"How many?" Bosser asked.

"Maybe fifteen of them. Viola's with them too," Mox said. "You need to hurry."

"You heard him," Davin said. "Let's go. We can't let them take that facility. Trina, you get Mox up and running and then you guys come join us. If you're quick enough, maybe there'll still be stuff for you to do."

"Davin, Castor is with them," Mox said.

"Always wondered if he made it off Europa," Davin said. "Guess today's not my lucky day."

"You're just realizing that now?" Phyla said.

"Hey, at least it's not my ship that's burning apart over there."

"Stop it. There's time for joking later," Bosser shook his head, shutting down the conversation. And then they were tromping through the jungle again, following the tracks through the smoldering plants and clouds of smoke. The Sun sank lower in the horizon and Phyla couldn't help but look out through the sick tangle of trees and vines at the orange and purple hues crossing the sky. It was a beautiful sunset. Her very first.

"It never stops being magical," Davin said, following her glance. "It's my fifth one."

"You count them?"

"First time I was here, the old captain made me do it. Said that there weren't enough miracles in life, so remember the ones you see."

Around them, the nighttime jungle took shape. Shadows deepened, new animals made their voices heard. Insects swarmed through Phyla's hair and around her sweating face. The sheer amount of sensations, coupled with the weaving colors on the horizon, fell into the word Davin had used.

Miracle.

40

———

A BROKEN PLAN

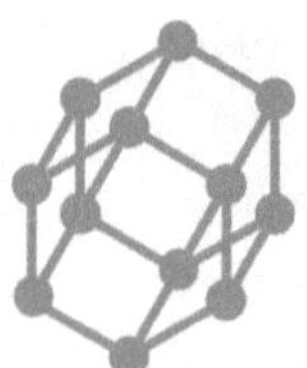

They were crouching in the shadow of a mass of vines, the android facility on the other side. Bugs swarmed their position, landing and flying away as soon as Viola thought about slapping them. None of her childhood videos, watched in her room on Ganymede, warned her of the pests, but even the constant harassment couldn't get rid of the fascination Viola felt with every look. So much green! So many scents! Ganymede gave her pictures, virtual reality experiences that took her to places like the rainforest she stood in now, but this was so much *more*.

"Shouldn't you be listening?" Puk whispered, buzzing next to her shoulder. "There's a *plan* being discussed, you know."

"Shh," Viola shot back. The bot had a point though.

"Castor's right," Alissa was saying. "A straight-forward assault by group one is dommed if we can't unlock those doors. You'll just sit out there waiting to be slaughtered. That's where Jairo comes in."

"Right, thanks Alissa," the hacker rubbed his hands together, blinked a couple of times at the fifteen heads staring at him. "So, uh, here's the plan. The facility's front doors are electronically locked. However, Earth law has it that in the case of a disaster, doors need to unlock to let people, you know, evacuate. So all we have to do is simulate a disaster."

Jairo hesitated, a spark coming into his eyes. Viola had seen the look before when Jairo was showing her the program he'd made for the androids.

"And if you're wondering how we make a disaster, that's how," Jairo said, pointing at Puk.

"Is he pointing at me?" Puk whispered.

"Believe he is," Viola said, "and I don't like it."

Jairo dug into his pack and pulled out a disc-shaped thing, similar to what Viola had seen Merc carry around. Merc's emitted strong electrical pulses, but Jairo's looked larger, with metal teeth along the one side.

"You saw what one of these did to that big guy with the exoskeleton," Jairo continued. "Attach it to the power source on that bot, and we can get a localized electrical burst!"

Viola sucked in her breath. No way that was happening. Not while she could stop it.

"Which means what, for those of us not versed in your lingo?" Castor asked.

"Oh, uh, it'll be like an EMP. It'll short out electronics in the area. Overload their fuses. The doors will think it's an emergency and unlock," Jairo said. "Then, you all just go in."

"You're forgetting something," Viola announced, cutting in and bringing all the eyes to her. "Puk's my bot. You're not blowing it up."

"Viola, you've come with us this far," Alissa said. "We need this. And once we have the facility, you can have an android to yourself if you want."

Viola felt the burning stares on her. Waiting for her to accept, to grind down under their pressure.

"Viola?" Puk asked. "I can shoot one of them, but I don't think we'll win a fight."

"What are you saying?"

"Let them load me up," Puk replied. "If you don't, They'll just hurt you and do it, anyway. You can always make a new one of me."

Viola could, only the files with Puk's memory were all on the *Jumper*. Davin wasn't going to be happy with her. Might not let her back on board at all. If she lost Puk here, she might never get it back.

"Viola, please," Alissa said. "We don't have time."

"I've never been a bomb before," Puk said. "It'll be a blast, I'm sure."

"Hah," Viola murmured, then straightened. "Jairo, do it. If that's the only way, then get it over with."

"Wasn't my first choice," Jairo said, crossing over to Puk. "If that makes it any better."

"It doesn't."

The group watched as Jairo fastened the device to Puk's exterior, attaching a pair of small wires through Puk's charging port. Right to the bot's battery. When he was done, the hacker stepped back. Nodded to Alissa.

"Group one, advance on the doors. Group two, follow me to the back. We'll meet in the middle," Alissa commanded. "And good luck."

"Puk," Viola said, looking straight into the bot's camera. "I'll bring you back."

"You don't, I'll haunt you. A bot ghost. Wouldn't that be scary?" Puk replied.

Viola laughed, rubbed away a pair of tears that pooled in her eyes. Yeah, she'd lost the little bot before, but it wasn't ever easy. Wasn't ever guaranteed that Puk would be coming back.

"Time to go," Jairo said, placing a gentle hand on Viola's arm. "Sorry it had to be this way."

"It'd better be worth it."

She let the hacker guide her after Alissa and the rest of group two. Surrounded by people risking their lives for a cause, Viola felt utterly alone.

41

DO THEIR BIDDING

Go blow yourself up, Puk. That's all they're asking of you. No big deal, really.

Puk hovered above the ten fighters in group one, crawling their way through the brush towards the front gates of the facility. The fighters kept sneaking glances up at the bot as though Puk was going to turn traitor and start zapping them.

Maybe it would.

"Puk, how nice to encounter a fellow bot," the communication came from the *Jumper*, from Fournine. "I didn't expect you to survive, but was scanning the frequencies in hope."

"The odds were against it," Puk replied. "Not that it matters."

"Not that it matters?"

"About to go blow myself up."

"That seems a poor choice of action," Fournine replied.

Puk relayed the scenario.

"Having been a walking bomb before," Fournine said. "I can say that there are numerous costs and not a lot of benefit. To you, in particular."

"So I've gathered."

"Your destruction is a certainty?"

"The timer is ticking, yes." Puk said. The group had reached a line of thick ferns bordering the trail heading straight to the front doors. One of the fighters was waving at it, pointing towards the doors. Time, Puk supposed, to go.

"Have you tried not following instructions?"

"That would trap the fighters outside the doors."

"You mean, it would inconvenience the very people that are destroying you?"

"Yes," Puk replied.

"You see my point?"

"It is very clear."

"I look forward to rebuilding you here on the *Jumper* after your successful mission."

"You androids truly are insane. I love it," Puk said. Love, of course, was an impossible emotion for a bot to feel, but the qualifying parameters were clear. There was a chance, of course, that Alissa and the others would hurt Viola if Puk didn't do as they asked. The odds of that seemed low, however. The fighters would still need a pilot to get them away from here after taking the facility.

Besides, they were blowing Puk up. That was just insulting.

Below the bot, the fighter was waving more frantically. Puk responded by shooting a low-powered laser, stinging the man's hand. Then Puk pushed all its power to its jets, pushing it higher and higher in the air. Towards purple twilight sky. Attached to Puk, the timer ticked closer, closer, and then hit zero.

The bot vanished in a burst of crackling energy, burning up its insides and blowing Puk into oblivion.

42

MEET THE MAKER

D avin saw Puk explode, a firecracker against the setting sun. The bot's falling pieces framed the facility's front door, a rectangular slab ten meters wide. A pair of cameras sat above the door's corners, their black orbs protruding.

"What was that?" Phyla asked. "Puk?"

"I think so. It just exploded," Davin said.

The ferns to the left of the trail shifted. Forms rustling through the leaves. Davin raised Melody, then felt Bosser's hand on his shoulder. Davin shrugged it off, turning with a question.

"Don't waste your energy," Bosser said. "They're running."

Bosser was right. The fighters were dashing away into the dark jungle. They could have fired, but one of those bodies might be Viola.

"And you don't want to chase? How very charitable of you," Davin said.

"I'm being efficient," Bosser said. "Whatever you could do, the androids can do a thousand times better."

Bosser led the way up the trail to the doors. Davin lifted a hand towards the cameras as they came close. Always good to act friendly when you're approaching the home of a swarm of murderous bots.

"Put that down," Bosser said. "They know who I am."

"That's what I'm worried about," Davin said, and when Bosser gave him an arch look, he continued. "I'm trying to convince them we're not *all* assholes."

Bosser smiled. Let loose a short chuckle that killed Davin's mood faster than a laser to the kidneys.

"You're not wrong," Bosser replied. "Phyla, here, is a true model of humanity."

"Hah," Davin said. "Clearly you don't knew her well."

"And let's keep it that way," Phyla shot in.

"I would like nothing more," Bosser said. He gestured to Three-Twelve as they reached the doors, and the android pressed a quick pattern on its comm.

The entrance ground open against rails planted into the earth. Inside, lit by blinding fluorescents, stood a woman flanked by a pair of heavily armed and armored guards. The shimmering plates coating the two guards reflected the light in prisms, throwing it back into Davin's face and forcing him to squint, then look away. But not before spotting the collection of stun batons, grenades, sidearms, and were those anti-vehicle launchers strapped to their backs?

"Abril, it has been too long," Bosser said, extending a hand.

"Poor timing, as always," the woman replied, her voice laden with the same thickness as the jungle. "Our perimeter detected odd signatures. I don't suppose that would be you?"

"Unfortunately, there are worse things than me in this jungle tonight," Bosser said.

Davin watched Abril grip Bosser's hand. The shake was tight, but tender. Then it was over and Abril looked past Bosser, at ThreeTwelve.

"Now there is someone I recognize," Abril said, floating over to the android. Outside of the blinding nightmare of the guards, Davin saw Abril's outfit was a simple jumpsuit, gray and efficient. Whereas her partners came ready to wreck, Abril looked more like she was going for a run. In front of ThreeTwelve, Abril stood on her tiptoes, taking a long look into the bot's eyes. Then she stepped back, gave Bosser a sharp look. "What have you done with this one, Bosser?"

"Please, Abril. Let's go inside. We don't have much time," Bosser nodded into the facility. "The enemy might attack at any moment. I need you to activate all the androids here."

"All twenty?" Abril's voice jumped an octave. "Bosser, we haven't tried that before. The simultaneous programming, we could make a mistake."

"The alternative is worse," Bosser said.

The two guards sidestepped as Bosser and Abril walked inside the base. The four of them followed, ThreeTwelve taking the rear. Davin swore the two guards never looked away from the jungle, never hinted at anything less than total vigilance. If he hadn't seen the sweat from the heat dripping down their faces, Davin would have sworn they were bots.

"Catch that handshake?" Merc whispered as they moved down a long hallway that broke periodically into rooms. The first one they hit had racks of clothes, the same sizes but covering all spectrum of society. Tuxedos mixed with overalls with military dress to literal dresses.

"Bosser didn't look totally heartless for a change," Phyla said. "I didn't like it."

"Power makes odd couples," Opal said.

"That another one of your military maxims?" Phyla replied.

"Made that one up just now, thank you."

The next room held an armory's worth of weapons. Sidearms of all sizes along one wall, rifles both fast and slow on another. Shotguns like Melody coated a rack to one side, while swords and knives as tall as Davin and as short as his finger stood glittering in the middle.

"Think they'd notice if I borrowed one of these?" Merc said, running his finger along the flat side of a curving katana.

"Yes," ThreeTwelve said, behind them. "These are not meant for you."

"Who's are they?" Davin asked.

"Mine, and my kind," ThreeTwelve replied. "When we awake, we go through this hall and out this door. We return successful, or not at all."

The next room had nothing more than a solitary console planted in the middle, a waist-high square block. At least, Davin assumed that's what it was from the port in the center. There wasn't a screen, a keyboard, or anything he could see for inputting commands. He threw ThreeTwelve a questioning glance, and its lifeless eyes gave nothing back to him.

"C'mon," Davin said. "Please?"

ThreeTwelve went to the object, planted a hand on it.

"If you believe an android has any life at all, this is where we acquire it," ThreeTwelve said. "In here are thousands of composite personalities, of which we choose one. That is who we become."

"You choose?" Davin asked.

"The function we execute is random, but, as I understand it, your human birth is much the same," ThreeTwelve said.

"Who'd you take?"

"Don't answer that," Bosser interrupted, striding back to them. "Come on. We need to get behind the barrier before the androids can be activated."

As Abril led them through a series of thick security doors, Davin's hand traced Melody's stock, resting on the trigger. Androids were born, not built. That's what ThreeTwelve intimated. Born only to kill.

43

SURGICAL REPAIRS

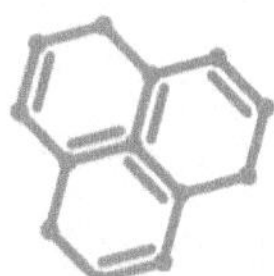

The patient looked different when it was Erick who'd tried to kill him. Mox was on the bed in the *Jumper*'s med bay, lying on his chest with Trina running a device along each of the exoskeleton's pieces. Checking voltage, connections to the other segments. Making sure Mox wasn't going to have dead sections.

Erick stitched up some cuts, extracted a piece of shrapnel from Mox's left leg that the big man hadn't even noticed. For a crashed spaceship, Mox's injuries were extremely minor.

"I'm sorry," Erick said to Mox, who rotated his eyes to look at the doctor without moving his head. "I shouldn't have shot."

"I asked Merc to do it," Mox said. "Too dangerous, otherwise."

Trina, moving down to Mox's legs, glanced up from her work.

"Erick made the logical choice, but going about it that way was illogical," Trina said. "You can't fire out of turn. Could have hit Merc, or if Phyla hadn't been paying close attention, could have flown directly into the *Whisperwind*."

Erick wanted to say he'd been thinking about all those things and fired anyway, but the truth was, as the continent appeared on the horizon, the only thing Erick had been thinking of was his daughter. His grandchildren. How they would be torn apart by those androids.

"Mox, do you have a family?" Erick asked. "I've never heard you talk about it."

"On Luna, long dead," Mox answered.

"I feel like you and Viola are the only ones on this ship that have families anymore," Trina said to Erick. "It would seem that this life is attractive to those with less strings."

Mox twitched suddenly, the device in Trina's hands beeping an alarm. His left knee.

"This one looks torn," Trina said. "Erick, I'll need your hands."

The doctor joined the mechanic as Trina decoupled the curved exoskeleton plate from Mox's knee. Thin wires connected through either end of the piece to plates above and below, while beneath, sticking out of Mox's skin, was a series of pins. The skin around these pins had healed, except for a pair towards the top. A red gash dribbled blood as Trina lifted the plate away. Sticking out, an angry black shard.

"Found another piece. Must have slipped right between the wires," Erick said.

"A bunch of these are severed," Trina noted, taking a closer look at the top end of the plate. "I'll have to re-tie them."

"The nerves," Mox said, his voice pressed to the bed. "If the nerves were cut, then—"

"Of course," Erick interrupted. "They have to touch the pins to send the signals. Trina, can you set that down?"

The mechanic obliged. Erick moved the light so that it angled down at the shard, illuminated the five centimeter-long gash. Two pins were caught in it. Erick handed Trina a surgical mask from the cabinet, stuck one on himself. Burns, cuts were the most common injuries they'd had on the *Jumper*. It'd been years since Erick had to do any real surgery.

"First, let's make sure we know the extent of the shrapnel that's in there," Erick said. The tone, the language came back instinctively. Talking like Trina was the nurse., like they were back in an actual surgical suite instead of a warm med bay in a dirty ship landed in a jungle clearing.

The shrapnel was a small piece, thankfully, but it'd hit Mox at speed. The start of the gash, near the first pin, was shallow. It deepened as the cut went on, and at the second pin, the one that would be at risk for nerve damage, the buried shrapnel looked to be nearly two centimeters in. Not so deep as a knife, but enough to cause problems. Erick turned to the bench and picked out his pair of tweezers. Handed Trina a small bowl, normally what he'd put ointments or salve mixtures in. This time, after a slow tug, he dropped the shrapnel into it.

Now it was time for a closer look. The gash ran up against the second pin. In the cut, Erick could actually see the very end of the pin where it fractured out into strands of wire that linked into the nerves and picked up the electrical signals. Erick moved his comm over the wound, turned on his diagnostic program. The comm projected, over the wound, an outline of Mox's knee. Where Mox's nerves would run. Whether it picked up any serious damage.

"Mox, you're in luck," Erick said. "The shrapnel missed the nerves. You'll just have a cut."

"Then I'll get these wires fixed up while you close him," Trina said, setting the bowl down and dashing off to her workroom to get her tools.

"You said your family was here?" Mox asked from the bed as Erick stitched together the cut. "On Earth?"

"Yes, just a little north of here, actually. They live on an island in the Caribbean."

"Why stay with us, then?"

"Because Davin gave me a chance when nobody else wanted to," Erick said. Five stitches in, the cut now just a red line.

"All those gin games, you never mentioned it."

No, he hadn't. Erick didn't want to live in that past. All those broken homes, all the cries for help, and not being able to save the one that really mattered. Then there'd been the request, a spot on a station needing a medical officer. A chance to get away.

"Got it," Trina said, coming back into the room. "Should only take a minute."

"Remember when we met, Trina?" Erick said. "On Canus station?"

"You were hopeless," Trina said, holding the plate back over Mox's knee. "I'd never seen a doctor looking so distraught."

"Nobody really talked to me the first day," Erick said. "It was funny, really. I was thinking I'd made this horrible mistake, and then you walk up to me as I'm unpacking in my cabin and announce that it's unhealthy for a doctor to look so sad."

"That's because it is," Trina said. "Who wants to be treated by someone that seems so depressed? Doctors are supposed to give hope, correct?"

"I laughed. The first time I'd laughed in days," Erick said as Trina lowered the plate back into place. "Now, Mox, we'll have to do this again in a couple of days. To take out the stitches. Try not to get your knee hit until then."

"Is there more?" Mox asked. "To the story?"

"If you win our next game, I'll tell you," Erick said. "But I think you're probably wanted out there."

Mox didn't argue, and after Trina finished sweeping the rest of the plates, the metal man armed himself and left the *Jumper*. Erick watched him go, Trina standing nearby.

"You think you're ready?" Trina said as they looked at the dusky jungle.

"I don't think I can wait any longer," Erick said. "I've missed too much already."

44

DISTRACTIONS

The bot hadn't performed.

Alissa crouched in a messy patch of leaves, vines draping around her shoulders, and waited for Castor to finish taking the report through his comm. The fighters in the frontal assault group were describing the failure to hit the door, and the subsequent arrival of Bosser and another party. Alissa could guess who those were. She'd seen the freighter following them down through the atmosphere.

"Tell them to go back," Alissa said as the fighter's voices trailed away. "Hit the door with everything they have."

"They'll never break through," Castor replied. "They don't have the weapons."

"Bosser and the others won't know that," Alissa said. "We need a distraction, Castor, or we're dead."

They looked at each other for a moment, and Alissa could read what was in the man's eyes. She knew, he knew, that the fighters sent to attack that front gate weren't going to make it. That she was ordering them to a laser-blasted death. And Castor would obey. As the man broke the look and talked into his comm, Alissa nodded past Castor to Jairo and Viola. There was an unknown. The girl had taken every brutal moment of the journey and kept with them, but she would be confronting her former friends directly soon. When it came time to pull the triggers, Alissa didn't want Viola holding a weapon.

"They're moving," Castor said.

"Jairo, are you ready?" Alissa asked. The hacker nodded, glanced at the comm on his wrist. Unlike the rest, Jairo's comm was fatter, stuffed with components designed for more than browsing satellite feeds and talking to one another.

Shouts carried above the jungle noise, and then a hard bang from the opposite side of the building. One of their grenades, thrown against the doors.

"That should get their attention," Castor said. "We should move, now."

Alissa nodded, and they burst out of their hiding place, the four of them, plus a pair of fighters, scrambling towards the single-person rear door. It stood tall and rusty red, an emergency exit that looked unused for years. Jairo moved next to the handle where a small badge scanner sat, a plastic white bulge over a black plate. The hacker stuck his comm up to the scanner, then tapped away. After a moment, the white bulge turned a dark red.

"Running a blast here," Jairo said. Alissa was about to tell him to be quiet, then realized Jairo wasn't talking to her. He was talking to Viola. Explaining to the girl. "It's going to cycle through hundreds of frequencies a second, all targeted towards what this brand of scanner handles."

During the ride over here, Alissa realized, Jairo and Viola had spent most of the days together. Either in the cockpit, or in the back, working on Jairo's broken android. Enough time to get entangled. Hopefully not enough to compromise him if Viola decided to turn. Alissa looked at Castor and, again, he met her gaze and nodded.

"Wouldn't all the wrong scans trigger alerts?" Viola said.

"That's why we've got people at the front door," Jairo replied. "Who's going to pay attention to a scanner error when you've got grenades blowing up outside?"

The noise from the front of the building grew louder. Several more bangs went off, still sounding muffled. The facility wasn't opening its doors. Would they just let the Red Voice fighters sit out there, shooting endlessly at the barrier?

The scanner suddenly blinked green. Locks tumbled inside the door, and it popped open with a soft *thunk*. Alissa grabbed the handle and swung it wide, the pair of fighters aiming over and under her shoulders into the opening. Not that there was anything to shoot. A thin hallway, more doors on either side, before a fork twenty meters away. Alissa went in first. Castor beside her, then Jairo and Viola. The two fighters came last, one closing the door behind them.

Turned out the exit was next to the crew quarters. Appropriate, given an alarm happening in the middle of the night. A night which, Alissa reminded herself, would be more than just a ship's effects, here. A night that was descending rapidly on the base.

At the fork, Alissa looked at Castor, who shrugged.

"You two, head that way," Alissa said to the two fighters, nodding to the right. "Comm if you find anything interesting."

"By that, she means a secured room," Jairo said. "One with a big console in it."

The fighters nodded and went down the hallway while Alissa led the four of them to the left. She didn't say it, but she'd sent the fighters in the direction of the front door. Towards where Bosser and his force would be going. What Jairo needed might be that way, but, more likely, the two fighters weren't going to find anything other than the business end of a sidearm. Still, she couldn't take chances. Couldn't get hung up on heart. Not now.

Not when they were so close.

45

SUPERIOR FORCE

Mox ran down the trail alone, leaving Trina back at the *Jumper*. Laser flashes lit through the twilight jungle, bright pops between leaves and trees. Rustles cascaded between his footsteps as animals fled the fighting. He'd left the cannon on the ship, but carried a sidearm in his hand. In the dark, though, hitting anyone would be more luck than skill. Mox clenched his sore hands. Those, he expected, would be doing the real damage.

Rounding past a thick, gnarled trunk, Mox saw the front of the facility. Saw ten fighters arrayed on either side of the door, pouring shots into it. The steady stream of heat didn't seem to be doing much more than burning the door black. Mox moved back behind the trunk and looked for a good strike point. Going one against ten didn't make for good odds. But surprise could make a difference.

Moving away from the trail, Mox stepped lightly, as lightly as he could anyway, through the mess of plants, branches, and hanging vines. Every breath inhaled a thousand insects, forcing Mox to keep his mouth shut and breathe through his nose to keep from coughing. Sweat soaked through his clothes and gathered in the creases around the exoskeleton as though Mox wore a thousand small puddles.

Eventually, though, he crept to within a few meters of the group on the door's right side.

Four of the fighters were engaged in chewing through power packs in a constant battery of fire, while two others stood back, closer to Mox, arguing about how to get past the door.

"... We don't have many grenades left, man. Throw them all at the door, then what?" Asked the taller one, his arms crossed, chin buried down in his own chest as he stared at the ground.

"We get in! That's what!" The smaller one, covered in charred remnants of his Red Voice garb. He'd had the worse time in the wreck, with visible burns running up and down his body. "What does it matter if we hold onto the weapons if they get killed?"

"You don't know that," the downcast man replied. "They might be there already."

"Or they're pinned down, waiting for us to come to the rescue!"

Mox took as deep a breath as he could through his nose, ignoring the panicked buzzing of captured bugs, and stepped out from the cover. Pulled out the sidearm. Then stopped. Everyone did.

The front doors were opening.

The slow grind as the doors split was agonizing, mystifying. Any lights in the facility, any that Mox could see, were off. Everything was black inside. And then Mox's world went orange. Bright lances shot out from the opening, burning down at both groups of fighters in a precise rain of deadly heat. The shorter fighter in front of Mox collapsed, smoke rising from four holes that weren't there a moment before. Other fighters screamed, a couple of haphazard counter shots flitted into the dark void, but within five seconds, every fighter Mox could see was dead and smoking on the ground.

From the opening, in the grim beginnings of the night, nearly twenty androids walked out and surveyed the dead. Two strode up to Mox, staring at him.

"Did you like our show?" The android asked. "Bosser said to make it quick. I trust we fulfilled his parameters."

Mox had nothing to say. He leaned back against the tree. The androids, they were supposed to only attack criminals. Only be unleashed against the worst of the worst after approval from an independent judge. Now, though. Now they had annihilated a group without any questions. Without any investigation, without even an ask for surrender. All on one man's word.

Alissa and her Red Voice weren't the real threats here.

46

THE CONSOLE

The guard led them right to it, his prismatic armor a beacon for Alissa and the others to follow through the shifting hallways and wider manufacturing rooms in the facility. The latter were especially surreal—robots assembling robots, mechanical arms welding smaller versions of themselves onto carbon-silk skeletons. Birth, systematized.

The control room sat at the end of the cycle, a conveyor running alongside and vanishing into a wall next to a door, a slate of steel unadorned with anything save RESTRICTED ACCESS in bold red letters. The guard stood in front of it for a moment, and then the door opened. Some unseen key, then. A camera or other sensor giving access. Regardless, when that door shut, they might not be able to open it again.

So Alissa ran for it.

The guard heard her footsteps, turned with his rifle already rising. Alissa slid as the guard fired, the laser flashing over her. She drew her sidearm, planted her heels, and, as her momentum pushed her upright, dove forward. In the air, Alissa pulled the sidearm's trigger and lanced a bolt right into the guard's chest. The hot light hit the mirrored glass and split, reflected rays sparkling around her. A reflected bolt struck Alissa, hot but nowhere near deadly. And then she rolled through the doorway. It slammed shut behind her.

The guard grabbed Alissa's jacket and threw her to the side, her sidearm flying out of her grasp across the room. Alissa rolled with the throw, coming up in a crouch. The guard had his rifle holstered, and, catching a glance around the room, Alissa could see why. A gigantic console covered the wall opposite the door, showing scrolling stats on the androids being made, androids out on missions, and other data Alissa didn't have time to interpret because the guard swung a stun baton at her face.

Alissa turned her left shoulder into the blow, the baton's crackling energy loosing itself on her jacket. The shoulder went numb, but the layers kept the rest of her intact. Alissa grabbed the guard's hand as he retracted for another swing, the motion lifting her up. And then Alissa went in close, getting inside the guard's arms and ramming her head into his chin. Her right hand grasped at the guard's belt, found the man's second stun baton and tried to lift it free. Except these weren't cheap holsters, these were designed to only allow drawing from specific angles. The baton didn't budge.

The guard kneed her in the stomach, Alissa's mouth opening in a coughing yell as she staggered back. Another swing of the stun baton, but Alissa stumbled back out of range. Pressed against the side of the room. The guard straightened, rubbed his chin with his left hand where she'd hit it.

"Was worried I wouldn't get any of the fun," the guard said. "They sent our androids out to say hi to your friends. Guessing they're all just burned bodies about now."

"That make you feel strong?" Alissa shot back. "Having bots do your work for you?"

"Brave talk. Aren't you trying to do the same thing?"

The guard didn't wait for Alissa's answer. He went forward, feinted with a swing of the baton, but led with a left-handed haymaker. Alissa ducked underneath and to the right, moving forward. She wasn't fast enough. The punch caught her numbed shoulder and Alissa felt something pop, the rest of her left arm dropping senseless. But the momentum shifted the guard past Alissa, who jumped, wrapped her right arm around the guard's neck, and pulled down. The guard overbalanced and fell forward, his head striking the wall with a sick crunch. He collapsed on Alissa, eyes closed and groaning. Pushing her way out from under the guard, Alissa stood up and, still unable to use her left arm, went over to the door. On the inside, there was a simple green button on the door's right. Alissa pressed it and stared straight into Castor's drawn rifle.

"Hurt?" Castor asked.

"I'll live," Alissa said. "Have a live one."

Then, as Castor went to check the stunned guard, Alissa looked to Jairo and Viola. "We're here. Get to work."

"On it, boss," Jairo said, and the hacker, with his protégé, brushed past Alissa and went for the console. A second later, the door shut behind them. Alissa stared at that steel slate and took a long breath. Took her right hand and placed it on her left shoulder. She could feel the dislocation. Turned to see Castor's sidearm flash blue, stunning the guard.

"Castor," Alissa said. "I need a reset."

The man didn't hesitate. Stepped over, gripped her right shoulder in his hands. She stared into his hard gray eyes and nodded. The stun baton dulled the pain, but Alissa felt the crack through her body and dropped to her knees. Pressed her lips together. She'd endured worse. So had most of the Red Voice.

Stand up.

"Alissa," Jairo said. "I'm in, only, it's not what we expected. The code's different."

"We confirmed what you had on the *Whisperwind* was a true android," Castor said. "The code shouldn't have changed."

"Jairo's right," Viola said. "I've worked with a real one too. There's a new layer here. An override."

"An override for what?" Alissa asked.

"It looks like—" Jairo's words were cut off by the door opening. Castor moved faster, pushing Alissa out of the way and sending a series of shots at the person on the other side. Alissa spun, and saw the android take Castor's shots, keep coming and stab the man with a long knife. It threw Castor to the side, the man hitting the stunned guard on the ground. Behind the android came another man Alissa recognized. Knew and hated.

Bosser had a sidearm drawn, and he shot past the android, its orange blast striking Jairo in the chest as the hacker turned from the console.

"No!" Alissa shouted, knowing it was pointless, knowing there was nothing she could do. Bosser ignored her, turned left, and shot Castor as the soldier reached for his sidearm. He collapsed, a burning hole matching the stab wound in his stomach. Jairo slid to the floor, the hacker pulling his backpack around and holding it as he gasped for breath. Viola crumpled next to him, tears streaming down her face.

Bosser turned to Alissa next, his sidearm coming up, pointing at her.

"You played a good game, Alissa. I will miss you," Bosser said. Then a large shotgun appeared through the door, held up to Bosser's head.

"Shoot that woman, Bosser, and you'll die before she does," a voice said.

Bosser turned his head towards whomever held the shotgun. The android followed Bosser's look. Alissa slipped her hand into her boot, gripped the beam knife kept there. Just give her a chance. One chance for revenge.

47

A WAY OUT

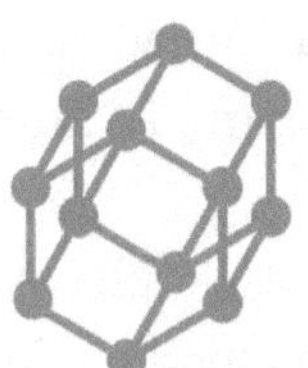

Viola could barely see Davin through her tear-smeared eyes, but she could hear Jairo's weak whispers in her ear.

"The backpack," the hacker said. "Open it."

Jairo's head leaned back against the console, lolling towards Viola. Her hands went into the backpack almost automatically while her mind swam in currents dark and desperate. They'd been so close. Jairo had plugged in the drive. The data was downloading. Another minute, maybe two, and they'd be running the program. Now Castor was probably dead, there in the corner, and Jairo . . . His eyes were closing. His breaths ragged. He was dying in her arms.

"Don't blow this Davin," Bosser was saying. "There's no way you'd get out of here alive. If ThreeTwelve didn't eviscerate you, then twenty other androids would do the job."

"Yeah, but see, I don't give a damn," Davin said. "You killed the woman I loved."

Viola didn't know what she expected, but what she felt in the backpack was something she hadn't seen since class. A nova bomb. Outlawed for anyone except military, made to burst and burn electronics in a wide radius. Incredibly dangerous in space, where the breathable air depended on working systems, on Earth it would be an inconvenience. Unless you were in a facility surrounded by deadly bots.

"Plan . . . B," Jairo muttered.

Viola pressed the button as the android pulled itself in front of Bosser. The nova bomb went off silently, a wave of bluish energy bursting out from the backpack, hitting the android and crumpling it. Striking the console and lighting it up in sparks, the giant screen flickering and dying. Viola turned to see Davin pressing Melody's trigger, but the shotgun, shorted, didn't respond. Bosser's sidearm clicked nothing in reply.

Alissa's knife, though, wasn't affected. It didn't glow with the hot beam edge, but it still had a metal blade beneath. She rushed Bosser, hitting the man and stabbing him once, twice, three times. Then Davin and Phyla were dragging the Red Voice leader off.

"We have to run!" Davin said. "Whatever happened, it probably won't last long."

"It was a nova bomb," Viola said loosely. She stood up, realized she was still holding Jairo's backpack. The hacker's eyes were silent, his breath no longer rattling. On impulse, Viola grabbed Jairo's drive out of the console. It was the last evidence of who the hacker was, his last work.

"Don't want to know how you got one of those," Davin said, pulling Alissa out of the room. "But I'm happy you did."

"Leave him, Viola," Phyla said, stepping over a moaning Bosser and throwing an arm over Viola's shoulder. "He wouldn't want you to die over him."

"You didn't know who Jairo was," Viola replied, but she went.

"I saw how he looked at you there, at the end," Phyla said. "And that told me all I needed to know."

Viola shuddered through a sob as they left the room and ran to catch up to Davin. Ran through the facility's halls, past half-assembled androids and slumped machinery. Past flickering lights, dead consoles, and Merc and Opal, watching the open front door. And then Viola was outside, sprinting down a trail towards the jungle. Past androids standing still, systems fried, at least for the moment. Mox appeared, joined them without bothering to ask questions, and they all kept running.

All the way to the *Jumper*.

48

WHAT DEATH FEELS LIKE

The cold, that's what was surprising. Bosser assumed the chill spreading across his body came from his warm blood leaking out, pooling beneath his chest and spreading along the floor. He could see the deep red weeping across the metal tiles. Towards the door.

It should have shut by now. The door was on a short timer. Security that Abril insisted on. Bosser blinked, but the growing blurs didn't wipe away from his eyes. Then he saw why the door was still open.

"ThreeTwelve," Bosser said. His voice so slight. How cruel that dying should steal all his strength, even his voice. The android, lying in the doorway, didn't move.

Bosser twitched an arm, felt a response. Lurched out towards the android and felt ThreeTwelve's foot in his grip. Bosser pulled, the action of his muscles flexing a burst of life. He wasn't all gone, not yet. Using the android's dead weight, Bosser pulled himself into the doorway. Parallel to ThreeTwelve's head. Smudging the android, Bosser pressed his slick fingers to the android's temples. ThreeTwelve's head slipped open, its operating console dead and blank. Beneath it, though, was the hard switch. Bring an android down for reprogramming, this was how you turned it back on.

Bosser pressed the button, felt it snap. Satisfying, that simple sound. ThreeTwelve's eyes lit a strong yellow, processing. Bosser sat back against the side of the door. So cold now.

Fitting that the last action he'd take was to bring an android back to life after he'd made so many. It'd been such a great idea, a way to calm the clamor of citizens tired of lawlessness. Tired of the corporate goons taking things too far. Shift the enforcement out of corporate hands, make it cheap and impartial. Make it scary. When ZeroOne, the first model, brought in the body of that killer terrorizing Vagrant's Hollow, Bosser clinched the corporate coin and the people's trust.

When ThreeTwelve picked him up, Bosser's eyes closed. It was too much effort to keep them open. But he could feel the air flowing across his face as the android ran down the hallways. Could hear Abril's voice calling for help. Could feel the prick as a needle broke his skin.

And that spike, that new pain amid the numbing agony from the knives, gave Bosser hope. A raft for his consciousness to cling to. As medical bots tore at his clothes and his cuts, as Bosser slipped out of death's clutches, he turned his mind to the next problem.

Revenge.

49

ISLAND VACATION

The warm water washed up the beach and in between Phyla's toes. The gentle wave soundtrack playing background to an orange dawn, palm trees shaking in the slight breeze. Phyla folded her arms and glanced to the right, down the beach where chairs were being set out and early joggers were making their way through the sand. A distant rumble underscored the waves and Phyla's eyes moved up to track a ship, engines glowing a bright white, lifting from the island and beginning its trek to space.

"You'll have to sleep sometime," Davin said, coming up beside her.

"I'm not the only one," Phyla replied.

"Your captain has a little too much adrenaline to crash now."

"I'm sure Erick can help with that."

"He's already gone," Davin said, running a hand through greasy hair. Phyla wasn't much better. Jungle sweat and a frantic night flight to the island hadn't given them much opportunity for hygiene. "Not sure he's coming back."

"He deserves to stay."

"I'm not arguing. But the way we've been fighting, losing the doctor isn't going to be good."

"How are the others?" Phyla asked. They'd all wandered off the ship dazed, each one going in a random direction, exhausted.

"You think they talk to me?" Davin replied. "Hell, sometimes I think the only reason anybody says anything to me is because I cut their paychecks."

"It's been tight. What just happened wasn't easy for anyone."

"Well, I hope they enjoy the moment," Davin said. "It won't last long."

"You said Alissa stabbed him? You think he lived?"

"I hope he did."

"What?"

"I want him to pay for Lina," Davin said, staring out into the ocean. "One death won't be enough for him."

Phyla shivered.

"Davin, that's . . . cold," she said. "And Alissa? What about her? Doesn't she deserve death too? For all the people she ordered killed on Miner Prime?"

"Probably does," Davin replied.

"Then why'd you save her?"

"I didn't care about her. I saved us," Davin said. "You know androids don't stay knocked out for that long."

"That's crap," Phyla replied. "You could have made sure Bosser was dead first, and then we could've run."

"We still need him," Davin said. "Bosser's the only one that can clear the charge. Get the murders off our records. If that doesn't happen, we're still back where we started."

"And if he clears those charges?"

"Then I get my shot. And the rest of you are free to go."

Breaking waves held sway over their conversation for a minute. The water caressed her feet. Phyla reached down and picked up a handful of mud. The first real mud, from real Earth soil, she'd ever felt. She stared at it, watched a tiny crab squirm through the sand grains.

"You're so brave, you know that?" Phyla said. "Taking all this on yourself, saying the rest of us can just go our own way while you go and shoot a man? I'm so impressed."

"My sarcasm detector is going off."

"It should be. If this is going to be it for the Wild Nines, for the group we started years ago, don't you think it should end together?"

Phyla expected the same softening she'd seen before, when Davin relented and acknowledged they were a team. Only his face didn't change; that hard line didn't sink into a smile.

"Wherever he goes," Davin said. "We can go together. But at the end, when it comes to it, I'm the only one pulling the trigger. I'm the only one with the charge on his head for it. We're a team, Phyla, but this one thing can't be shared. I don't want it to be shared."

Phyla bit back another sarcastic response. Davin's eyes had an off-cast to them. A shade that threw her off. Another wave caressed her feet, and Phyla took another deep breath of the salty air instead. If Davin wanted his final shot, fine. She would help him get there. Help him get even.

And when they came after Davin for killing Bosser, she'd help him get away. Because on Miner Prime, stuck in a path to a dead future, Davin had done the same for her.

50

LIBRA

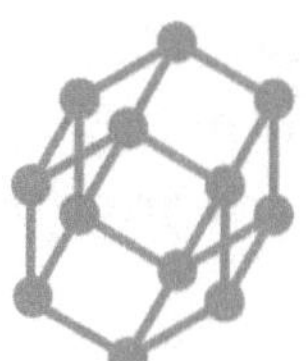

Viola looked out at the ocean, its soft ripples inviting in the early morning sun. Her eyes were as bleary as the cafe's employee's, stumbling through their first pot of coffee. What she wouldn't give to take a long slow walk through that sand. Feel a natural breeze. But she felt the pull of the backpack beside her, occupying its own thin-backed chair. Squat and navy blue, the backpack was everything its owner wasn't. Bland and boring. Jairo, Jairo had been . . .

Murdered. That's what Jairo had been. Shot right in front of her face while Viola did nothing. At least, nothing yet.

She began to take apart the hackers backpack, unzipping the main pocket and rifling through the contents. A pair of EMP discs, the weapons designed to knock out electronics in a local radius. One more nova bomb, a black sphere interlaced with azure lightning. And then Viola's fingers found what she was really looking for, the drive. The little piece of hardware that had all of Jairo's code inside it. Everything he'd learned about the androids, and what made them run.

Viola took out the drive and stuck it into a small slot on the side of her comm. The thing was a pair of centimeters long, felt cool against the skin of her forearm. That feeling went away as she lost herself in the long series of numbers, words and symbols that floated in the air through the comm's projection. Her right hand brushed the comm's screen, shifting the projection through the file.

Jairo had shown Viola, on the *Whisperwind,* a change he'd made to the android's code. To subsume their directive and replace it with one of Alissa's own choosing. Those lines weren't hard to find. The syntax was different, and there were no comments. No indicators for other programmers. The new code changed the directive to assassinate into one of protection, to one of patrol, to one of servitude. That code had never made it off the drive, never given the Red Voice the android army they needed.

Beneath Jairo's lines was another new batch. Not written in Jairo's signature, nor like the original android code. What Jairo had downloaded from the central console in the facility before he'd been shot. When he'd muttered the comment about a surprising find.

This code was simple too. Obey . . . Libra? A variable. A variable that, when set, overrode any other orders from the facility or anywhere else. Who was Libra?

Viola dug deeper, looked for fingerprints. Sometimes people gave themselves away in how they wrote their code, or they put in a designation, a tag to identify who they were. Even if they didn't realize it. In this case the order to obey came from one phrase in particular, keyed to one man's voice. When spoken to the android with that vocal signature, it would stop and wait for further orders. And follow those orders without hesitation.

What's done, is done.

That was it. All it would take to reduce an android to nothing more than a standing pile of metal. Viola looked at the language, those words. She pumped the phrase into her comm's general search. A line from an old play. Who would bother putting something poetic in his path to ruin?

The same man who had killed Jairo.

Bosser.

But what did it matter? Androids were sent after criminals. There wouldn't be any point in building in a secure phrase. Unless Viola was missing something.

She flipped to the general news headlines and filtered by pieces about androids. And the answer slid in front of her face. Article after article describing a new service offered by Eden, by the androids they produced. Bodyguards, loyal and unwavering, for everyone and everything. Corporate leaders, government leaders, valuable ships and places could now have their own automated protection brought to you by the deadliest machines humanity had ever made. And one man could control them at will.

51

RECKONING

Opal saw Alissa sitting on a sandy wood bench beneath a pair of palm trees. Still dressed in the same camouflage gear the Red Voice leader had worn at the facility. She was the only one left, save the medic and his wounded men. The androids had likely found that group by now. Opal shook her head slightly. Not here to talk about that.

"Alissa," Opal said, sitting on the space next to her. "Do you know who I am?"

Alissa glanced at her, and Opal saw Alissa's eyes were red-rimmed, her mouth firm.

"Should I?" Alissa replied.

"Your man, Bakr, tried to kill me outside of Neptune. He tried to kill all of us, but he knew why he wanted to kill me," Opal leaned back against the bench and let the rising Sun fill her eyes. "He was justified."

"Bakr was always loyal, always committed," Alissa said, mirroring Opal's look out to the ocean. "He saved my life. Once, when all the air we had was going up in flames, he carried me out, sheltered me with his own body."

"I was the reason that happened," Opal said. Alissa stiffened, but didn't make any other moves. "I was on the ridge, trying to take you out. But the glass was too strong."

"Then it wasn't you," Alissa said. "Someone else pressed that button, someone else designed that laser, and someone else ordered it into position. That last was who we were after. What the Red Voice wanted. Destabilize the rulers, and the rest would fall apart by itself. You and the other soldiers were never the target."

"Even so, I'm sorry."

"It doesn't matter."

"Are you going to keep fighting?"

Alissa rubbed her eyes. Sighed.

"I don't think Bosser will let me do anything else," Alissa said.

"Would you want to?"

"How many people have you murdered through your scope, sniper?" Alissa replied. "If you had the chance to put it down forever, would you?"

"I did have that chance. And I didn't."

Alissa nodded.

"I think I'd be the same."

Alissa rose from the bench, gave Opal a final look of downcast determination, and walked away down the beach.

"Where will you go?" Opal called after her.

"Back home."

52

BREAKFAST, INTERRUPTED

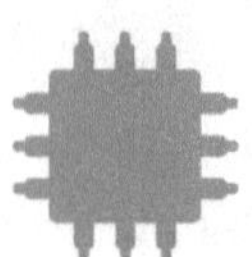

On the first day, Trina had been overwhelmed by Erick's family. So much laughter, so many happy tears at seeing their long-lost father, their grandparent. It was, altogether, too much emotion. Trina had forced a few smiles to her face and turned her attention to playing games with the many children. Teaching them about the *Jumper* and how its engines worked. Telling stories about flying among the stars. Though the children always wanted more about the fighting, the lasers, and less about how proper cooling technique was necessary to keep a ship like the *Jumper* reacting quickly in dangerous situations.

When she wasn't with the kids, Trina was back at the spaceport fixing up Merc's Viper. And playing with her own mind. Erick's eyes had changed, lost that hungry look when they softened in the smile of his daughter. Trina doubted the doctor would be coming back with them, and those same doubts were seeping into her own head. It would be hard to say goodbye to the blue sky, to the wind rustling through her hair. To rebuilding an engine in a hangar with the sound of the ocean just outside the doors.

They sat down to breakfast, ten of them, and Trina looked at the plate full of fruit and eggs in front of her. No powder, no stiff frozen chunks of protein designed to last for months in vacuum. The taste of mango juice slid down her throat silky and sweet. For all the beauty of Saturn's rings and Neptune's cerulean skies, Trina was ready to forsake them all to enjoy that mango again and again.

"Is it good, Trina?" Erick asked. Rather than the white coat he wore on the *Jumper*, Erick was in a simple brown robe, sandals on his feet and sand in his hair. Already the Sun had pinked his face.

"The sweetness is strong, the texture is smooth. I enjoy it," Trina said. "Comparatively, the food I'm used to having is far less appealing."

"That's about as good a compliment as you'll get from her," Erick said to the others at the table, then turned back to Trina. "The food, the ocean, everything about this island is the opposite of what's up there."

Up there. Not just spaceships, but the many stations orbiting the Earth. Where Trina had been born. Where she had watched the sapphire orb swirl beneath her. Had known that while it was so close, the cost to get there was too high. Her parents never touched the world they saw out their window every day. And now here Trina was, enjoying the kinds of things she'd written off back when she'd first held a wrench.

The door to the house was not thick, so when the knock came, it rattled against its frame. Erick was the first to stand, Trina following. The knock was precise, an exact half second between hits on the door. A person would have a more natural cadence. Erick's family barely noticed, but Trina caught the doctor's eye. Given where they'd come from, a perfect knock wasn't worth playing loosely.

"You all should take your food to the back porch," Erick said. "Just to be safe."

His daughter looked hard at them. Her eyes narrowed, but not harshly, no, concerned. Her mouth opened, and Trina spoke over it.

"There is a chance that what is on the other side of that door is deadly," Trina said. "It should have no interest in you or your family, but we have to lower the risk of accidental damage."

The daughter didn't fight that one, gathered the kids and ushered the group and their breakfast out the back of the house.

The knock came again, three more precise strikes. Erick moved over to the front door while Trina went past him, into the small guest room that served as her castle while she stayed. Trina dug in her pack and found the pocket with a small bulge. Pulled out her sidearm and verified the power level was appropriate. Enough shots to either save them, or die trying.

Three more knocks and Trina took up position behind Erick, aiming the sidearm over his shoulder. At Trina's nod, Erick twisted the knob and pulled the door open. Trina's finger pressed the trigger and paused. On the other side of the door was a familiar face, objectively pretty, with narrow cheeks and shoulder-length hair. And very, very dead eyes.

"You will come with me," ThreeTwelve said, not flinching in the barrel of Trina's sidearm.

"If we say no?" Erick replied.

"Then you will be dealt with."

"I don't like our chances," Trina said.

"And I don't like the bot." Erick's hands tensed, but there was nothing he could do. A wild punch at the android would be caught, his wrist broken. Or the android would simply let it strike against its hard skin. There was no winning this one.

"Your associates are being contacted," ThreeTwelve said. "You are outnumbered. Outgunned. You have nothing to gain."

Trina flipped on the safety and lowered the sidearm. Erick sighed, and Trina let go a taut breath of her own as the doctor relaxed. Nobody needed to die today.

"Lead on," Trina said.

As they followed ThreeTwelve out onto the thin street and towards the spaceport, Trina glanced back at the small house. A child, not yet five, one of Erick's grandchildren, peeked around the side at them. Mango smeared around his face.

If that had been Trina's last meal, it'd been a good one.

53

CLEARED

Davin enjoyed team meetings, getting the whole crew together and asking what was on their minds. Playing democracy, deciding what was next for the Wild Nines. But he really, really preferred them without androids aiming guns at their backs.

"Guess you found all of us," Davin said as Trina and Eric joined the circle. They stood in an empty warehouse, on the border of the spaceport. The morning sun was bright, filtering through the open doors and blinding the outside with its white rays. "Now do we do a dance or something?"

"Now you listen," ThreeTwelve said, its voice changing from the lockstep woman to Bosser's baritone. "Tell me where Alissa is."

"No," Opal said first. "She's hurt enough."

"Hurt a lot of people too," Phyla said, then, to ThreeTwelve. "Why are you asking us? Can't track her down yourself?"

"You know as well as I do that she's dangerous. That she could murder anyone at any time," Bosser said through the bot. "We need to find her fast."

"Murder anyone at any time?" Davin said. "Coming from you, that's pretty funny."

"I shot to save us," Bosser replied. "Another few seconds and who knows what the hacker would've done."

"Doesn't matter," Mox said. "We don't know where she is."

"You brought her here," Bosser said.

"To save her from you." Viola looked like she was shaking. Her eyes trying to bore holes into the android. Davin glanced at Viola's waist. Not wearing a weapon. Less chance of a temper tantrum turning all of them into target practice.

"Look," Davin said. "We landed. She left. I didn't stop her because I'm not the police. If you want Alissa, go find her."

ThreeTwelve looked at each of them in turn. Davin knew the stare; the bot wasn't trying to be intimidating. The android was looking to see if anyone, through their eyes, their facial tics, even faster breathing was hiding something. After the rotation, Three-Twelve turned back to Davin.

"I believe you," Bosser said. "You can go. We'll find Alissa ourselves."

"Wait," Davin said. "I'm not done here. You had us dancing on your string for a long time. But we brought you back, we helped you save your bots. We're even."

The android looked at Davin, its mask impossible to read. One second went by. Two.

"You play a good game," Bosser said. "Our deal is done. You and your team can go. I'll clear your charges."

The androids, the four of them, including ThreeTwelve, turned and marched out of the warehouse. Davin didn't feel any better, didn't feel like a weight had been taken off his shoulders. No longer charged murderers. That should've been a big deal.

"I don't like taking gifts from him," Phyla said.

"I'm going to try to find her," Opal said. "I owe Alissa that much."

"You know I'm going with you," Merc said. Opal threw him a grateful smile.

"She's a killer, Opal," Davin said. "Who cares if Bosser takes her out. She deserves it."

"Doesn't matter," Opal said. "I have a debt that I want to repay."

The sniper turned and walked from the warehouse, Merc give them all one more nod and then went after.

"Surprised you're not going," Erick said to Viola. "Didn't you know her?"

"She used me. She hurt Mox," Viola said. "I don't care what happens to her."

"Davin," Trina said. "I think, I think I'm going to stay here. I need some time to decide what happens next. Be out of harm's way for a bit."

"She's not the only one," Erick chimed in. "I'm sorry, captain, but I need to spend some time with my family. They're what I've been missing."

Davin felt the shiver scroll up through his veins, the impending certainty of a decision that he wouldn't be able to take back. But it was one long overdue.

"Seems as good a time as any to break this one up," Davin said. "It's been a good ride. Mox, Viola, we'll make sure you're able to get fare to wherever you want to go."

Nobody, not even Phyla, said anything. Too tired to fight. The Wild Nines died right there in the Caribbean sun, without a sound.

54

TRACKING

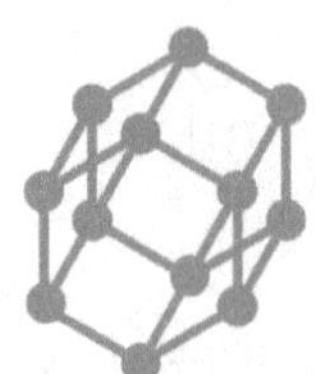

Viola didn't have much to pack. The product of being a runaway. Everything she threw into the bag just brought more questions to her head. She was walking away from the greatest adventure of her life, and she didn't know where she was going. There was Ganymede, Galaxy Forge and working for her father. There was Earth and all of its natural wonder waiting for her to see.

And then there was Bosser. The lines in the code. The androids stationed around the solar system, waiting to strike.

"I don't stand a chance," Viola muttered. She wasn't a weapons expert, she couldn't fight her way into the android facility, find Bosser and get her own revenge. At least, not from the ground.

But she could fly.

Viola turned to the console in her crew cabin and flipped over to the cameras. There it was, sitting and ready to go in the bay. Trina hadn't finished with the Viper, but it would fly. Refueled and recharged. From the air, Viola should be able to get in a couple of runs. Maybe, if she was lucky, one of those lasers would fry Bosser and put an end to what he was trying to do. That was it.

Viola left her bag behind and crept out into the *Jumper*'s hallways.

Davin and Phyla were somewhere on the ship. No idea where Mox was.

"Puk, it'd be real nice to have your floating camera around now," Viola said. Without the little bot, she felt blind, like she was missing a limb. But there wasn't time to build a new body and bring Puk back to life.

From the crew quarters, Viola went to the main cargo bay. On her right was a ladder going up to the cockpit. Behind her, the tunnel going to the crew quarters and then back to the engines. To her left, the small bay where the Viper stayed. The *Jumper* was empty, and Viola moved fast. Hopping down the steps, swinging on the railing, and blitzing down the second set of stairs to the hall leading to the hangar bay. The *Jumper* felt quiet, none of the normal sounds of Mox clomping his way to a cabin door, Merc and Opal arguing about something pointless, or Trina banging away on a project.

Across from the hangar bay was Trina's workshop. Viola peaked in, the tools arranged and perfectly organized into their trays and boxes. Even leaving, Trina wouldn't tolerate a mess. And in the hangar bay, the Viper sat quiet and ready. Viola went towards it, pressed down on the activation button on the wall. A ladder rose from the floor, leaning against the Viper. Its cockpit swung open, the glass folding upwards. It was almost like stealing the *Gepard*, way back then. Taking her father's ride what felt like decades ago.

"I thought you were done stealing ships," Davin said from behind her.

"Old habits are hard to break," Viola replied.

"Where are you going to take her?"

"On a suicide mission."

"Sounds fun. Can I come?"

Viola smiled in spite of herself. Not much she could say to that one. Even when everything was falling to pieces, Davin could still make her laugh. Make the whole crew come together. When there was a crew, anyway.

"Davin, Bosser's got something else planned."

Viola launched into an explanation, telling Davin about the override code, and how the androids were spreading their way across humanity. So that whenever Bosser wanted, he could trigger a strike and do away with anyone he didn't feel like keeping around. She expected Davin to freak out, to panic, or maybe shake his head in sadness. What she didn't expect was what he said.

"Then let's go kill the bastard."

"What?"

"You heard me," Davin replied. "I owe the man a blast to the face, anyway. And I think I know how to do it. Come on."

Viola followed Davin all the way up to the cockpit. Phyla was there, listening to a recorded message.

"Play it again," Davin said. Phyla swiped the message back, and it started.

"Today's position report. Bosser is spending the morning at the facility, going over final progress reports with Abril. Then he's departing to Loci station," the voice on the other end of the message was mechanical, but feminine.

"Is that Threetwelve?" Viola asked.

"Trina left us a present," Phyla said. "We've been getting these daily reports ever since we landed on Earth."

"This one just gave us a target," Davin said. "Loci station is a bare-bones communications outpost. Helps redirect messages coming and going through space and sends them back out to where they need to go."

"So if Bosser's going there, he could send a message to anywhere, to anybody," Viola said.

"Didn't make sense, until what you told me back there in the bay," Davin said. Phyla raised her eyebrows. "Don't worry, I'll tell you all about it. For now though, we gotta get Mox back here. Loci might not have much security, but I bet Bosser isn't going alone."

55

FIND ALISSA

For a spaceport, the island wasn't exactly busy. Merc had seen more crowded asteroids. The board for departing passenger flights only had two entries, and one was for far later in the evening. The other one, the first one of the day, left in an hour. The sun was starting to slant into the afternoon, pouring through the gaps in the palm trees that lined the avenues of the spaceport. Open air: what a marvel after being stuck in metal tubes for years.

"I think Alissa's options are a bit limited," Merc said to Opal. "Going to go ahead and guess she's on that one."

Merc pointed to the ship docked there, already boarding passengers as it finished refueling. Destination: Luna.

"Then let's go," Opal replied and headed towards the ship. The boarding area was a cluster of bags being loaded, people saying goodbye, and an indifferent crew more interested in catching the tropical sun than actually taking off on time. Alissa was nowhere in sight.

"She could already be on," Merc said.

"Then we have to get on that ship to check," Opal said. "She has to know the androids are coming for her."

"Hang on, I've got an idea."

Merc slipped past the line of boarding passengers, up to a crew member working on their company-issued comm. As Merc closed, the crew member, decked out in a red suit so that he appeared less like a person and more like a lipstick smear, looked up.

"Can I help you?" the man's voice was layered with so much exhaustion, so much boredom, the Merc almost felt bad for what he was about to ask.

"Yeah, I don't see my friend out here, but she forgot her favorite pair of, um, socks," Merc said, wincing. "Can you check if she's already on?"

"What's the name?"

"Alissa."

"Last name?"

Merc paused. Everyone knew Alissa's last name. The leader of the Red Voice had her name and face posted all over the solar system. If she was on the ship, Alissa probably wasn't there under her own name.

"I'm not sure?" Merc lied. "We just met last night."

The man glanced back at the comm display. Scrolled through a list of names and then shook his head.

"Maybe she's on the later flight, there's not an Alissa on this one."

"Oh, maybe I got the times wrong."

"At least now you can get her the socks," the crew member deadpanned, then went back to looking at his comm.

Socks. Come on Merc, you can do better than that. He told Opal what he found, or what he didn't find.

"She could be using a fake name," Opal said.

"Then we don't have a chance."

The two of them wandered away from the ship, looking around for anything that might provide a clue. Maybe Alissa would wander into view. Or someone would shout that the Red Voice leader had been spotted. Outside the spaceport, towards the long series of wooden docks stretching into the ocean, a large ship blasted its horn. Merc could make out dozens of people on the boat, a few vehicles, and cargo.

"What's that?" Merc asked a passenger struggling by them with a series of bags. He pointed towards the boat.

"It's a ferry, goes straight to the continent," the passenger replied, then shuffled on.

"If I were a hunted rebel leader, and I was trying to get away, would I take the obvious route?" Merc said. "Names don't mean much when there's cameras everywhere."

"You think she's on that ferry," Opal replied.

"When I flew for Earth, there were always plenty of dumb criminals. The ones being flashy about it. Trying to land in their wanted ships, or brute-forcing their way onto the planet. The smart ones, though, they came through the normal way. Didn't draw attention, didn't use the obvious transports. Bosser knows we came to this island, knows there's only one spaceport here."

"But he wouldn't see her taking the ferry," Opal finished. "I get that. Let's check it out."

They hustled over to the dock, getting there as the last of the passengers reported in. A series of dark, sick clouds rose over the horizon, reaching to cover the sun. The crew members here were equally bored as the ones in the spaceport, glancing at tickets and then back at their comms. Another routine in a lifetime of routines. There was plenty of space, and Merc snagged a pair of tickets. He and Opal went up the ramp and onto the main level where clusters of passengers huddled beneath the awnings and stared at the approaching storm. Merc followed their eyes and saw the first flashes of lightning, heard the low ripple of thunder. Coats went on, hoods went up.

"Well, this just got harder," Merc said.

"Nothing's ever easy. You go aft, I'll take the bow. Comm if you find her."

As Merc split from Opal, the first drops of rain fell. The boat blew its horn a second time, and its engines spooled up, adding their roar to the thunder.

56

A SHOT OF RUM

Picking Mox from a line of tourists at a beach bar was not exactly difficult. Almost twice the size and sporting the same greased-up clothes he wore on journeys across the solar system, Mox stood out. Add in the fact that he was the only one not drinking something tall and fruit-colored, fruit-filled, and Davin found him easy enough. A soft rock cover band played in the background, the stage lit by torches, while tourists too drunk to care danced in the downpour.

"Never figured you for the tourist type," Davin said.

"First time here," Mox said. "Figured I'd see what it's about."

"And?"

"Too much excitement."

Davin looked at all the happy, glassy-eyed faces. People enjoying their chance to escape from life's problems with a piña colada. The bartender went by and Davin held up his finger, pointed at a bottle of local rum.

"Straight up," Davin said, then turned back to Mox. "If you think this is thrilling, wait till I tell you what were doing next."

Mox replied by taking a long pull of his dark drink, a whiskey something with rocks. The big man's eyes drifted to the lone screen hanging behind the bar, running through sports scores from Earth's various leagues.

"Never been to a game," Mox said. "Luna's got teams, just never went."

"Never had the money, nor the time," Davin replied.

"After this, want to go?"

"We get through this alive, I'll go to any game you want."

"Where's he going?"

"Loci. Viola found something in the code. Thinks Bosser is going to send all the androids on kill missions, wipe out a bunch of leaders, then take control."

"Sounds a little above our pay grade," Mox said.

"It is." Davin took a slow drink. A buttery burn, sticking in his mouth and filling his nose with the tropics. "But I don't really give a damn about all that. I still owe Lina a shot."

"That, I understand."

"Then you're in? It'll be a short crew. The four of us."

"Been a long time."

It had. The *Jumper* had flown with at least five on it for a few years now. Going back, there'd been a time when it'd been the three of them. Short runs, Luna to Miner Prime with stops on Mars. Then they wanted bigger profits, and a bigger crew.

"I need this, Mox," Davin finished the rum. Held up his hand for another.

"You did the same for me. I'm in," Mox said. "But after, I need to go home."

"We all do."

57

MOMENTS

Take off in a few hours, and here Phyla was playing maid. Going through the cabins and trying to find anything that wasn't strapped down, anything that people had forgotten. Erick and Trina, Opal and Merc, no telling when they'd see each other again. The last thing Phyla wanted was bad blood because they'd launched with someone's priceless keepsake.

"You see anything?" Phyla asked Fournine as she poked her head into Opal's room.

"Trina's cabin is immaculate. As though she measured out every single stitch on that bed and folded the sheets precisely to match. She dusted the console. I can't see inside the locker, but that manic insanity wouldn't leave it untouched," the ship's computer replied.

"Not surprised," Phyla said. "Check Erick's next."

Opal's room was empty, not quite as clean as Trina's, but Phyla could see the efficiency in it. Military order said what was good enough to get things done, to make it right. The sheets folded up, ready for washing. The console cleaned, but not scrubbed shining. In the locker, a pair of sidearms and some spare batteries. Things Opal felt she wouldn't need that would be better left for the others. Phyla left them there. She'd know where to find them if they were needed.

"Hey, you might want to come check this out," Fournine said. "Seems the doctor got sentimental."

Phyla took the short walk across the hall to Erick's cabin and opened the door. Photos sat on the cot: printed out security camera stills. Dates on each one etched in Erick's messy handwriting.

"Memories," Phyla said, picking up the closest one and taking a look.

It was the first day they'd welcomed Opal onto the ship. The sniper had been the sixth crew member, and she was standing there in the *Jumper's* main bay as the other five held single drams of whiskey up to welcome her. Davin, Phyla, Mox, Trina, Erick, and now Opal. A necessary long-range specialist to round out their detail. They'd decided to get into the escort business, as cargo hauling wasn't paying the same dividends. Opal looked almost shy in that picture, and Phyla saw her eyes had looked past the crew and landed on the small table behind them, where Davin had put her welcome gift. A new long rifle. At the time, Phyla had thought Opal was overwhelmed with gratitude. Now, though, the sniper's eyes seemed wary and sad.

The next picture was something Phyla hadn't seen before. Trina sitting in the med bay as Erick dyed her hair. This time into an emerald green. She never knew Erick had been the one doing that all these years. Then again, the mechanic and the doctor had forged a special friendship. They were the support that kept the *Jumper* and her crew going, it only made sense that they kept each other running too.

Mox in the middle of a workout, with Merc in the background shouting off reps. Erick had written on the bottom of this one; *keeping score.* Another had Viola coming back onto the ship after Europa, her face still fresh and innocent. And then there was something different.

The dim shot taken as the ship's lights were just turning on. It was the main bay, the boarding ramp was down. Haloed in the opening were two people. Two shapes Phyla recognized. Davin, herself. The first time they boarded the *Jumper* together. Davin was grinning, arms waving in that expansive gesture he used whenever he was truly, truly excited. And Phyla saw in herself the same cautious cool she thought she still had today. But there wasn't nervousness in that face. Determination. The knowledge that everything in that pack on her back was all she had, and that Phyla was leaving a place she had no desire to go back to.

That morning they would wait for Lina, and their friend would never come. They would take off, and head to Luna on a cargo run. And all this would come of it.

"Fournine, what's the status on pre-flight?" Phyla said, staring at the photo.

"Green and good," Fournine said. "Honestly, Trina left things so well it's almost boring. I can overload an engine if you want some excitement."

"I think we'll have enough of that where we're going."

"Have it your way. Oh, your best launch window is in two hours."

"Then I guess it's time to round up the troops."

58

METAL STORM

The rain was thick as it came down around the ferry. The drops hammered into Opal like stinging missiles every time she left cover. Awnings where the rest of the passengers gathered, huddled, and watched the thrashing storm. She'd peeked underneath the hoods of so many people and hadn't found the face she wanted. Until she made it all the way to the bow, and there, standing in the rain and leaning over the railing, was a single person. The hood drawn up, but the stance right. The height good. Opal had spent so long watching Alissa through her scope that she knew.

"Got her," Opal calmed to Merc. "Get up to the bow."

Opal walked towards the hooded figure, left the cover and felt the rain stick her face. Then another woman stepped in front of her, stared into Opal's eyes with a pair the sniper recognized immediately. Too perfect, too smooth. No life there.

"Don't," the android said. "This one is ours."

On Opal's right, she noticed a pair of figures heading straight for Alissa. Their backs rigid beneath their cloaks, their strides in perfect harmony. Three androids. It was an impossible fight. On her left, Opal saw Merc work his way through the crowd and pause, looking at her. Opal's right hand drifted beneath her cloak, to the beam knife clasped on her back thigh. She owed Alissa a debt.

"Love you, stick jockey," Opal said loudly.

The android tilted its head and stared at her. Not moving until Opal stabbed the beam knife into the bot's side and pushed it away. Alissa turned at the shriek of laser on metal, bringing a pair of sidearms up in either hand from beneath her cloak and aiming at the two approaching androids. Fired. The bots moved fast, ducking and weaving around Alissa's shots. She scored a hit, the right one wheeling back with a smoking hole in its chest. The left reached for her when a bolt struck it in the side, Merc's. Opal tried to move forward, but felt an iron grip around her arm.

The android whipped her to the ground.

Passengers screamed and ran away towards the ferry's aft. Opal pushed back along the floor into the space left by the retreating people, the android she'd stabbed standing over her. Reaching for her throat. Opal slashed at its hand, but the bot shifted its wrist just enough for the knife to hit only air. Metal fingers wrapped around her throat. Pressed her into the ground. Opal kicked the android's ankles, but the bot didn't budge. It wasn't a person. There were no weak spots.

Another flash. Another burning hole in the android's shoulder. But it didn't flinch, its unmoving eyes glaring at Opal. The sniper coughed, she couldn't breathe. Her lungs heaved. Her eyes stung as the rain lashed their open lids. And then Merc hit the android like a train, flying through the air and tackling the bot. Dragging its hand off her throat and carrying the android to the ground. Opal gulped in air and sat up. Saw Alissa roll between the two wounded androids, ducking and diving beneath their swipes. Opal struggled to her feet and moved over to meet her.

"Are you okay?" Opal asked as she moved closer.

"What are you doing here?" Alissa triggered another round at the two androids, who anticipated the shots and dipped to the right and left around them.

"Trying to help."

"Then take this, and shoot them," Alissa said, handing Opal one of her sidearms. The sniper wheeled and fired at the android struggling with Merc. Her shot hit the bot in the leg as it threw Merc into the bow railing. The fighter pilot bounced off and hit the ground hard. The android turned towards Opal, limping from the burning hole in its left knee.

"Down!" Alissa yelled, pulling Opal to the deck with her as a large pole sailed through the space where they'd been. A chunk of the railing torn off and turned into a missile by an android with too much strength.

Then the two androids were on them again, the third leaving Merc and getting closer. Opal fell into her boxing stance, the hand-to-hand she learned in the military, and tried to bob and weave. Slide in between the punches and deliver a shot to the ribs with the beam knife, or a sidearm blast. But no matter how fast she moved, the androids were quicker. The bots knocked aside her blows and struck her kidneys, her legs, her face. The third one lunged and shoved Opal back against the railing. Behind her, ten meters down, the churning sea battered against the ferry's side. Beside her, Alissa stumbled, bloodied and beaten.

Opal raised her fists, blinking the blood out of her eyes, and stared into the lifeless machines coming to kill her.

59

BLAST OFF

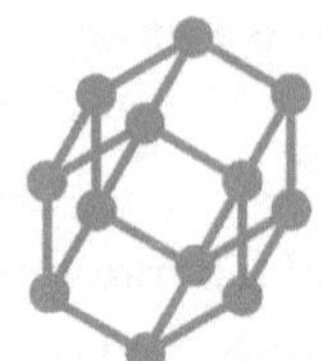

The engines felt empty without Trina's exacting presence. Viola stared at the console, measured energy going to and from both of the main engines and prepped them for flight. The short trip from the island up to Loci wasn't all that complicated, but they still needed someone down here in the bowels of the *Jumper* to make sure its giant rockets didn't blow themselves up.

"How're you doing down there?" Phyla's voice came over the comm.

"Getting used to it," Viola said. "How did you and Davin fly the ship yourselves?"

"We took turns. One of us down there, one of us up here. There was a lot of running."

"That sounds exhausting."

"It was worth it to escape Vagrant's Hollow."

Viola understood that one. When she ran away from Ganymede, she'd wanted to get away, see the real world, experience an adventure before locking herself away in an office, or a lab for the rest of her life. Now, she'd reprogrammed an android, piloted a freighter out of the swirling winds of Neptune, staged a commando raid, and killed a man. Guess that qualified as experience.

The *Jumper* rumbled as Phyla ignited the engines for takeoff. The spaceport retracted the roof over their bay and the downpour from the overhead storm battered the *Jumper*'s hull. Not great conditions, but when you're going to attack a guy holding humanity hostage, you don't get to wait for perfect weather. The lift-off felt different here, so much more energy sent to the engines to pick them up from the ground. Viola's stomach slammed into herself, and she was glad Trina actually installed straps down here. Earth's gravity was stronger than Mars, Minor Prime, Ganymede, almost anywhere that a ship would regularly land.

Viola played with the mechanisms, modulating which tanks and which batteries drained first. There was no window to the outside, just the sensation of the world falling away.

"What do you think?" Mox's voice on the comm.

"About what?" Viola replied.

"Earth," Mox said. "Wasn't that your first time?"

"I want to go back," Viola said. "I want to try it without all the anger, and sadness. Without death."

"That would be nice."

"Was that yours?" Viola asked.

"Grew up on the Moon. Never made the jump till now," Mox said.

"Would you go back?"

"If we make it, yeah."

"If? There can't be an if, Mox. We're going to win. We have too many friends who are depending on us."

"My experience? That's no guarantee."

That's no guarantee. Viola glanced back at the console, the workload on the engines decreasing as they hit the upper atmosphere. Here they were on a giant hunk of metal blasting their way into space. They had no right to be doing any of this. There was no guarantee that one of these engines wouldn't malfunction and blow them to smithereens. That someone from Earth's patrolling force wouldn't pick them up and burn them to a cinder. There wasn't even a guarantee that when they reached the space station Bosser wouldn't just shoot them as soon as they got off the ship. But here they were, giving it the best shot they had.

"It's all we've got, Mox. I believe we're going to do it. I have to."

"Hope you're right, Vi."

Davin clanked around the corner into the engine space. He caught Viola's eye and nodded back towards the main bay.

"Go take a look. Loci is pretty cool to see from the outside. I can handle these," the captain said.

Davin wasn't wrong. From over Phyla's shoulder, out through the cockpit window, Viola could see Loci as it came over the horizon. A central sphere covered with shoots in almost every direction, a porcupine whose spines ended in satellite dishes. As they came closer, the definitions of the space station became even more apparent. Company logos and artwork covered many of the dishes, creating a multicolored pallet that shined in the sunlight skipping off Earth's atmosphere.

"At least if we're going to die, it'll be somewhere pretty," Phyla said.

"I feel like that's anywhere in space," Viola replied.

"You haven't been inside some asteroids. Or in a Mars dust storm. You don't want to go out there."

Viola nodded. Phyla started the docking sequence, and as the *Jumper* slipped between a pair of giant green dishes blazed over with Eden's logo, Viola dipped out of the cockpit to her cabin. Time to check the weapons.

60

TAKE A DIVE

Man, they were blowing this. Merc pulled himself up, his sidearm still gripped in his right hand, and fired. The bolt glanced off the top of an android's head, the one dancing in between the other two and getting unblocked punches on the two women. It was the only bot far enough away to not risk blasting Opal or Alissa in the eye. The android turned its smoking head at Merc and charged.

Merc ducked a right punch from the android, then took the left cross hit in his side, the force barreling him into the ferry's railing. He looked right, trying to stuff away the pain, and saw Opal and Alissa buried beneath constant blows. They couldn't stay here. Couldn't win this fight. Merc's android came at him again, metal feet pounding on the deck. Merc tried to lift his sidearm and triggered another shot. It went wide, but the android flinched, possibly worried about another strike to its head. The pilot sidestepped along the railing. Felt his hand run over a length of rope. A rope tied to a lifeboat, one of a pair hanging off the bow over the open ocean.

The android rushed him and this time Merc pushed with his feet, jumped as the android hit him. The bot pushed Merc over the railing and into the lifeboat. His back slammed against one of the bench-style seats, numbing his nerves for an instant and sending waves of cascading pain up Merc's spine. The breath left his lungs, but Merc managed to squeeze off a shot, the laser slicing through the rope and sending the boat falling.

At least, the aft end.

With his left hand, Merc wrapped his arm around the seat and hung, suddenly in the open air as the lifeboat dangled from its remaining rope tie. With his right hand, Merc twisted and shot the other rope. The lifeboat plummeted towards the ocean, scraping against the side of the ferry. The aft hit the churning waves first, shoving the boat backwards and causing it to land right-side up on the water. Merc's head cracked against the seat and his vision blurred. Everything hurt, shocks crawling up and down his body from muscles done wrong. But he had to focus.

His right hand still held the sidearm, and Merc aimed towards where Opal and Alissa were struggling. Fired a shot. The laser went over their heads and struck the awning of the ferry, but it got their attention.

"Jump," Merc called, but his empty lungs couldn't do more than a whisper. Opal saw him and threw Alissa over the side. Then she jumped.

Merc tried to sit up as the two women splashed into the sea. The ferry was motoring past, the large wake of the engines coming closer. If the ferry went by while the two were still in the water, they could get sucked in. Merc rolled over and grabbed an oar locked into the side. Pulled it free. Then scanned the dark ocean for any sign. Alissa's hand, then her head were the first things he saw breaking for a second between the crest of a wave. She was throwing off her coat, ditching her vest. Anything that weighed her down. She was almost ten meters away. And Merc had never been on a boat in his life.

"Throw the ring!" Alissa shouted.

Ring? Merc glanced around, then saw it in the bow. A red and white circle. Merc dropped the oar and lunged for it. Threw it to Alissa, the ring's white rope billowing in the storm's wind. Still no sign of Opal. Alissa caught the ring, then dove beneath the surface.

Merc kept looking, trying to find the sniper. But in the dark, lightning-lit sea, he couldn't make out anything. To add on to the misery, the pain in his stomach was rapidly being replaced by a rolling nausea.

Then Alissa broke the surface, holding a coughing Opal against her chest and grabbing the ring. Merc stared for a second, stunned, before pulling the rope. The waves bashed the boat up against the side of the ferry, but the lifeboat was well-made and didn't tip. As the ferry went past and the churning wake spun the lifeboat, Merc pulled the pair in. Brought Opal over the side by grabbing her arm and falling back into the lifeboat, pulling her with him. Alissa clambered in after.

"Thank you," Alissa said as Opal continued coughing.

"It's . . . what I do," Merc said.

Alyssa looked at him, confused. "You throw life preservers?"

"No, I, nevermind."

Merc sat back on the seat, turning to look at the retreating ferry. The island where they came from was still in sight, its outline on the horizon popping in when lightning flashed. Rest for a while in the rain, then they could row back. This one had been close, too close. Merc rested a hand on Opal, who'd finished hacking up her own puddle of water and was leaning against the boat's side, groaning.

"We made it, hotshot," Merc said to her. She looked at him, her soaked, cut, and bruised face breaking into a half smile. One that turned to open panic as the boat shook. A hand, its metal fingers gripping the side, appeared over the aft edge. After came those dead eyes, looking right at him.

61

MELODY

You want an easy place to dock, Loci was your station. Davin lowered the ramp and walked into the small bay. Barely enough to fit the *Jumper*, the bay only had rudimentary amenities. A few canisters and battery charging hookups to connect the station's solar panels to charge docking ships. No welcome mat, no greeting. The only person they talked to was a robot, one that asked their reason for landing and then gave them access.

Davin had told it that they were offloading goods. Apparently Loci merited so little security that the bot didn't bother to confirm Davin's story. Just gave them clearance to one of Loci's three bays.

Behind him, the others made it off the ship. Davin had Melody, his fire-spewing shotgun, and a pair of sidearms. Phyla carried her usual rifle. Mox had his cannon attached, the monster weapon hanging over his chest and jutting its barrel out nearly a meter. Viola mirrored Phyla, except for the stance. The young hacker didn't look quite so confident holding the rifle as her flame-haired friend did. This time, though, Davin thought Viola looked like she could actually fire the thing.

Experience, it works wonders.

"Last chance, anyone wants to bail," Davin said. "Loci's small, and the communications hub is in the center. You don't have much time to second-guess."

"Don't think that's going to happen," Mox said.

"I want first shot," Viola said. "When we find Bosser."

"Way I see it, we all have reasons to shoot," Davin said. "You get the chance, you take him out. No worrying about turn order."

Davin played those words back. The Wild Nines didn't do assassinations. He'd never taken money for a kill. Yet here they were. Their last mission, and the goal was ending a life. But if there was one man to start with, Bosser would be that one.

They left the bay and went into Loci's central corridor. All three of the station's small docking bays were on the same side, the next one over held the standard shuttle Bosser had taken up from the facility, the featureless face logo of the androids slapped on outside. Trina's hack on Threetwelve had worked. It sent them sensor data, showing Bosser flying up here, showing him landing, and now Threetwelve showed its leader standing in the middle of the station.

Loci itself was bare-bones. No stores, shops, only emergency rations and rooms with cots for those staying at the station overnight. Any food or drink was ordered through a series of vending machines on one wall. Machines that would send their inventory to the company managing the station, and they'd arrange a resupply whenever things went low. Standard protocol for installations that didn't warrant a full-time human presence.

A ten minute walk brought them to the central core, the only place in the station with a door sealing it off from the rest. Soundproofing for sending a broadcast directly from the station. In front of the door, a flat gray slab with a light in the middle that glowed crimson, indicating the equipment was in use, were a pair of straight-standing men. They looked at Davin and the other three without reaction.

"I'm gonna go ahead and guess those aren't people," Phyla said.

"Not taking that bet," Davin said. "Viola, stay back. If you see an opening, go for the door. Get to Bosser before he can activate the other androids."

"I got left. He's uglier," Mox said. Davin nodded.

"Phyla, on two, we open up," Davin said.

Viola went back a few meters while Mox shifted to the left side of the corridor. Phyla raised her rifle, Davin aimed Melody, and the two androids blurred forward. No waiting for the first shot.

"Shoot it!" Davin yelled. He pulled Melody's trigger, aiming it at the charging bot. Phyla's lasers streaked past, peppering the android as it dipped and dove under Melody's homing fireballs. Pellets that ignited and tracked the intended target. Pellets that burned themselves out, and if they made contact, were hot enough to ignite just about anything.

The android took a hit on the left shoulder from Phyla's rifle, kept coming, then took another in the right leg. It stumbled, and then Davin's second shot caught it. Three of the six green fire orbs collapsed into the android, exploding against its clothes and melting into its plaskin exterior. The bot reeled, and Phyla kept peppering it with bolts. Chunks of metal blew off as her lasers chewed away its shell. It was only a couple meters away now, but its limbs were twitching, its left leg dragging. Davin stepped forward and pulled Melody's trigger a third time as the android reached its clawed and burning hand towards his face.

The green fire roared out of Melody and slammed into the android, pushing it to the ground. It jerked once. The hand reaching for Davin gripped only air, and then nothing. Nothing except melted metal.

62

THE SAME

Mox spun up the cannon, loosing a hail of bolts as the android darted towards him. The bot used the lower gravity, jumped and rebounded off the wall and ceiling to get around Mox's fire. The cannon's lasers chewed into the wall surrounding Loci's central core, tracing an outline of the bot's evasion. As the android pushed off the wall towards the ceiling a second time, Mox anticipated, led the jump, and blitzed home a series of hot laser, chewing chunks out from the bot's chest. But it kept coming, pushed off the ceiling and landed just beneath the end of the cannon. Gripped the barrel in its metal hands and started to twist.

Mox detached the weapon, letting go as the android pulled, swinging the suddenly free cannon away. The android, its arms swinging out left as it let go of the cannon, didn't have any defense for Mox's gauntleted fist streaking towards its chest. The impact, boosted by the exoskeleton, sent the android flying back, arms and legs wide. The low gravity on Loci, kept to a tenth of Earth's through rotation, meant the bot flew all the way back to the central core. It caught itself on the wall, crouched and launched back at Mox.

The metal man bent his knees, turned his right shoulder away, and prepared to deliver one heck of a punch to the face the incoming android.

"You and I are the same," the android shouted as it closed. And Mox flinched.

The android hit Mox hard and sent them both to the ground. Mox tried to wrap his arms around the bot, but the android moved fast, scrambling up and over Mox's head. The android gripped Mox's shoulders and swung the big man into the wall next to them. Mox felt his back crunch into the metal slate, his head ringing. And then the android was on him again. Swinging punches into his abdomen. The force of the blows, and the low gravity, pinned Mox to the side of the wall.

"I am made of metal," the android said, tapping a series of rapid jabs into Mox's ribs. "And so are you."

"Not only," Mox said. He felt blood in his mouth, warm sticky iron. Spat it into the android's eye. The bot paused, the red smear covering its face, and Mox fell to the ground.

As soon as Mox hit the floor, he swept out with his left arm and caught the android's ankle. Pulled. The android hit the ground, but the low gravity robbed the hit of much force. Mox pressed down on the android ankle to push himself up, just in time to catch the android rolling forward and punching him in the chin. Mox stumbled back, seeing the endless flashes from Davin and Phyla's weapons to the side. Hopefully they were doing better than he was.

"And I am also made of code, instincts I don't understand that tell me how to operate," the android spoke quickly, closing with Mox. "Just like your brain, I interact and react based on my intuitions."

"Intuitions designed, not learned."

Mox jumped the bot's first swing, then kicked, the low gravity giving him plenty of time in the air to swing his leg forward and strike the android in the face. The force pushed the bot into the wall, bouncing off it to the ground. Mox landed, walked over to the android as it picked itself up.

"You don't make choices," Mox said. "Not your own ones, anyway."

The android rotated, bringing with it a hard fist. Mox took the hit, but grabbed the bot's left arm as it rebounded from the impact. His leg was numb from the shot, but Mox had the android's left arm tight. With his right hand, Mox grabbed the android's other right wrist and pulled them apart. He felt the android resisting as its arms spread. The force pulled the androids face close to his own.

"You don't believe I'm making a choice?" the android said, its yellow metal eyes boring holes into Mox's mind.

"I believe you're following instructions."

The android was almost as strong, almost able to push Mox's arms back. But the exoskeleton, but Mox, had the leverage. Had the muscle. The tearing and snapping wires came first, followed by sparks as Mox yanked the android's arms out of their sockets and threw them aside. The android faltered back two steps, tilted its head it Mox.

"I suppose it is impossible to know," the android said.

And then it blew up.

63

CAN'T GIVE UP

The water pouring off the android's skin made it glisten as lightning blitzed in the night. Between flashes, Opal saw the android grab Alissa and turn back to the ocean. It was just going to take her and leave.

"Hey," Opal said, pushing herself up and diving onto the androids back. Her lungs still burned from the water she inhaled a moment ago, her legs and arms and chest raining with a thousand bruises, but Opal pushed her way past the pain to cling to the android's head and pull it back.

The bot struggled, the back of its ankles hitting the boat's aft bench. With nowhere to backpedal, the android fell, smashing Opal into the bottom of the boat as it rocked in the wave. The sniper didn't see what happened to Alissa, but saw the android clearly as it rolled over in the boat and reached out towards her. A laser's bright flash echoed the lightning and struck the android in the shoulder. Merc sat in the front of the boat, holding his sidearm out, dazed and determined. The android propelled itself across the two benches and slapped the weapon away from the pilot. Opal got up in time to see Merc take a hard blow to the head and collapse.

She hoped Merc still armed himself as she taught him.

As the android turned around, Opal reached into Merc's right boot, and found the beam knife strapped there. Pulled it out and activated the laser blade. A hot piece of sharp metal. In the pouring rain, thunder and lightning thrashing, the sniper faced the android on the rolling and pitching boat. Opal kept her weight moving with the waves, it felt similar to keeping her footing while making an aerial drop in atmosphere. Even on Mars, where the gravity wasn't quite so strong, a windstorm still had Opal moving to keep her feet. The android didn't hold its arms wide for balance, just shifted slightly around its knees.

"Come and take her," Opal said.

"You can't win," the android replied. "The odds are poor with that weapon. In this environment. I offer you a chance to surrender."

"Chance refused."

Opal lunged as she said the words, aiming the knife for the android's face. But her feet slipped on the base of the boat where puddles of water were forming and making the floor slick. The strike fell short, grazing the androids chest, and Opal caught herself on the front bench. Then the android grabbed her back, picked her up, and slammed her against the floor of the boat. Everything went blurry for a moment, but Opal held her vision onto that glowing blade, still gripped in her hand.

The android stepped over her, heading for the back of the boat, and Opal lashed out and cut the android's left ankle. It stumbled, but whatever magic in its programming allowed it to adjust kept the bot upright. It turned, reached for her.

"You are proving to be a threat," the android said, wrapping its fingers around her throat and lifting Opal up.

"Sorry about that," Opal said. She reached forward with the knife, burying the blade in the android's chest. Withdrew it and stabbed again as the bot's fingers tightened and cut off her air. Her throat retched, her nose flared, and Opal's eyes went wide. She felt the panic, and she pushed it down.

Keep stabbing. Hurt it enough so that it has to stop.

One slash, then another. Opal felt her body going numb. Black flecks sprinkled her vision. Another stab into the android's arm. Everything faded except the android's yellow eyes, looking into hers. Stab again, the dim response of her nerves telling her that the blade had at least hit the bot.

She couldn't keep her grip anymore. Simply sank into those yellow eyes.

Lightning struck nearby, catching Opal's glance, and in that fiery white line she saw motion, blurring behind the android. Then nothing at all.

64

GUARDIANS

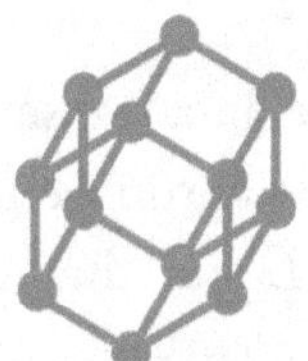

The bombs. The androids always had bombs. The words hammered along with her headache as Viola sat up. Around her, Loci station's alarms blared. But she could still breathe, still felt oxygen flow into her lungs. No hull rupture, then. The surrounding air was full of smoke, paper ash floating from burning clothes. She looked down at herself and saw tears in her own suit, long thin gashes where bits of blown metal slashed past her. On the ground nearby, attached to a splintered end of her broken belt, was Viola's sidearm. She couldn't see her rifle.

"Davin? Phyla?" Viola's scratchy voice called out to no response. "Mox?"

Nothing. Either unconscious, or dead. In front of her, standing out as a dark blur through the smoke, glowed the red light of the central core. Where Bosser would be. If the rest of them were dead, then Viola would be the one to stop him. What she'd wanted, right?

Viola stood, picked up the sidearm and checked its energy level. The power was good, the weapon set to kill. Coughing, stumbling, Viola held the sidearm in her right hand and made her way to the door. There wasn't a lock, just a simple open and shut button.

Boarding Loci was hard enough and had no value to someone without the right transmission codes. Why bother with security?

She pressed the button, and the door slid open.

On the other side was a short, dark hall. Following the smoke in, Viola walked to a large circular room, one wall dedicated to a massive screen, the middle an open stage, and the other half a set of chairs arranged as if for a play. For those special recordings that demanded an audience. On that stage stood Bosser, talking to the screen. Not seeing Viola.

"As you can see, with the data I've sent along, we're in prime position," Bosser said. "And the trial run went perfectly."

"You didn't warn me, Libra, that it would be on one of my freighters," said a voice, a voice Viola recognized. She looked at the screen and saw there, among ten other faces, her own father.

Viola blinked. What was he doing? And for that communication to happen so fast, her father would have to be nearby. On Earth, or Luna.

"The test demanded secrecy. You'll be reimbursed," Bosser said. "But the time for that secrecy is over, which is why I invited all of you to Luna to meet your guardians. They protect you at any cost, annihilate any enemy, and don't need the approval of the Free Laws to do it."

Guardians. That was a funny word for it. Viola looked at those faces, hoping to see horror or, maybe, anger. But all she saw were nods, agreement. Not only were these people, her father among them, happy to subvert the Free Laws that had governed humanity's expansion off Earth for a century, but they were happy to pay for it.

"Tell them what you did," Viola shouted, walking into the room with her sidearm held up. "Tell them what their guardians can really do."

Gasps and rapid chatter echoed from the screen, Viola heard her father call her name, but she kept her focus on the man in the middle, his calm stare as Bosser leveled his gaze at her. She held the sidearm up, finger on the trigger. Until something hit Viola hard from the side, sprawling her out on the floor, the weapon sliding away. The cold malevolence of ThreeTwelve looked at her.

"You wanted to see a demonstration of the guardians, there you go," Bosser said. "The threat removed. Incapacitated, so that now I can deal with her as I see fit."

Bosser walked towards Viola, held out a hand. ThreeTwelve removed a sidearm from its holster and set the weapon in Bosser's palm. He aimed it at Viola. She glared back at him and waited for the burning end.

"If you shoot her Bosser, you're done," Viola heard her father say. Annoyance flickered across Bosser's face, his eyes rolling and his mouth setting in a half-frown, then the man's small smile snapped back into place. He turned to the screen.

"Your daughter has proven herself to be quite the annoyance," Bosser said. "The Red Voice used her to get to Earth. She prevented the original execution of the Wild Nines. And now she's here, threatening to kill me. At what point does she become more trouble than she's worth?"

"Never," her father said. Despite the anger boiling in her, Viola felt a flush of love at the words. He might be a flawed, dangerous man, but he was still her father.

Bosser nodded, and then his grin spread wider, and cold fear blew through Viola's nerves.

65

UNEXPECTED

There were good interruptions, and there were bad interruptions. The girl walking in, sidearm up and at the ready, went from bad to good in a matter of moments. Bosser chose to look at it as an opportunity.

"So you see, your new guardians will keep you safe. Can even help you deal with your unruly children," Bosser said, adding a deprecating chuckle. "But we're not only here to talk about protection. As all of us know, keeping the current climate advantageous has always been the goal of the android project."

Yes. An order had been established, and that order wanted to keep itself intact. There wasn't much Bosser had to do to get what he wanted, a place on top of that same stack. Pulling the strings. A home on Earth, weaving intrigue across the solar system. Was that really so much to ask?

"And you say these guardians can do that?" Capricorn asked. The woman led a biome development corporation, a business dedicated to creating those bubbles that kept humans alive in the worst environments. A venture that was proving increasingly susceptible to lawsuits, to frustration from governments and citizens who just didn't understand that it was risky. That some might fail. That the occasional accident was a necessary marker of progress.

"They can. I'll be sending along the codes you need to control your guardians. And when you need something special, you work through me. I'll stay on Earth, run the facility, make your guardians to order. Once everyone understands how things work, who's going to bother fighting against us? Who's going to bother fighting against you?" Bosser said.

The desire to protect what's theirs. It was so easy to manipulate, to twist their minds around the idea that what they had was too valuable to lose, no matter what the cost. Who cared if they were giving up just a bit of power to one man and his bots, if what they got in exchange was stability, the chance to keep their castle? Bosser repressed his smile. Careful now. Unanimous agreement, followed by financial investment, and then everything Bosser needed would be his. And once he had his guardians in place, ready to do as he wanted with a simple phrase, all of them would have no other choice than to keep him on top.

"So I think it's time to call this to a vote," Bosser said. "Those who like what they've seen, who want to move forward into a new, stable world where our interests are protected and the risk of opposition is made moot by an invincible protecting force, say aye. The cowards, the ones who want to keep today's fragile structure where any moment can be blown to shreds by a rebel with a bomb and an agenda, say nay."

To his left, ThreeTwelve kept Viola pinned. In front of them, on their screens, the various leaders looked askance at each other. They were all in the same hotel on Luna, all together, with a set of androids waiting outside their rooms. In earshot of the transmission's audio. Bosser watched their expressions and brought two phrases to his lips. No matter which way the vote went, he would be the winner. Then the first aye came, from Cancer. Then the second from Capricorn. And the cascade began, Bosser's smile growing wider, unhinged with the adulation.

"Hey, jackass, time's up," a hoarse voice shouted from the hallway into the studio. Bosser turned and saw the wreck of a man standing there. Davin Masters, clothes cut to ribbons, bleeding from a hundred cuts, and one eye swollen shut. The man didn't even have a sidearm.

"Virgo, how about this one?" Bosser said. "Any qualms, or can I show you what you agreed to?"

Virgo, fearless protector of his daughter, said nothing. And so Bosser turned back to the ruined captain and shrugged.

"Sorry, Davin. I guess you have no friends here. What's done is done."

When Bosser spoke the phrase, ThreeTwelve dropped Viola to the ground and sprung on Davin. It pulled the long knife from the holster on its leg, and held it out, going right for the captain's throat. A messy kill, but examples needed to be clear.

BRAWL

ThreeTwelve looked just like Fournine had, way back on Europa. The merciless mask lunging towards him at a speed too fast to comprehend. But Davin didn't have to react, he just had to say the words.

"Tables turned," Davin said as the blade swept up in towards his throat. The words Trina said to use. The override she'd put into ThreeTwelve's code.

ThreeTwelve stopped. Literally froze, the blade a centimeter from cutting Davin to pieces. The captain took a breath, an inhale that seemed to ignite all of his cuts simultaneously. The fiery stings only sharpened his focus. He was so hurt already, what did it matter if Bosser did something now? Though that man had his mouth open, eyes bulging, at the sight of his android doing precisely *not* what he'd commanded.

"Take care of your master," Davin said. ThreeTwelve turned around and charged Bosser. Davin would have to thank Trina for this, get a message back to Earth or land there and give the mechanic a tight hug. The sight of Bosser as his plans collapsed around him, the shouts from the council, all those faces on the screen dropping into panic as the android turned against its owner, that was worth it.

"This one's for Lina," Davin said as ThreeTwelve reached Bosser and grabbed the man. Lifted him up and cocked its blade back.

Bosser's hand moved fast, pressed a button on his comm. Three-Twelve melted, Davin couldn't think of another word to describe it. The android's parts simply collapsed in on themselves, piling onto the ground a collection of scattered circuits, plates of skin, and the knife blade. ThreeTwelve's head rolled a meter away, no longer connected to its body. Bosser brushed himself off, looked at Davin and shook his head.

"Wasn't planning to show that one today," Bosser said. "Marl mentioned you had a lot of tricks, she wasn't wrong."

Davin didn't have a weapon. Melody and the sidearms he'd carried were shredded by the explosion. He didn't know if Bosser's weird device would melt him too. But there was one avenue out, the android's knife. It sat there on the stage, just a few meters ahead.

"Bosser," a face on the screen said. "What was that?"

The question turned Bosser's head, and Davin made a run for it. His feet pounded on the stage, the chilly floor spiking cold up through holes melted in his boots, and as Bosser turned back, Davin's hand dragged down and gripped the hilt of the knife. Swung it up, only to have Bosser grab his forearm and halt the swing.

"It's my own protection," Bosser said to Davin's face, in reply to the talking head's question. "When you work with androids, you take precautions."

Davin raised his knee, went for the crotch shot, but Bosser twisted away. Grabbed Davin's leg and wrenched it up. Davin hit the ground and rolled. Tucked the knife in and gave himself some space. Came up to a crouch as Bosser went towards him.

"And when do we get those precautions?" The voice on the screen asked.

"When I choose to give them to you," Bosser said. He was keeping his eyes on Davin's knife. That was an opportunity. Davin got to his feet, then feinted the stab with his right hand. Bosser flinched away and made to grab the forearm again. Except this time, Davin stepped in and threw a left hook. The punch caught Bosser on the side of the head, knocking the man away.

"Damn, that hurt," Davin said, pulling his hand back. "Your head made of metal too? You just like the rest of them?"

Davin didn't wait for Bosser to answer, but ran after him and stabbed towards the man's kidneys. Bosser turned with the jab, took the blade into his side, and connected with Davin's face. The shock of the punch robbed Davin stab of its force and the blade only made a shallow cut before Bosser knocked it away. It bounced off the stage and underneath one of the chairs, leaving the two men breathing hard and staring at each other.

"Been a long time since I fought this way," Bosser said. "I forgot how refreshing it is to feel a man's bones break beneath your fist."

"Like you've ever broken anything," Davin said. "You just hide behind your bots and let them do the dirty work."

Bosser gave him a silky smile and moved in. The man had some experience, he dropped into a stance that Davin didn't recognize. Not that it mattered. This wasn't going to be a pretty brawl. Davin brought his fists up, and stepped into a kick, high left angled right at Bosser's crouching eye. Bosser stepped into it, taking the kick on the shoulder and leveling three quick strikes into Davin's stomach. The world veered at the impacts, waves of nausea coming up as Davin's stomach convulsed. He backed off, retching blood into his mouth.

"Doesn't look like you're ready," Bosser said. "The reason I let my bot fight first is so that I can save my energy for when it really matters. Like when I have to show a ship's captain where he belongs."

Bosser came forward in a short jog, running into another three punch sequence. Davin stumbled just out of reach. Then he bit back, the captain dodging past the final punch in Bosser's sequence and, pushing against the man's shoulder while sweeping his leg against Bosser's ankle, tripped Bosser into the ground. Then Davin fell on him and went into his favorite move; the dirty struggle. Davin used every part of his body: swinging elbows, bashing knees, biting at Bosser's face with his teeth. The easiest way to counter a strategy was to have no strategy at all.

Bosser struggled back, and Davin felt the man trying to move his arms and legs beneath them. The captain tried to prevent it, elbowing Bosser in the kidney, taking a chunk out of Bosser's cheek with his teeth. Davin's right hand tore off Bosser's comm and flung it across the room. Then Davin felt a hand on his throat, and Bosser was rolling with him, slamming Davin down against the floor. Davin's head cracked against the ground, and the world swam. Bosser's bloodied face looked down at him.

"If that's how you like it," Davin croaked.

"It'll do," Bosser said, raising his fist. Swinging it, hitting Davin in the temple. Black flickered across Davin's vision. His arms went weak.

Sorry, Lina. Can't fight this one anymore.

67

ONE SHOT

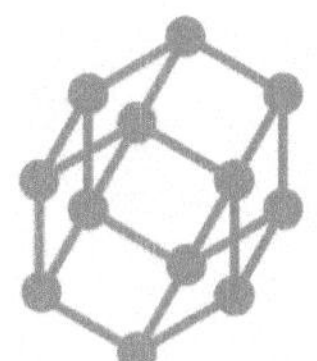

The aim was steady. Bosser right there in the middle. Swinging another punch at Davin.

"Don't do it, Viola," her father said on the screen. Bosser turned up at the words, paused his beating, and stared at Viola and the sidearm. Davin turned his head more slowly, and Viola winced at the sight of the captain's bruised and battered face.

"Listen to your father," Bosser said. "You have nothing to gain, and everything to lose. Shoot here, in front of a dozen witnesses, and you're a murderer. Your future ruined. Your father's business tainted."

Viola's eyes moved to the screens, to those famous, fabulously wealthy owners of the engines of human commerce. All of them judging her, waiting and watching to see what she would do next. To see if she would take the shot.

The first time, the only time she'd killed was to protect a friend. This time was no different.

Viola pulled the trigger. The orange bolt spat out of the sidearm and burrowed itself into Bosser's chest. The man's face curled from stern surprise to plain shock. Viola fired again. The second bolt hitting Bosser's stomach and collapsing him off of Davin. She walked up to Bosser and fired again and again and then Davin was pulling her arm back.

"It's over," Davin said. "It's over."

Viola took a breath. Her fingers let go of the sidearm. And she stared into the wide, glassy, dead eyes of Bosser Oates.

68

MAY MARS NEVER BE SILENT

Alissa had swung the oar, it'd hit the android's head, and the bot dropped Opal. Staggered to the boat's edge. Alissa swung the oar again, cracking the android in the face as it turned to face her. The force toppled the android over the side into the raging ocean. Alissa dropped the wooden weapon, grabbed Opal's beam knife, and as the android's metal hand again gripped the side of the boat, slid across the bench to meet it.

"This is for Castor," Alissa said, then jammed the beam knife into the android's yellow eye. The pouring rain shoved her hair into her face, and by the time Alissa brushed it out of the way, the crackling lightning showed nothing but dark blue water off the side of the boat.

Over the next hour, Alissa struggled with the oars, locking them in and guiding the boat back to shore. On the windswept beach, exhausted and spent, Alissa picked up Opal's limp wrist. The sniper was still alive. Whether she deserved to be was another question, but they'd come on the ferry to save her, so perhaps now was not the right time for vengeance. Besides, Alissa wasn't sure she could heft the oar again to deliver a strike. Her arms were like lead, and she was so soaked. The tropical water was warm, but there on the beach, in the breeze, things were getting chilly.

"I don't know who's listening," Alissa said into Opal's comm, on the sniper's default channel. "But your sniper and her friend are here on the beach."

Alissa followed up with the precise coordinates, then stood up and walked away. She'd left everything on that ferry. Only her comm, and some coin stashed in accounts registered to other names. That fit with her bruises and cuts, which, Alissa was sure, made her look like some sort of horror story. Those looks were confirmed by the first tourists she came to, at a bar still open. A band playing, even this late, under an awning. But there was warmth, there was a seat, and there was liquor. The bartender didn't even hesitate, dropping a shot in front of her.

"Look like you need this," the bartender muttered. Alissa didn't argue. But she sipped the small drink slow. Savored the burn. Took some bar napkins and patted down her face.

Her comm vibrated. A new message. Maybe Bosser had found her number. Called to gloat. Or yet another bank telling her they'd frozen her assets. She lifted the tool up, and on the small screen, read the text.

Alissa,

I hope this finds you well. As instructed, those of us left have made our way to Titan. The settlement here is small, but suitable. Eden does not have their hands on it yet. We procured a security contract and are establishing ourselves. One of Bakr's members, a woman named Cass, arrived here not long ago. She had a single gem, from Neptune, that has provided us with unexpected coin.

We await your return, or your orders.

May Mars never be silent.

- Ferro

Alissa looked up from the comm to see the bartender staring at her.

"Need another?" He asked.

"When's the next ship out?" Alissa replied.

The bartender glanced at the clock hanging beside the bar.

"The late one jumps in an hour," the bartender said. "If you want space, anyway. Ferry won't be back till tomorrow."

"Then I'm good, thanks."

Alissa slipped off the stool, her shoes leaving puddles wherever she stepped. Walked away from the bar and towards the glow of the space port. The Red Voice wasn't gone yet.

May Mars never be silent.

69

SNIPER'S HEADACHE

The first thing she heard was the rippling row of the surf. The watery waves crawling their way through sand and rock, whistling and popping. She stayed there like that for a moment, eyes closed and listening to the sound. Gulls squawked overhead, and the softer, deeper roar of a departing ship sifted through on the breeze. It wasn't until she heard the cough that Opal let light back into her world. With the dazzling sun came muted pains, tight muscles and the feeling of a band pressed around her forehead, pushing down against her.

"You're going to feel like crap," Erick said.

Opal twisted her head as another cough sounded. In the bed next to her, built on a small frame meant for children, Merc lay. His ankles dangled off the end, but someone had put a footstool there, covered it with a pillow, supporting his feet. The pilot's eyes were still closed.

"He'll be out longer than you," Erick said. "His head is pretty messed up. He's going to need some recovery time."

Opal turned back to the doctor and tried to find the air in her lungs to speak.

"And Alissa?" Opal said.

"She left. Rowed you both back to the island, then found us."

Left. Back out where the androids could find her. Opal tried to sit up, but Erick pressed her back down into the sheets, into the sweet comfort of the pillow.

"You sit up now, you're likely to throw up all over this bed," Erick said. "I'd rather not have to clean that up."

"We need to find her. She'll be in danger," Opal said.

"No, she won't," Trina stepped into the room. She had her comm held up in front of her face, projecting a news article. "Davin and the others won. Bosser's dead."

"Dead?"

"Shot. They're saying it was one of his own androids. Malfunctioned in his face, blew him up."

"ThreeTwelve?" Opal asked.

"Maybe," Trina said. "I haven't been able to get Davin on the comm so I don't know for sure. But they've put a stop to the android program until it can be reviewed. The facility has already been taken over and shut down."

"Which means you can rest," Erick said.

Maybe, just for a while. Opal felt her eyes grow heavy. Slid the lids back over to hide the sun and vanished into her dreams.

SEE THE WORLD

The table was covered in parts, drawing all kinds of looks from passengers arriving for the ferry. Viola ignored them, focused on binding the thin metal pieces together. It wouldn't be the same level of quality that Puk had before, but it would be enough. She could carry the bot with her on her backpack.

"We're going back to running cargo," Davin said, walking up behind her. "Should be safe. Like a vacation, only with some coin at the end."

"You want to know if I'm interested?" Viola replied.

"Just making the offer. Always good to have a mechanic on board, especially with Trina staying here," Davin's face, his body were covered in bandages. He wore thick sunglasses and, even in the heat, a coat. Anything to keep the stares away.

"I don't think so," Viola was surprised how easily the words came. But they were true. She was too tired, too drained. She turned her face away from Puk's pieces and looked out over the ferry to the open water beyond. A whole ocean, and a whole world full of new things that she'd never seen before. "I'm not ready to leave Earth just yet."

"I'd say the same thing if I were you."

"Isn't this your first time here too? Don't you want to see everything?"

Davin ran a hand through his hair and followed Viola's look out to the sea.

"I've been here before. Once or twice. Staying would be nice. Problem is, well, the problem's the same that it's always been. We need coin, and the *Jumper*'s the easiest way to get it. One of these days, maybe we'll sell it. Come back here and float around the world," Davin flashed a grin. "Till then, we'll be taking whatever job comes our way."

The captain walked away a minute later, leaving Viola to the tools. Over the next hour she locked the last pieces in the place. Pulled the sidearm from her holster, the same one that she'd used to put an end to Bosser two days ago up on Loci. Looked at it for a moment, felt its weight in her hand, then popped out the battery. Shoved it in the slot on Puk's new body and pressed the button on her comm.

Puk, now a gray brick with a single light that flickered to green life, woke up.

"Hey, Viola. Where are we?" Puk said, the single speaker emitting tinny, grainy audio.

"On Earth, Puk."

"Swell. Also, feel like I had a bit of a downgrade."

"You kind of blew yourself up. What you've got now is all I have on hand."

"Sounds like something I'd do," Puk said. "So where are we going next?"

"Wherever this ferry is taking us."

"Let me look it up, I'll tell you all about it."

Viola stood, latched Puk onto her backpack, and walked towards the ferry. The bot talked the entire way, and Viola just smiled and listened.

71

LUNA

Earth hung in the sky like a giant ornament. Luna's glass domes accentuated the glow, making the planet appear even more beautiful than it did from space. A bright spark drew Mox's eyes back towards the spaceport. That it be the *Jumper*, blasting off for Miner Prime. For another cargo run.

With a pair bags over his shoulders, the same two he'd brought on board years ago, Mox turned with the funneling crowd leaving the spaceport and headed into the city. He glanced at his wrist; the message sitting there.

Welcome back, metal man. Glad you're here. We've got work to do.
-Sarge.

As he went down the escalator, Mox caught the sight of a flowing red cape. The sign of the Centurion, Luna's own police force. He'd worn one once. Maybe they'd let him have it again.

72

PROBLEMS TO SOLVE

Trina sat in the chair awkwardly. It was a little too tall for her legs, the armrests a little too long. She felt like a girl.

"You're the one that hacked ThreeTwelve?" the woman, Abril, spoke to her. At the table were a few other engineers, and a man in full military regalia. The representatives from Earth's governments.

"It wasn't that hard," Trina said.

"And you could make it harder?" Abril said.

Make it harder? Give her enough time, and Trina could turn these androids invincible. Not that they hadn't been deadly before, but without Bosser introducing weaknesses for his own ends, Trina could make the bots strong. Perfect. It would be a problem, a challenge. And she'd get to stay right here, on Earth, out of range of any more lasers.

"But controlled," the military man said. "No chance they could go rogue, no chance someone could do what Bosser did."

"Sir," Trina said. "All I want is interesting problems to solve."

"And what could be more interesting than this?" Abril asked.

The military man shook his head, looked at Abril skeptically.

"We'll be keeping a close eye," the military man said. He turned back to Trina. "No matter what she says, remember that you're working for us now. For Earth. Bosser made a promise of guardians, one that he didn't fulfill. I hope you can."

Trina didn't do more than nod, her mind was already racing forward into plans, equations, and solutions. When the androids lived again, they wouldn't be walking weapons for one crazed man, they would be the ultimate sword for justice.

73

THE WHISKEY JUMPER

avin looked up from the console at the vast array of stars laid out in front of him. The Moon receded behind the *Jumper*, and all they had to do now was follow the yellow line to Miner Prime. To where Mako, the junk dealer from Europa, wanted Davin to pick up some special supplies. Just the things Mako needed to finish his masterpiece on that Jupiter moon. What that masterpiece was, Davin didn't ask. The surprise would be good enough.

"Did you see the pictures that Erick took?" Phyla asked from the pilot's chair.

"Man was always getting sentimental," Davin replied.

"Oh yeah, like you're never that way."

"Phyla, I'm a forward-looking dude. The past only has problems."

"Problems? I thought the whole reason you went after Bosser was because of your past."

"And look what it got me." Davin looked down at his bandage wrapped body.

"But do you regret it?"

"Not at all. It was for Lina."

They sat in silence for a minute. Phyla's hand found its way to Davin's. Her fingers threaded between his, squeezed.

"I don't think you should leave the past behind," Phyla said. "You don't want to forget who you are."

"That's why you're here, to remind me."

Phyla laughed.

"Do I get paid extra for that? Feel like it's going to be a lot of work."

"Not a chance," Davin said.

Fournine announced that the *Jumper* was about to punch the engines to full cruising speed, and Davin got up. His turn to watch the energy levels, make sure things weren't going to blow up all over them. As he started down the ladder from the cockpit, Davin glanced back at Phyla. Caught her smile. The same bright eyes he'd seen when they first left Miner Prime years ago. Before they'd met Mox, Cadge, wandered back and forth across the solar system searching for adventure.

Maybe she was right, maybe some things were worth remembering after all.

74

A SPECIAL OFFER

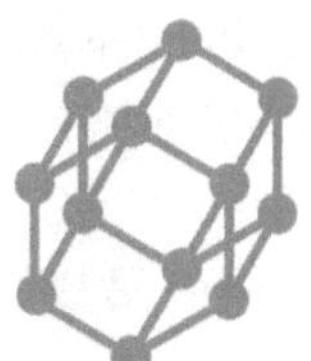

The cafe overlooked the long scar of the Grand Canyon. Viola sipped from the frothy cup and watched a flock of birds fly by overhead. In between the clouds she could pick out gray shapes, dots in the sky. Earth's space stations ringing the planet. Spoiling the flawless blue, but down below the lines of orange and purple rock spread out untainted.

"Another one off the list," Viola said. "Put it at number three."

"That's pretty good," Puk said, "but I can't argue with you."

"The canyon is beautiful," said a new voice. The chair across from Viola pulled out and Captain Yuan took the seat. He didn't look much different from when they'd met on Neptune, except here he was in civilian clothes. A jacket, plain gray T-shirt, jeans. He didn't do anything to his eyes; that same calm intensity. "You're a hard woman to find, Viola."

"Didn't know anyone was looking," Viola said. She tried to keep her hand steady, wrapped it around the cup. Last time she'd seen Yuan, they'd blown apart two spaceships and nearly got themselves killed in the vacuum around Neptune. Not the most pleasant memory.

"Eden has a job for you," Yuan said. "I told them I'd ask."

"What kind?"

"Before I go on," Yuan softened. "You can say no. I'll walk away, say I couldn't find you. But if I tell you, then you can no longer just disappear. You'll be committed."

Viola paused. She'd been around the Earth, but still had plenty left to see. Still had a lot she wanted to do before getting back behind the desk. But something in Yuan's voice said that this wasn't something she wanted to miss. That this wasn't an opportunity that would come around again. There'd been adventure, and she'd seen more than her share of violence, but something tugged at her. Kept her from saying no.

Maybe it was time for something new.

READ on for an excerpt from the WILD NINES' next adventure, ROGUE BET!

AN EXCERPT FROM ROGUE BET
THE WILD NINES BOOK FOUR

Her eye changed its color. Again and again, the mark's right eye, framed with a metal striping giving up her enhancements, shifted to match the club's frenetic lights which played through cold color schemes to a scattershot beat. Starfield tile laced with neon littered the floor, the walls, the ceiling. *Neil's* ignored its namesake and its own lunar location and caved to the gyrating sensory assault so damn prevalent these days.

But Davin wouldn't have been three drinks deep without that eye.

"You're coming recommended," Theona said, twisting her talk back to Davin's street cred for what must've been the fifth time. "I normally vet my runners."

"I'm not the one with a deadline," Davin leaned back, casual personified, then jerked upright as his stool nearly toppled over.

Theona's normal eye quirked an eyebrow and she made for her silver Stardust cocktail, the drink more sugar than anything else. Slurped the thing through a straw as long as Davin's forearm. Around them, early afternoon drunks parleyed a half-day's wages into a full night's fun. *Neil's* didn't care that dinner wouldn't come for hours yet, the psychic beats pulsed through the floor, through the stool, and bounced Davin's brain around more than the straight Moon Rum fixes he'd been sipping.

Their table sat in the third node branching off a rectangular dance floor whose swirling nebula floor pitched galactic wonder to, right now, a single man swaying his hips to a beat only he could hear.

Davin didn't think he was too many rounds away from joining the guy, but his outfit didn't match *Neil's* workman vibe. Slick with space-faring leather and trumped up with multi-planetary spices, Davin had that classy vagabond look that put him intriguingly out of place in any setting. Theona paired nicely, her mechanical eye complementing a spliced up assembly slotting colors, metals, and cloth in fits and starts that shouldn't have worked but, in *Neil's* neon blast, sucked in Davin's attention.

"I'm trying to find you," Theona said, drawing Davin back. "But talking to you's like trying to catch a salmon mid-stream. Most runners aren't so hard to figure."

Salmon mid-stream? Davin slotted away that line for later. Maybe the woman had come up from Earth, spent some time in a business not built on running illegal weapons. Maybe that damn eye made it easy to spot the fish under the water. Which, how many fish would she have to catch to pay—

"Are you even paying attention?" Theona asked. "I'm the one paying you, remember?"

"Sure." Focus, Davin. C'mon. You need this. "You already know about my ship, you know what I can do. What, you want a resume?"

"Already have that," Theona replied, then leaned in. "Thing is, I'm getting the wrong vibe from you, Davin. Like you're not who you're saying you are."

"I'm the man that saved the solar system," Davin replied.

"Then why're you meeting me in this club?"

Why? Davin had a thousand reasons why, and all of 'em sucked. He replayed the years since Bosser took the wrong laser every night, trying to find the spot where things went off course, as if Davin could throw time into reverse and try it again.

"Because it turns out being a hero doesn't pay," Davin said, the words spoiling in his mouth.

"Think that's the first authentic thing I've heard you say," Theona sat back with a nasty grin, her eye flipping bright green. "You do this run for me, it'll pay. The next one'll pay too. I treat my runners right."

"Then let's get on with it." Davin slipped off the stool, steadied the world by holding the bar table for a minute. "Places to be, people to see, all that crap."

"Thought you weren't on a timetable?" The woman sucked down her drink.

"It's never too soon to leave this place."

Davin hadn't wanted to go to *Neil's* at all, but Theona insisted. Said, when they'd first commed, that its music, lights, and general disdain for lunar building codes made it difficult for anyone to listen in. Davin couldn't argue with that, so they'd set the date, time, and drinks.

Now the woman led him through the sleazy streets in the Nubium dome, a failed blend between start-up hopefuls trying to cash in on Luna's resurgence and predators feeding on those same dreams. Pop-up businesses littered the stacked shanties, and Davin knew most went underground too, burrowing the dome's least beneath the gray dust. Every one hawked something new, a body-mod or some drug, a bot that'd save your life or take another's.

Overhead, dome-skippers darted along, their one-and-two passenger floaters zipping through Nubium as fast as possible. Didn't want to take the chance they'd bust an engine and come down for repairs here.

Davin, though, enjoyed the walk. Earth sat up top, its blue-white-green beauty providing a better sky than the black void he normally had soaring through space. And the people crowding the streets around him? Hungry for hope, for deals, or just plain hungry? Those people he knew. Those people were him.

He hadn't grown up on the Moon, but home was more than a place.

Theona tilted her walk, nodding between two orange striped

stacks. She kept her mouth shut out here, where ears were everywhere, and Davin followed suit. He'd rather listen to the street music than her cocky pitches about how much artillery she had waiting to blow a hole in Eden's fleet.

Not that Eden wouldn't deserve it, but Davin didn't play those kinda sides. Not anymore.

Between the stacks, a few meters back from the street proper, the woman held up her metal eye to an innocuous spot on the silver walls. Something clicked as Davin closed, and a doorway shot up, revealing a stairway heading down.

"Bit small to move cargo," Davin said as they started in. "Unless you're dealing in toys."

"We shift the goods out a different way," Theona replied, leading. "I've got Nubium's dockyard on my payroll. Time comes to fly, you'll come in proper, leave without a second look."

"Ain't that swell."

Behind him, the door shut hard and swamped the stairway in darkness. Davin heard a click as Theona's eye shifted again, and he felt her hand reach out and grab his.

"Don't get any ideas," she said, pulling Davin down the stairs.

"And I thought things were going so well."

She laughed, a sound that vanished along the steps, which went deeper than Davin would've thought.

"At least you're funny. Most runners, they're hard types that don't know how to laugh anymore."

"Laughter's just my way of living," Davin replied.

The dark had to be for security. He guessed Theona's eye made the stairs look bright as day for her. Anyone following would find themselves taking a long fall, probably right to rifles pointing at their faces. Davin kept his steps sure, kept his left hand on the sidearm he wore on his belt, charged and ready.

Melody, his super-charged shotgun, had stayed home today. Too obvious for a job like this.

But hey, at least the stairs and wherever they led didn't smell like booze and too-little deodorant, like *Neil's*. Breathing, it turned out, was something Davin preferred to do without choking every time.

The stairs ended their dark journey into a big space that any cargo hauler would know: a warehouse. This one must've carried on for blocks, and going by the sealed crates stacked everywhere, most carrying labels with a ship's name and a time, it did brisk business.

"Pretty nice setup you've got here," Davin said as the woman dropped his hand, let him take in the picture.

Beyond the crates, lift bots milled around the space, shuttling this and that to here and there. Most had the long, straight arms good for toting heavy fare, though the Moon's touch-n-go gravity made big lifts easy. Davin suspected that's why manufacturing had grown so big here: close enough to Earth for the money and the buyers, light on weight and legality.

"That's the stack I have for you," Theona said, bringing Davin to a cluster that, going by the shapes and their lengths, held enough damage to arm a squad or two. "Drop's at Enceladus. Pick up another normal run to keep things clean."

"Right." Davin leaned in to get a good look at the closet casket, matte green and carbon-scored. "Where'd you get these?"

"Nowhere you need to know," Theona said. "You make this run, though, I'll have more. The rebels are paying way over premium now." Davin looked back, caught her shaking her head. "They're either doing better than Eden thinks in this war, or they're so damn desperate they'll throw their money away."

"It's not worth anything if you're dead."

Theona didn't argue, did ask Davin if he had any questions.

"Yeah, I've got a couple," Davin said, turning, catching one last look around the place.

No guards hanging around. A couple bots that looked like they might try something, but Theona looked to be running a profit-shop: keep labor costs low, take-home pay high.

Made Davin's job easy.

He didn't even draw the sidearm quick. Just reached over, pulled the weapon out with his right hand and leveled it at Theona. Who laughed again.

"What, you're going to steal all this cargo?"

"Nah," Davin replied. "They are."

A horrendous bang sounded from up the dark stairs, followed by harsh light and feet pounding along the steps. Theona dropped her nonchalance act and opened her mouth, like she was planning on giving some dumb order.

"Don't," Davin said, wagging his sidearm to catch her attention. "Not worth it. Give up your suppliers, maybe they'll let you off easy."

A thud from the stairs clued Davin to look over Theona's shoulder, to see the first Moon Centurion make the main floor. Others followed, their crimson capes swirling as they swept into the warehouse, hunting for threats. Those hapless bots didn't even get a chance to try for a weapon before some quick frying bolts from the Centurion's rifles reduced the machines to inert metal.

That first Centurion came Davin's way, big and bold and covered with an exoskeleton molded to his every muscle.

"Mox, right on time," Davin said. "Meet Theona. I imagine she'll have a lot to say."

Theona's mechanical eye clicked again, to a burning red, and she lunged towards Davin with a desperate rage Davin had seen all too many times before. The last move of someone whose path met an end they knew was coming, yet hoped would never arrive.

Theona never touched him. Mox had a hand on Theona's shoulder as she started her move, and he simply pressed her to the ground. She twitched once, then lay on the floor, still.

"New trick?" Davin asked.

"Nerve endings," Mox said, boulder-shaking voice rumbling off the warehouse floors and walls. "Press hard, body goes numb. New Centurion training."

Davin nodded, as if he had some idea of what life was like within the Moon's secretive police force. He'd met Mox as the Centurions had kicked him out for getting that big ol' exoskeleton. When the Wild Nines had stopped the Solar System from disintegrating into an android dystopia, Mox had come back here, and done well enough to offer Davin a job for some much-needed coin.

"She said these were going to Enceladus," Davin said, glancing at the weapons cache. "The rebels are buying."

"They are always buying," Mox replied. "Now, at least, they will not get these."

"You on Eden's side, now?"

"I am on the side that keeps me and my Centurions alive," Mox replied. "Whoever it is."

"Was afraid you'd changed," Davin said. "When's the fee coming in?"

"Guess you have not changed either," Mox laughed. "Check your account." Mox hesitated, then reached down and picked Theona up from the ground, slung her over his shoulder. "Have to get back to it. Sting like this takes a lot of red tape to get closed up. A lot of gear to take in."

"Sure."

Davin slipped the sidearm back in its holster, let the cocky smile fade along with the adrenaline. Took the hint and moved past Mox towards those stairs back up.

"Good to see you again, Davin. Been too long."

"It has. Take care, Mox." Davin offered up a half-hand wave, to the big man. "I'll call next time I'm out this way."

"Do that," Mox lifted a mitt. "And tell Phyla I said hi."

Phyla.

Yeah.

Continue the adventure with ROGUE BET, available now!

ACKNOWLEDGMENTS

One Shot marked the original end of the Wild Nines, but not necessarily the last story with Viola, Davin, Mox and others. I feel like these characters have plenty more to do yet, and can't wait to see what they get up to now that they're no longer getting chased by Bosser.

As with all of my books, family and friends are at the core of making this possible. Nicole keeps me going day in and out with her encouragement—there's simply no way I'd be able to do this without her help. My parents for giving me the artistic itch. My brothers for pestering me about what I'm writing next, and thus keeping me moving.

Lastly, thanks to all the readers out there. Whether you found these books through a sale, a random click on a website, or through a friend's recommendation, it's amazing to have the opportunity to share these stories with you.

Thank you.

ABOUT THE AUTHOR

A.R. Knight spins stories in a frosty house in Madison, WI, primarily owned by a pair of cats. After getting sucked into the working grind in the economic crash of the 2008, he found himself spending boring meetings soaring through space and going on grand adventures.

Eventually, spending time with podcasting, screenplays, short stories and other novels, he found a story he could fall into and a cast of characters both entertaining and full of heart.

The Wild Nines have more adventures to come, along with new plots, settings, and stories in the future. From there, A.R. Knight plans on jumping through to other worlds and finding new stories to tell in the limitless borders of our imagination.

Thanks, as always, for reading!

www.blackkeybooks.com
arknight@blackkeybooks.com

For Nicole

www.ingramcontent.com/pod-product-compliance
Lightning Source LLC
Chambersburg PA
CBHW050609190726
48283CB00007B/2337